CAIN
HERETIC SON

Beth Hildenbrand

ISBN 978-1-955156-54-7 (paperback)
ISBN 978-1-955156-55-4 (digital)

Copyright © 2021 by Beth Hildenbrand

All rights reserved. No part of this publication may be reproduced, distributed, or transmitted in any form or by any means, including photocopying, recording, or other electronic or mechanical methods without the prior written permission of the publisher. For permission requests, solicit the publisher via the address below.

Rushmore Press LLC
1 800 460 9188
www.rushmorepress.com

Printed in the United States of America

"The essence of sin is temptation."
-Lucifer

PROLOGUE

The darkness was unyielding. Cain stood untouched in the eye of the storm. Outside the vortex, nature unleashed its fury. The winds were so violent trees uprooted to fly like great arrows discharged from a giants' bow. Flaming balls of hail hail, the size of a man's fist punched down from the sky torching every growing thing, leaving behind a land now barren and scorched. The earth split open like a rotten melon giving the ground the appearance of torn ragged flesh.

Rising above the unrestrained symphony of destruction a thunderous Voice reached out to Cain. The Voice melding to become one with the forces that it unleashed.

"Where is your brother?" The Voice demanded.

Cain raised his head. His strong jaw pushed out defiantly. A snarl curled his full lips as he growled out rebelliously, "Am I my brother's keeper?"

"Your brother's blood cries out from beneath the ground. His blood is on your hands. You are cursed. You shall be a fugitive and a vagabond to wander this world forever alone."

"Everyone who comes upon me will seek to slay me." Cain snarled.

"I will mark you. Whosoever would seek to slay you will face my vengeance seven-fold. Your fate is sealed."

"Nooo wait." Cain cried out.

No answer came. The Voice was now lost to Cain forever.

A bolt of lightning rent the darkness striking the ground at Cain's feet illuminating a pool of water to make the surface appear like glass. For an instant, Cain was granted a glimpse of himself reflected in a flash of light. He was being shown his mark. Instinctively he covered his face. His body thrummed with rage. His heart turned black.

The Mark of Cain. Eyes that burned a hellish scarlet. Blood red, to remind him and any who saw him of his brother's blood he had so jealousy spilled.

Cain threw back his head. He screamed to the heavens. "If it's a monster you would make of me, then it's a monster I shall become." He vowed.

It would be many centuries before Cain would come to regret the vow he made in anger.

Eventually even a cursed immortal longs cursed immortal long for redemption…

CHAPTER ONE

Cain Adamson exhaled a deep sigh of contentment as he slept. In his dream, he was not alone in the massive antique four-poster bed.

A sultry brunette straddled his back. She was gloriously nude. Waves of thick chestnut hair fell to the small of her back. Tight rosy nipples tickled his skin as she stretched to massage his broad shoulders. He moaned with pleasure. This was the good life. In reality, it was how he spent his nights off. Tonight, however, he had been busy sending two particularly nasty demons back to the pit where they belonged. So, for the moment he would have to make do with the dream. He was enjoying the tender ministrations of his nameless seductress when his dream began to shift and go dark. The soft skin riding his back turned rough as sandpaper. The deft fingers working his shoulders raked his skin drawing blood. Cain turned to see what the hell was happening when a sharp pain impaled him in the base of his skull.

Cain bolted upright. The quick stab of pain was a warning. A swift but painful way of alerting him that something unnatural was close. His other senses awakened coming back online, bringing with them the overwhelming stench of brimstone. The smell hit his sinus cavity burning like acid. Not a pleasant way to be roused from sleep. Truthfully, it pissed him off. Demons always did have shitty timing.

The bedroom was dark. Only a few slivers of moonlight made their way past the heavily draped windows yet Cain knew with absolute certainty the identity of his intruder. His mark gave him enhanced night vision. The drawback was a sensitivity to light which was easily overcome with sunglasses. He was a cursed immortal, not a vampire. Demon hunting was best done at night which fit into his nocturnal habits perfectly.

The impertinent intruder had made himself at home. He sat relaxing comfortably in a nearby armchair. Tricked out in Armani with a superior air he acted as though he had every right to be there.

"Insufferable ass." Cain muttered. He had caught the creature's reaction when he suddenly roared awake. For all of his show of arrogance, his unwanted guest was fearful. He damned well should be.

Blank milky eyes regarded Cain intently. Demons all had white eyes. Upper-level they were able to alter their host's eye color if they chose to do so. This one had not. They could also manipulate their host's features up to a point. Choosing A host with the desired coloring, height, and build wasn't too difficult. To achieve replicating an actual person the host would also need the superficial bone structure of whoever the demon was attempting to mimic. In this case, it was the face of Cain's brother. The asshole was pulling out all the stops to get under Cain's skin. It was a wasted effort.

"Good Morning Grandfather." The demon greeted him.

Cain reclined into a sea of black bed pillows. His shoulder-length raven hair disappeared into the cloud of inky down. A sheet covered him to the waist molding against his long muscular legs and thighs. Cain was built like a warrior. His abs and chest ripped. There was not an ounce of fat to be found on his body. His chiseled features held an otherworldly beauty that some would call almost feminine. Long dark lashes and red lips were saved by the masculinity of a square jaw. That particular feature is now covered with a goatee in an attempt to camouflage his perpetually youthful features.

Cain reached for a pack of Marlboro reds lying on the nightstand. Clamping a cigarette between even white teeth he lit it with a thought then slowly inhaled a long satisfying drag.

"My grandson died before the village of Nod crumbled to dust. I should know since I'm the one who slit his throat. You're nothing but a punk ass demon carrying his memories."

"I am what you made me." The demon fired back.

Cain stared at the mockery of his brother's face. Of all the children born of his cursed bloodline, this one haunted him still. Even now the inner wounds of this one's death remained raw and bloody. What should have scarred over in time kept fresh by his own guilt? The "if only's" would drive him mad if he allowed himself to examine the memories. Right now, he needed to keep his head straight and focus. The beast seated before him was just that…a beast. Hell-bent on corrupting and defiling souls to serve up to its Master.

"I didn't put the blade in your hand and force you to kill an innocent man and child. Suck it up La Mech."

"La Mech is dead. My name is now Magnus."

"Damn, seriously?" Cain cringed. "Just exactly how long has it been since you've been topside?"

"Four hundred years." Magnus drawled out.

"No shit?" Cain blurted. He rose up nude from his bed. The moonlight casting a glow on his golden skin. If this encounter turned into a brawl which was the most likely scenario, well now, Cain had fought bare ass'ed before and come through it intact. However, he found it to be a lot less distracting when his package was safely tucked up.

Cain started across the room past Magnus. He was in no hurry. Magnus watched unaffected by Cain's blatant exhibitionism.

Cain chuckled," I know it's a lot to take in. At least that's what they tell me."

Magnus grimaced. If the demon could have rolled those blank eyes he would have.

Reaching into a dresser Cain removed a pair of soft faded jeans. He tugged them up muscled thighs taking special care as he pulled up the zipper. He had every right to be cocky. As the first-born son of the first two perfectly created beings, he was a little piece of heaven himself and had been well endowed by the Creator.

Already bored with the family reunion, Cain took a seat on the twin to the chair Magnus was seated on and got comfortable. He was determined to get things moving along and would be more than happy to push a few of the demon's buttons to goad him into spitting out what the hell he was up to this time.

"So how did you manage to get yourself back above ground Malcolm?"

"It's Magnus." The demon snapped. "I had hoped you would be pleased by my return Grandfather."

Cain ignored the familial crack. "If I remember correctly the Old Man put you on time out after you screwed the pooch with that sweet young thing in Prague. Hotshot Incubus couldn't seal the deal"

"The bitch would have been mine if you had not interfered." Magnus spat. "Lucifer was very forgiving. More than you ever were."

"Lucy, forgiving?" Cain snorted. "Yeah, I hear he's a real Angel."

"The first Angel. You should show more respect. I doubt he would appreciate your pet names for him."

"Poor little devil will just have to suck it up. What's he going to do kill me?" Cain taunted.

"There are worse things than death," Magnus growled with a very Billy Idol like sneer.

"Speaking from experience?"

"Four hundred years' worth" Magnus stood and began to wander around the room. He paused when he reached a 1920's era bronze floor lamp. The lamp was handmade by an artist Cain had discovered in New York. The body of the lamp was made in the shape of a slender woman her back arched and her arms raised above her head. He bought the thing immediately upon seeing it and paid an outrageous price. It was the tiny face of the women that had drawn him to the lamp. The delicate features had so reminded him of his mother that he could not leave it behind. Now as Magnus ran his hand over the sculpted body Cain felt as if it was being defiled.

"It was nothing in comparison to the pain of your betrayal Grandfather. It was thoughts of seeing you again that sustained me during my punishment."

"I'm flattered." Cain had not missed the venom in his voice. Magnus wanted him to suffer. The feeling was mutual.

Magnus turned back to Cain. His handsome face wore a mocking smile. "Now that we've been reunited, I thought we could spend some time reminiscing over the good old days. Maybe have a drink at the local tavern."

The hairs on the back of Cain's neck stood up. There was only one bar in town. Over the centuries the family that owned it had become very important to him. Magnus must know this and that was his reason for bringing it into the conversation. Cain kept his face blank.

"I think I'll pass. If I remember correctly you never were a fun drunk."

"What a shame. This is such a friendly little town. I'm sure I would have found the locals entertaining."

"Yeah, whatever, Marvin. Since I have no intention of becoming your new BFF. Why don't you just get on with it and tell me why you're here?"

"It's Magnus." He hissed. His milky eyes began to glow like headlights.

Cain's inner imp was doing the happy dance. He was getting under the assholes' skin and causing him to lose his temper. Demons weren't known for their patience.

Magnus strode over to stand by the fireplace. He rested his arm on the marble mantle his glowing eyes glaring at Cain. Despite his anger, he spoke slowly and deliberately. "What I'm up to is bringing you to your knees. It's time for a reckoning. You butchered my wives in front of me. Then you slit my throat. Tell me who the demon here is. You owe me lives and I've come to collect."

"Wives?" Cain asked incredulously. "I gutted two demon whores sent to seduce you. You, in your bedeviled mind believed every evil word they whispered in your ear. You were played for a fool. I see time has not increased your intellect."

"Adah and Zillah were good women." Fueled by rage Magnus was unable to maintain his new form. The darkly handsome facade slipped reverting to its true pasty grey demonic mask. Flecks of saliva oozed from the corners of his lips while spittle dripped from his fangs.

Cain's face remained indifferent. "They were who re-spawn."

The cold fireplace burst into white-hot flames. Magnus flew at Cain. Cain had been anticipating the attack and was faster. He lunged to his feet. The two stood nose to nose. Cain's ruby eyes spitting hellfire into the milky white eyes of the demon.

"They were two women I loved. It's time to finally settle our account. You will watch as I send the souls of those you care about to the pit. I've already brought one of your precious humans under my influence." Magnus poked out his pointed tongue sweeping it along black lips. "I've been taking special care of her. This time you won't stop me."

"You've got me real scared, boy."

"You should be an old man. As we speak, she sleeps touching herself and crying out my name. She is only the first. This town will be drenched in innocent blood before I'm finished with you."

"For shit sake. You sound like some B movie villain. You're all talk. What are you going to do next twirl your mustache?" Cain taunted.

"Mock me while you can. I wonder will you be so smug when you watch as I rape her soul."

Cain's control snapped. He hissed as his own fangs descended. Bloody talons tore free from his fingertips. In the blink of an eye, he wrapped his hands around Magnus's throat. Cain lifted him from the floor slamming the dangling body into the nearest wall. Plaster crunched a spider webbing an outline around his body.

"This time when I send you back to hell I'll make damn sure you never see daylight again," Cain promised.

Under the pressure of Cain's crushing grip, the demon's face managed a contorted grin. "Go for it." He rasped. In an instant, he vanished with a dramatic pop.

Cain glared at the ruined wall. "Fucking Rocky, really."

Faith Martin crept as silently as her Nikes would allow. She kept her fingers crossed on both hands as she entered the bedroom of her seemingly comatose roommate. In her mind, she was pleading with her best friend "Please don't wake up, please don't wake up."

Faith had sworn to her friend she would check in before she took off on her latest self-appointed mission. Of course, her good buddy slept through her departure Faith could at least argue that she tried.

"I'm out." she whispered."

Heri's hopes of a clean getaway were dashed as Jami Archer expelled an aggravated groan and shook her ash-blonde head. Her hair swung wildly obscuring her pixie-like features. The blue lighting from her Bates Motel night light cast an eerie glow. Looking at her friend, Faith's fertile imagination conjured up images of Scooby-Doo witches. "Crap!" she blurted. Her dreams of an easy escape turned into an epic fail.

"What time is it?" Jami croaked.

"Six a.m. and life is beautiful." Faith cringed.

"You did not just go there," Jami groused.

"Sorry." Faith apologized not really meaning it. The only thing she was really sorry for was getting caught.

"Sure Yes, you are. I didn't get to bed until four. Damn it Faith. What the hell are you doing up at this unholy hour?"

"Ack! See." Faith barked. "I knew you would forget. I never should have promised to check in with you. I'm going to the War Memorial…remember. Some atheist group wants it torn down because it's in the shape of a cross."

Jami wearily pulled herself into a sitting position. "We discussed this last night. I stupidly thought you had seen reason. You cannot be praying on State property." Jami argued. "It's against the law. They will throw your psycho ass in jail."

This was exactly the conversation Faith was trying to avoid. "I realize that." She snapped obstinately. "So, I spoke with Miss Myrtle Moyer a sweet understanding lady who lives across the street. She has no problem with me squatting on the edge of her lawn for the day."

"Crap!" Jami blurted, pissed off that Faith had outsmarted her.

"Ha!" Faith chirped in triumph. Her leaf green eyes lit up at outmaneuvering her friend. "You know J, they want to speak out about respecting all religions but let them see a cross and all hell breaks loose."

"I appreciate what you're doing. But aren't you getting a little carried away with all of this? You're on a one woman crusade. Last week it was the Fire Department."

"They should be allowed to fly the American flag on their truck. This is America."

"You baked them red velvet cupcakes with white and blue icing."

"By the way, they won that. They were granted permission to keep the flag on the truck."

Jami took a deep breath and looked down to her hands folded on her lap. She had been holding her tongue for weeks now not wanting to have the conversation she knew would hurt her friend. It was at the point now that she was starting to worry about Faith's mental and physical health. Her pale skin now verged on translucent with purple smudges circling her eyes. Jami knew she wasn't sleeping well. Her golden blonde hair had lost its luster hanging lifelessly down her back. She was becoming a shadow of the outgoing girl Jami had known all her life. Everyone deals with grief in their own way. Faith had been hit hard when she lost her father. Jami was determined to bring her back to the world of the living. Resigned she spoke from the heart. "You are not your father. You don't have to do this for him."

Faith jerked back as though she had been slapped. Turning her face from Jami she weakly replied, "Maybe I just want him to be proud of me."

"He was always proud of you." Jami went on earnestly. She took Faith's hand. "He was proud of who you were. He would want you to follow your conscience, not his. Be who YOU are."

"I'm not sure I know who that is anymore."

"Well, I remember a girl who busted her ass and opened her own bookstore before she was twenty-three. She was always there for her friends. She loved music, books, and the shooting pool. She loved her life and she was happy. That is what your dad would have wanted his legacy to be."

"I gotta go." Faith announced abruptly.

"Ah shit. Look, would you please just think about what I said?" Jami pleaded.

"I will." Faith sighed tiredly.

"Promise?"

"Yes, I promise."

"Try to keep your butt out of trouble and call me if you need bail money. Now getcha crazy -ass outta here and let me get some sleep. I've got to open the bar this afternoon."

Faith grinned at Jami's goofiness. "Will do." As she walked to the door she called back to her friend. "J?"

"Yeah?"

"I'll pray for you." Faith giggled, ducking to avoid the pillow flying at her head as she hurried out the door.

Jami snuggled back into her soft cocoon of quilts grumbling about psychotic roommates. As soon as her eyes closed and her mouth shut, she was sound asleep.

A mountain of a man appeared beside the bed. Unruly white-blonde hair was covered with a cowboy hat. He was comfortably dressed in a white t-shirt, jeans, and hard-worn cowboy boots. Strapped to his hip totally at odds with his good old boy persona rested a sword that shimmered with an otherworldly light.

His face held a lethal scowl that softened slightly as he took in her girl's peaceful slumber. Had he ever slept that peacefully? If he had he carried no memory of it.

Her hair was a mess of tangles. Her darkly arched brows stood out against her pale skin and ashy hair. She had a small pointed nose and cupid's bow mouth that snapped open and began snoring loudly.

Before coming to this room, he had checked in on Faith. What he found there was far from the peace he found here. The darkness that haunted Faith was a vacuum pulling everything good from the room and leaving behind the indelible stain of damnation.

Unlike her friend, Faith's delicate features had been pinched in pain as she slept. When he engaged with her subconscious, visions of the demon assaulting her nearly brought him to his knees. Her mind held the tell-tale wounds of demonic influence. He could see she was a fighter. He felt the battle that was raging inside her. Still, without intervention, it would be only a matter of days until the damage became irreparable and her soul would be lost.

He laid his palm gingerly on Jami's forehead. He knew she wouldn't wake having lulled her into a deep sleep when he first entered the room. What he was doing was an invasion. It was also necessary.

Easing into her subconscious he immediately hit a wall. Stunned, he pushed harder. Ah, there it was.

Well hell, wasn't this a surprise. He allowed himself a rare smile. They might come out of this alive after all.

CHAPTER TWO

Faith spent the day sitting cross-legged on Miss Myrtle's lawn. By afternoon she was stiff, cranky, and exhausted. She found she was wearing down so easily these days. She blamed depression or maybe she was coming down with something. Lately, she felt like she was living in an older woman's body instead of that of a young twenty-four-year-old woman.

From this vantage point, Faith had an excellent view of the memorial. She was surprised that Miss Myrtle had not come out to chat. She had the impression that the elderly woman was lonely. When they spoke on the phone Faith had a devil of a time trying to end the conversation. First thing when she arrived Faith had knocked on the door to say hello but there had been no response. She assumed the lady was out for the day.

At this point, Faith was ready to call it a day. For someone who had driven all this way to pray she had done a lousy job of it. Instead, she had spent the day ruminating on the wake-up call Jami laid on her and how correct her best bud had been.

How long did it take to get over the loss of the most important person in your life? Why hadn't some shrink come up with a timeline? You will be over your grief in eight months, one week, and four days. Or maybe a magic spell. Sculpt a wax effigy of your lost loved one. Insert a wick. When the wax is burned your pain will be gone. Yeah, if only. It had been over a year. She did need to make an attempt to pick up the pieces and try to get back to her life. Gah, if only she had the energy to do it. She had foolishly assumed after going through the first year and having all of the first holidays, birthdays, and such, pass it would get easier. These last few weeks had left her feeling even more worn down and depressed than anything the last year had dealt her.

As she began to repack her things, she caught a shadow coming up beside her just a second too late. Faith threw out her arms to brace for impact.

"Ack. I'm so sorry." Apologized to a nice-looking young man. He stumbled over her and was pin wheeling his arms while bobbling from foot to foot trying to regain his balance.

Faith righted herself. "Are you okay?" She asked peering up at him.

"Yes actually," He responded. "Thanks for asking. Although I think I'm the one who should be asking you that question."

"No harm done." Faith assured him while brushing her grass-stained palms off on her jeans.

The young man appeared pleasant enough even if he was kind of klutzy. He smiled down sincerely from under the brim of a snazzy straw fedora. He looked like he was in his early twenties. Faith guessed he was probably a local college student. He was dressed in khakis and boat shoes. Hipster fashion was in these days and he filled the bill. A pale blue checked button -down, red, blue, and yellow argyle vest, and good grief a yellow silk bow tie completed the ensemble. Faith mentally thanked the heavens his sable hair was not sporting a man bun.

"May I?" He ventured, pointing to where Faith was sitting in the grass.

"Be my guest." She held out her hand offering up a piece of lawn.

His shocking ice blue eyes twinkled as he sat down beside her and began to speak. "I got distracted and lost my footing."

"No worries. It happens to us all." Faith assured him trying to ease his obvious anxiety over almost crushing her.

"I can't picture you stumbling and bumbling around. You look like someone who always knows where you're going."

"I used to think so." Faith spoke quietly. "Now lately I'm not so sure."

"Well trust me we all get lost but if you hang in there you will find your way again."

"This has become a very odd conversation."

"I tend to bring that out in people." He smiled brightly.

"You should be a psychiatrist."

"Heaven forbid." He shuddered playfully.

Faith laughed. It was an honest laugh and made her think she needs to start doing more of it.

"It was nice meeting you Faith."

Faith took his extended hand and shook it. "Nice to meet you too."

She had meant to ask him his name. The thought vanished from her mind as a wonderful warmth engulfed her hand spreading up her arm then flowing through her until her body was filled with it. She suddenly felt better than she had in days.

He released her hand and stood up.

"Take care of yourself, Faith. Remember just because we lose our way doesn't necessarily mean we're lost."

He gave her a cheeky grin and went off on his way.

"Weird." Faith whispered. She gave herself a little shake. It wasn't until he was out of sight and she stood up with her bag that she realizes she never told him her name. Or had she?

Cain paced his kitchen, cursed, and paced some more. If he kept this up much longer, he would wear the warm honey -colored varnish off the hardwood floor. The inactivity was driving him crazy. He had blown up his cell trying to contact the few beings he spoke to in the supernatural community. The few he managed to pin down were not even aware Magnus had resurfaced. The rest he had left text messages for. Now he paced and waited.

It was too early to head out to Archers Bar. They would be open but nothing would be going on this early. He threw his cell onto the butcher block table and poured himself another cup of the dark Colombian roast he preferred. Leaning against the marble counter top he decided to think through what he knew so far.

Magnus wanted revenge. Anyone who got in the way of that was cannon fodder. He had obviously been haunting Archers or he would not have brought up the whole getting a drink thing since Archers was the only bar in the small town. Magnus had also said her was preying on a woman. That made sense since he is an Incubus and their MO was to prey on women. That being said Magnus was already feeding off an innocent woman who had a connection to the Archers. There were only a few women who mattered to Cain and they were all connected to Archers Bar.

It was a long time ago that Cain made his promise to Levi Archer. Levi and Caroline had been the first of the Archers to settle in the area. The area had still been untamed wilderness at that time. Cain had become friendly with the Archers out of necessity. The Archers had been such good people that closeness had grown before Cain could prevent it. He promised his friend he would watch over his family and he always had. True he would have to leave every few years and come back as his own son or cousin so the family and local folks wouldn't catch on to the fact that he never aged, but he always came back. He had foolishly allowed himself to get too close to this latest crop of Archers. They were a weak spot for Magnus to take advantage of. Damn it, he knew better than to get so attached to mortals. A lesson he had learned the hard way centuries ago. He had no intention of letting his friend down now. Especially since he was the one who led the wolf to their door.

"Fuck" Cain growled. It would be at least two more hours before he could leave. Cain refilled his coffee mug, rechecked his phone for messages shoving it into his pants pocket when he saw there was nothing new on the damn thing.

A shower was in order. The time spent with his demon kin had left him feeling dirty. It would help to kill the time and maybe clear some of the cobwebs from his mind in the process. If he got lucky maybe one of his contacts would have hit him back by the time he finished showering.

Thirty minutes later Cain stepped out of the shower. He wrapped a towel around his lean hips without bothering to dry himself off. Careless of the water pooled on the marble floor he went to stand in front of the vanity. He swiped a hand over the mirror to wipe away the condensation from the steam. Cain usually avoided mirrors. Today he forced himself to look at his wavering reflection. He had not changed much since the time he was cursed and those changes were only superficial. He still appeared to be in his late twenties. The last two years he had grown out a goatee to age himself for the mortals. Otherwise, was still very much the same. The same square jaw, blue -black hair, full red lips. Any relevant changes were on the inside. Sighing, Cain walked away from the mirror and the memories before was pulled into remembering too much. His memories, much like the Great Flood, were so consuming if he allowed them to, they would drown him.

Magnus was bored. For hours he had been watching as his target sat on a lawn praying. Occasionally a pedestrian would pause to speak to her. Most just ignored her. No wonder so many souls turned to sin. Religion was just so boring.

He had to admit he lucked out when it came to Faith. She was an appealing young woman. The wholesome all American girl next door type. Coincidentally that was just his type. The more innocence for him to devour the tastier the meal. Hair the color of sunshine, petite build, and daddy issues. Yum.

He remembered Lucifer sending someone to pull him out of that hellish cell. He had not questioned it. He gratefully accepted the assignment. He would have done anything to be released from the centuries of torture he had endured. Centuries spent planning the vengeance he would deliver to Cain had whetted his appetite for revenge more than ever. Cain.

As he watched the five-foot nothing slips a girl he began to wonder what threat she could possibly pose to the Big Bad. Then he discovered her relationship with Cain. After that, his plans changed. Yes, Lucifer would get the girls soul but Magnus would also make sure he got his own vengeance.'

Magnus was enjoying himself playing the tender lover in her dreams. It was exquisite torture draining her little by little. His hunger to finish her was getting harder and harder to keep in check. That was the reason for the visit to Cain. The time had come to draw him in. The final act would soon play out. When Faith physically took him into her body, he would finish the contamination of her soul. He wanted Cain there to witness it. To see his face when Faith's soul went dark and was marked for Lucifer. Then he would have her slit her own throat right before Cain's eyes just as Cain had done to his wives.

Magnus already had another of Cain's cherished mortals under his control. The rest were being watched as he awaited an opportunity to use them. They were all puppets and he held the strings. When the old man was weak and hurting from his loss losses, he would take him out. What did the Almighty's wrath matter to him? He was already in Hell. The real question was why Lucifer wanted Cain alive. Not that it mattered. He had already faced down the worst imaginable pain and torture Lucifer could dish out. Cain was going to die. And the Devil be damned.

Faith walked down the street to where she parked her sensible blue Cavalier. She made a decision. Jami was right, so was the klutzy hipster with the Guru complex. She needed to get her shit together. Her father had been a great man. A true patriot who gave his life for his country. He had been raised in a strict Mennonite household and though he disagreed with their beliefs as Conscientious Objectors he left the church he took his faith with him. She had been trying to live happy life. The causes she was pursuing should be uplifting her spirits. Instead, she had never felt so soul-sick. They were good causes and deserved to be pursued. They just weren't her causes.

She opened the car door and tossed her bag onto the passenger seat. Going around to the driver's side, she glanced forward noticing a man leaning against a tree staring in her direction. She swung her head around to see if he was watching someone nearby. Nope, she was the only one on the street.

"Oh my." She purred.

Mr. Yummy was watching her and he was sooo hot. He looked at least six foot tall dressed all in bad boy black. Expensive black by the looks of it. Not that she could tell the difference between designer threads and Wal-Mart duds. But damn, even the cut of his midnight hair screamed money. She wished she could see his eyes but he was too far away and wearing sunglasses. As if reading her mind, he removed the sunglasses and flashed her a smile that radiated pure sex.

Faith recoiled. An odd sense of recognition rolled through her. Her stomach rolled and she broke out into a cold sweat. What the hell. As hot as Mr. Sharp Dressed Man was, she should be getting the warm tingles. There was nothing warm about the shiver of icy fingers slipping down her spine.

Like a frightened rabbit Faith jumped into her car and took off without even looking for oncoming traffic. A green SUV honked its horn as it just missed nailing her right quarter panel. Faith shrieked her hands trembling on the steering wheel. As she drove past the spot where he stood, she dared a peek out of the corner of her eye. He was still standing there smiling at her. Too damn creepy.

Jami went into her mother's office. The bar was already running low on change. She bent down unlocking the drawer that held rolls of coins. She reached in and grabbed two rolls of quarters and one of the dimes.

Against the wall across from the desk stood an old metal rack of shelves. The top shelf held Mom Archer's ancient twelve-inch television. It only had reception on one channel. Right now, that channel was blaring the local newscast.

"...this afternoon in a quiet neighborhood in York County... here in this house directly across from the highly debated War Memorial..."

Jami's head jerked up the small screen in front of her demanding her full attention. That annoying K.G. wannabe news anchor Jessica Landry stood in front of the same damn Memorial Faith had gone to that morning. She felt the hair stand up on her arms. A premonition of what she was going to hear making her tremble.

"No way." Jami groaned in denial.

The newswoman continued on with her story. It became a buzz in Jami's ears. Her heart sank to her stomach. She forced herself to focus and listen to the rest of the news report.

"...after receiving an anonymous call to the local police Myrtle Moyer was found brutally murdered in the bathroom of her home. Police are looking for a blonde woman in her mid-twenties for questioning. Neighbors say the girl spent the day sitting on Myrtle's front lawn."

A pencil sketch of Faith appeared on the screen. Thank God it was generic. A telephone number flashed beneath it.

"...police are asking anyone who might recognize this woman to contact the York police at the number on the bottom of the screen."

"Crap! Crap! Crap! No fucking way. Key-rist Faith." Jami ranted.

She pulled her cell phone from her back pocket. With her fingers shaking, she smacked frantically at a picture of Faith, impatient as last, the damn thing read that it was dialing.

"Fuuuck." She growled, now even more worried as she was dumped straight into voicemail. "Faith call me immediately. I mean it. What the fuck is going on? Call me damn it."

Jami knew it had to be a coincidence. Faith would never hurt anyone. Her friend was a gentle soul. Her worries were that maybe Faith witnessed something she shouldn't have. This was why she worried. Faith had no concept of self-preservation. At the moment all she could do was wait for Faith to return her call or maybe she would get lucky and Faith would come straight to the bar before going home.

Shoving her phone back into her pants she grabbed the change she had dropped on the desk and headed back to work. Passing the jukebox Serenity by Godsmack was playing. Jami laughed ironically. She could use some serenity herself right about now.

Seated in a booth at Denny's with a steaming cup of tea in front of her Faith was already feeling less spooked about the stranger. It was hard to feel freaked cocooned in the normalcy of a busy restaurant full of people. The chattering voices, the sound of dishes chinking, waitresses bustling by, the sights and sounds washed away any lingering willies plaguing her.

Checking her phone watch, she realized she wasn't going to make it back in time to close up her bookstore. She dug out her phone to make a call to her one and only employee.

Katie answered on the second ring. "Martins Books." She chirped.

Faith could visualize her assistant. Katie would be seated behind the counter on an old bar stool donated by Mom Archer. Her carrot colored hair would be a mass of unruly curls framing her heart-shaped freckled face. Horn rimmed glasses would be sliding down her nose. Her head would be bent over a book.

"Hey, girl. How did we do today?" Faith inquired hopefully.

"We made enough money to keep the lights on this month."

"Woo Hoo." Faith mock cheered.

"There is some excellent news. The new Kim Harrison came in. I'm already reading it."

"Of course, you are?" Faith teased. "Being able to get your hands on the new releases is the only reason you work for me."

"Not true." Katie denied. "It's the big bucks you pay me. Seriously though, I priced them, entered them into inventory, and made an awesome display in the front window."

"Wow. I hate to ask you to do more…" Faith began.

"But…"

"But since you're so indispensable would you mind closing up and making the bank deposit for me? I'm running late and I'd love to go straight home."

"Hmmm sounds like a good time to ask for a raise," Katie teased.

Faith sighed. She would love to give the girl a big fat raise. Katie was as devoted to the store as Faith. Unfortunately, he wasn't making enough money yet. If things keep going this well in the next six month months, she might be able to swing it but she didn't want to get Katie's hopes up. "I'm sorry sweetie. If anyone deserves a raise it's you. How about you keep the book, you're reading as a bonus. That way you'll have the entire series in hardcover."

"Yes!" Katie squealed jubilantly. "You knew that's what I was really angling for. Since you are such a generous mood boss, I will be glad to lock up and make the deposit for you."

"You're great. Thank you."

"Yes, I am."

"I'll call you later. Be careful."

"I always am." Katie assured her.

CHAPTER THREE

Archers Bar was a local institution. Owned and operated by the Archer clan for generations. Cain had been a regular since the original owners Levi and Carolyn Archer built the first Inn on the property in 1762. It was the one place on earth Cain could go and feel welcome and at ease in a crowd full of mortals. He was accepted unconditionally and treated like family. Now after all the friendship they had shown him he brought evil to their home. Lousy way to repay their loyalty. All he could hope to do at this point was to keep an eye on them and hope like hell he took Magnus out before he finished carrying his demon games out to their deadly conclusion.

Cain pulled the thick handle opening the heavy oak door. He stepped inside ridding himself of his sunglasses. The darkness of the barroom barely affecting his glamoured blue eyes.

Cain smiled genuinely when he saw the girl behind the bar. Jami was his favorite of this current generation of Archers. She had a sweet smile and a generous heart. Something about her made him think of a curious pixie emerging from a forest. She hid her kindness behind a tough as nails exterior. Having grown up with three roughneck brothers had prepared her to deal with the most obnoxious bar patrons. She had a quick temper and woe to those who unleashed it.

A tug of recognition pulled at Cain from the corner of the room. Before he could address it Jami nodded him over to his regular stool. He hadn't even taken his seat before she placed a frosty mug of Budweiser on the bar for him.

"Thanks, J." Cain took a healthy swallow and smiled at her with appreciation. "That's just what I needed tonight.

Jami frowned at him, concern written on her face. "You look tired tonight. Your eyes are bloodshot. Everything okay?"

"A little too long staring at the computer screen." He lied. "Nothing to worry about."

She gave him a look that said she thought he was full of shit. "You really should hire someone. You run a billion-dollar company from your home house for pity's sake. Your very large house where you are alone way too much." She lectured.

The Archer children used to come out and do yard work for him when they were younger. The whole family had been to the mansion in the woods at one time or another. They were the only mortals who could actually locate the house. It was spelled to where anyone else would walk right by and never know it was there.

"I'm alone because I like it that way. We have had this discussion before."

Brushing aside his comment she lectured on undaunted. "Why don't you hire one of the boys? Micah hates working in the bar. He only stays out of loyalty to Mom and Pop. Well, that and the easy pick-ups. He would love to work for you. Mom and Pop wouldn't fuss because he would still be working for the family."

Cain warmed at her shameless flattery. That didn't stop him from changing the subject.

"I hear Mom and Pop took off for Virginia to see your brothers' new baby."

"How did you find out?"

"Sam texted me and sent a picture," Cain informed her pulling the picture up on his phone for her to see. Sam was the eldest of the Archer siblings. His son was the first grandchild for Mom and Pop. They had their bags packed and waiting for weeks. The second they received a phone call that the next generation had arrived they were out the door and in their car on their way to Virginia.

"Isn't he adorable?" Jami gushed.

"He looks like a wrinkly little old man." Cain blurted honestly.

Jami looked crestfallen. "All babies look like that." She snapped. "Still, he's much cuter than most babies."

"He's a very handsome little old man." Cain amended. "Better now?"

"Much."

"So, anything else going on around here? You seem a little antsy." Cain questioned her. She had a smile on her face but he could she was jumpy. Her usual mannerisms were off-kilter, like she was forcing herself to behave normally.

Jami's face instantly became guarded. "Other than Grey being late it's all good." She lied refilling his beer.

Cain could tell she was keeping something from him but it would have to wait until he could talk to her alone. "He will turn up and I'm sure he will have a good reason for being late," Cain tried to settle her down then glanced over his shoulder for the third time.

"He better." Jami huffed. Cain's distraction had not gone unnoticed. "I'm sorry. Am I boring you?"

"Of course not. Why would you say that?"

"If you keep looking behind you like you've been doing you're going to give yourself whiplash. Do you know that woman over there or are you just looking to pull one out of the herd tonight?"

Jami glared at him. Cain could see her body radiating indignation. He was clueless as to why she would be angry with him. He had been picking up women in Archers since she was a kid and it never made her snappish before. He had been alive since damn near the dawn of time and he still didn't understand women.

"That's Ennie. She's an old friend. If she's come here looking for me there must be a good reason. I should get my butt over there and say hello."

"Please do. I wouldn't want you to be rude." Jami oozed sarcasm that was wasted on Cain.

Cain approached the exotically stunning woman seated alone at a corner table. No matter how many years separated them she remained as beautiful and unchanged as the day they met. Her dark auburn hair fell past her shoulders. She was wearing it straight now. Her mocha skin and almond eyes gave her the look of a heathen

Goddess come to visit the unworthy mortals. A soft butter yellow sweater clung to her feminine curves. Every man in the bar was fixated on her. In return, her eyes told them, No Chance.

Pulling out a seat across from her Cain gallantly took her hand and placed a feathery kiss on her palm. "It's been a long time."

"Too long." She agreed. "I was already on my way when I got your call."

"What do you know?"

"Not much." She admitted. "It started out as a whisper about ten days ago. Now it's loud, demanding, and driving me insane."

"Tenacious little spirit is it?"

"Not funny." Ennie scowled at him. "If this guy wasn't already dead, I'd strangle his annoying ass."

"Tell me."

"He claims to be a friend of yours. Says his name is Josh. He just keeps repeating "Tell Cain guard Faith. Does that mean anything to you?"

"Yes. It does."

"Explain, please. If it's not too much trouble."

"Josh was a friend who used to help me out from time to time."

"And just exactly what did this guy help you with?"

"He was an exorcist." Cain sighed. He rubbed his eyes with the heels of his palms. "About twenty five twenty-sixyears ago Josh a typical Mennonite kid met a girl."

"There's always a girl." Ennie shook her head.

"Quit interrupting and let me get through this."

"Forgive me. Continue."

"Bethany was a troubled young thing. Josh felt for her. He wanted to help. The kid managed to pull off an exorcism on his own. While all this was going on of course the two of them fell for each other. He was shunned. Excommunicated from the church. They married and had a daughter. Bethany wasn't strong. The baby was three when another demon took advantage of her weakness and made itself at home. That one killed her. Josh raised the baby on his own. About fifteen years ago he approached me. He told me he had seen the other side and knew I was something…other. He had been watching me. He offered his help. I took him up on it. He had true faith and was damn good at dealing with demons. A little over a year ago he was killed in action overseas. Before he left, deployed he asked me to be guardian to his grown daughter Faith. To keep an eye on her without her knowing. It was a moral responsibility, not a legal one. If it's Josh contacting you it must be Faith who's the target."

"What target? You need to catch me up."

"La Mech paid me a visit this morning. He told me flat out that he is here for payback. He plans to use anyone close to me to get what he wants."

"Bastard." Ennie snarled. "Isn't its Magnus now?"

Cain growled. "Are you shitting me?"

"I hear things." She shrugged. "So where do we start?"

"Right there." Cain pointed to Jami.

"The cutie behind the bar? She has been staring daggers at me since you sat down."

"She's in a mood," Cain grunted.

"Is that what you call it?" She smirked.

"For shit's sake Ennie can't you damn women ever say what you mean?"

"You are stump stupid when it comes to women. Let me spell it out for you. That beautiful young woman is in love with you dense ass."

"What?" Cain barked, floored by the thought.

"Shush, keep your voice down." She scolded. The bar was beginning to fill up and several heads turned at Cain's outburst.

Cain did as he was instructed, primarily because he lost his ability to speak.

Grey had arrived at last. After taking the time to bust his ass for being late Jami left him to take over behind the bar and started waiting tables.

Trotting over to where Cain and Ennie were seated she took a moment to give Ennie a good once over before asking for their order. "Can I get you two some refills?"

"Absolutely." Cain answered.

"Yes please." En answered, shooting a reproachful glance at Cain.

"Oh." Realizing why he had gotten "The "Look" he introduced them. "Jami this is an old friend of mine Ennie. En this is Jami Archer."

"Nice to meet you." Jami offered.

"Nice to meet you too." En offered in return, fully aware that the girl was only being polite. "I met your parents years ago. They're great people. I'm sorry I'll miss them on this trip."

The reference to her parents and the genuineness behind it managed to thaw Jami a bit. It's difficult to dislike someone when they are being thoughtful. "I'll be sure to tell them you asked about them. Be right back with your drinks."

Jami made her way to the bar. While her back was to them, En reached over and gave Cain a quick pinch on his arm.

"What the hell was that for?"

"Jami."

"Yes…"

"Open your hellish eyes and take a good look at the girl."

Cain turned his attention to Jami as she stood at the bar waiting for Grey to give her their drinks. She was five foot five, thick almost silvery ash blonde hair fell past her shoulder blades, very nicely rounded ass as well. He kept up the appraisal as she walked back toward them. The front view was damn fine too. Going by experience he would say high round perfect B cups.

Jami sat their drinks on the table. "You want me to keep you wet?" She asked.

"Huh." Cain dundered.

"You want me to keep them coming?"

"Yeah, that would be great."

Jami left them. She headed for a table of regulars coming in for their after-work relaxers.

"You got moves." En chuckled.

"Bite me. "Cain snapped.

En was watching Jami. Jami threw a quick glance back her face puzzled. When she saw En was looking she gave her a friendly smile.

"I'll be damned." En spoke up. "She's shielding us."

"She can't be she's mortal." Cain argued, frowning at En's second outrageous suggestion of the night.

"Are you seriously doubting ME about this? When she looked over here just now, she let her shield slip. I'm not sure SHE realizes what she is or what she's doing."

"No way. I would have sensed it by now."

"Sure, you would Mr. Observant. How have you survived all these centuries without me? I hate to break it to you big guy but she can see you. The real you. She's a Witch."

"Fuck."

"How do you want to handle this?" En asked.

"With a bottle of bourbon." He snarked.

"I can get on board with that. It's not what I meant though."

"We can't do anything right now. I'm sure she's keeping something from me. We're going to have to wait it out. We will corral her at closing at convince her to spill what she knows. She's got to be aware something is going on with Faith. She's trying to protect her. WE will have to make her see that is what we want too."

"Okay. It's your call. I'm just along for the ride."

CHAPTER FOUR

Two days of weather in the high sixties had the town folk flocking outdoors. As Katie Made her way to the bank, she dodged Big Wheels, scooters, and bicycles while waving to neighbors. Husbands mowed lawns while their wives swept porches and kept hawk eyes on their rambunctious offspring. Katie couldn't help but be cheerful. The town was jumping for joy after a long snowy winter making the short walk to the bank a pleasure rather than a chore.

Inside the bank, Katie made her deposit. She took a few minutes to chat with the teller about, what else, the weather.

She must have been inside talking longer than she thought. Stepping outside, she was surprised to see the sun had gone down. The crowded sidewalks were now barren.

Katie started the walk back to her apartment. Faith had given her a great deal on the three spacious rooms above the store. It wasn't much but it was cozy and Katie adored it. The living room had one wall that had been converted into bookshelves. So far, the bookshelves were only half full but Katie knew without a doubt she would see them filled. For now, the empty spaces were filled with bric-a-brac.

Turning onto the side street where the bookstore was located, she became aware of footsteps approaching behind her. Thinking it was a neighbor loathe to retreat indoors she turned to say hello. She was puzzled when she found herself alone on the sidewalk.

"Good grief." She mumbled to herself. "Now I'm hearing things." Katie continued walking but put a little more pep in her step. Again she heard the fump, fump, fump of heavy footsteps. This time they were more distinct.

It was full dark now. There were no street lamps on her short side street. Afraid to look back a second time she took off at a fast walk. Reaching the store, she bolted up the outside stairs to the safety of home. Her hand safely on the doorknob she braved a glance down to the street. It was empty. Her hands shook as she fumbled with her keys to unlock the door. Launching herself inside, she turned to re-lock the door and turn the deadbolt. She pulled the curtain on the small door window back a fraction to take one last quick peek. The street was empty and quiet.

"I've got to stop reading about Witches and Vampires." She chuckled nervously. "Yeah right. Like that's going to happen."

Katie switched on every light as she made a check of her apartment. After deciding all was clear she changed into her pajamas 'and made herself some hot chocolate and two slices of peanut butter toast. She curled up on the couch with her dinner and her new book. Katie lost herself in the drama of the paranormal. After a few pages, she forgot all about her earlier fears.

Katie's stalker kept himself out of sight blending into the shadows of an early-blooming willow tree.

Magnus had ordered him to watch the girl. It had become a snooze fest real fast. As far as he could tell all the girl did was work and read. She rarely even turned on the television. This chick had no life.

He had decided to rev things up. Tonight, he had wanted to scare her and he had. He lapped up the sound of her hard breathing, her frantic footsteps, and the hammering of her heartbeat. He grew aroused at the sound of her jangling keys as she struggled to lock herself away from him. It was a raw feast for his senses.

Fear had her turning on the lights before changing her clothes. The sight of her full breasts with their nipples hardened from adrenaline and her plump ass silhouetted through the sheer curtains made his mouth water. His borrowed body was throbbing with the desperate need to taste her fear as he tasted her body.

That bastard Magnus had forbidden him any direct contact. Tonight, he would have to hunt soon. He had quickly learned that inn these modern times it was easy to find a lonely woman who was willing for some time with a man. Yes, he would find a way to feed his beast.

    Faith walked in the front door letting the familiar comfort of home wash over her. The constant light from the television cast shadows across the living room. A commercial for a new wonder drug that had only a dozen side effects provided background noise. Jami insisted on the t.v. always be left on. They both came and went at odd hours. Jami didn't believe either one of them should walk into a dark quiet house.
    She went into the kitchen and dumped her keys and purse on the kitchen table. Opening the door of the ancient sunrise yellow refrigerator she grabbed a bottle of sweet tea and headed upstairs to her bedroom.
    Faith put her tea on the nightstand and flopped down on her bed. She loved her bedroom. She and Jami had helped each other decorate when they first moved into the rental house after college. Any person with taste would find the fFuschia curtains and comforter an affront to their senses. Motley Crue, Metallica, Avenged Sevenfold, and Papa Roach posters dominated the walls. The empty spaces were filled in with things like the Jack Daniels mirror her dad won her at the fair, feathered roach clips, and various other music paraphernalia. Jami referred to the room as the Aqua Net Palace. Tonight, Faith didn't notice her beloved decor. Her mind was still occupied with the mystery of the stranger she encountered as she was leaving the Monument. The man had seemed so familiar. The best explanation she could come up with was that they had crossed paths at Archers. Over the years she had seen a lot of faces pass through. Their small town was the Antiques capital of the U.S. Literally thousands of out of town folks flooded in on summer weekends. Yes, she decided, that had to be the explanation.
    Satisfied she had solved the puzzle she pushed herself up off the bed. Putting on comfy pajama bottoms and a tank top she set off for the kitchen to forage for sustenance.
    Ten minutes later Faith was sitting cross-legged on the second-hand crushed velvet lime green sofa in front of the t.v. A paper plate

balanced on her lap held half a roast beef sandwich leftover from the night before. Faith nibbled as she paged through the morning paper. A story on the second page caught her eye. As she read her stomach started to churn. Her appetite gone she set the barely eaten sandwich on the coffee table.

This would be the last one she told herself as she made plans to take off in the morning. Picking up her phone she called Katie and asked her to take care of the store again tomorrow. Katie was thrilled about the extra hours. She was saving every penny in the hopes of starting college in the fall.

Katie's father had been the notorious town drunk. After years of abuse Katie's mother up and vanished. Cain and Pop Archer were discussing it one night and Faith had overheard. She could tell that they were concerned Katie would become her father's new punching bag. Faith had pushed herself into their conversation. She came up with the idea of giving Katie a job and the small apartment over the store. That night escorted by the two men they knocked on the door of the rundown trailer Katie called home. The girl jumped at Faith's offer. She packed up her few belongings and left with Faith and Pop. Cain had stayed behind and Faith had never questioned it. The next day, Katie's father was gone. No one spoke about it. To the town, it was good riddance.

Faith loved Katie like a kid sister. They were devoted to each other and the store.

Ten o'clock rolled around with Faith snuggled under her comforter. A paperback hung limply from her fingers. Her eyes were heavy. She drowsily laid her book on the nightstand and switched off the lamp. Then, enter sandman, she was dreaming.

"Finally," Magnus growled impatiently. He had been watching and waiting under Faith's bedroom window for hours. He had been furious after seeing her reaction to him this afternoon. Tonight, as she slept, he would have to play the tender lover and banish her fear of him. He hid in the shadows until she was in a deep sleep then materialized himself into her bedroom. Smoothly he laid himself next to her slender body. He was quite adept at slipping himself into women's beds as well as their dreams. He placed a hand over her eyes willing himself into her dreams. He created the dream world to his best advantage. With a whisper, he called her to him.

Faith was lying on the softest bed she ever felt. Even in her dreams, the fact that she was nude brought a blush to her cheeks. Her legs were tangled in white silk sheets. Loving the feel of the silk she twisted her body enjoying the erotic sensation against her bare skin.

She went still as her eyes locked with a pair of golden ones fringed with impossibly long dark lashes. She lowered her eyes to look at his face. He was beautiful. Truly the man of her dreams. There was no fear as she lay totally vulnerable with him. Just the opposite. She felt warm, safe, and protected.

"Tell me your name." She whispered, lost in his incredibly hypnotic eyes.

"I am Magnus."

"Why are you here?"

"I came to you because you need me. You're hurting. Your pain called out to me."

"We've been together like this before, haven't we?"

"Many times, my darling." Magnus crooned, stroking her hair.

"Is this real or am I dreaming?"

"It's as real as you want it to be." He murmured. Magnus dropped her hair, he ran his hand down her neck to the top of her breast. "You're my girl, Faith. I'll never leave you. I want to free you."

"Free me?" Faith shivered, curious about his words but needing his hand to go farther.

"Free you from the cruelty you fight against. To take the burden of your morality away. Free you to enjoy the pleasure only I can give you." Magnus cupped her breast. He rubbed his thumb over her hard pink nipple. She moaned moving into him wanting more. Needing to feel his touch on her skin.

"Life is more than pleasure." she groaned, hating herself for arguing when all she really wanted to do was let herself go, let him give her the pleasure he offered.

"You've given enough. Let someone else shoulder the responsibility. Let go and allow me to take care of you. Don't you deserve some pleasure?"

Before she could reply he silenced her with a kiss. He was gentle at first but quickly the kisses deepened demanding more from her. Faith felt her body growing hot. She was melting for him. She cried out in frustration when he pulled his mouth away. The cry turned into a moan of satisfaction as he took her breast into his warm mouth and began to suck teasing her nipple with his tongue. His hand moved up the inside of her thigh. Faith let her legs fall apart giving him access to the place throbbing for his touch. She groaned his name burying her hands in his hair. Magus chuckled. He slowly ran his finger up and down between her moist lips. She thrust her hips against his hand wanting it harder.

"That's it its Faith. Take the pleasure only I can give you." Magnus began to work her harder building up the friction while she worked herself against his fingers.

The world spun out of control. Faith bit down on her lip to halt the scream as an orgasm tore through her.

The sound of the front door closing viciously ripped Faith from her dream.

Magnus hissed, ready to kill over the ill-timed interruption. Knowing he would ruin everything if Faith woke up to find a fresh kill corpse, he resisted the urge. Snarling he flashed himself out of the house.

Faith woke sluggish and drained. It had only been a dream. She was alone in her bed. She tried to recall the face of the man in her dreams. No matter how hard she tried he remained elusive.

The disorientation began to dissipate. Her head becoming less logy, clearer she remembered what woke her. She heard the front door. Her alarm clock glowed 12:10. Jami would still be at work. Shit, someone was in the house. A jolt of fear induced adrenaline shot into her. Her mind instantly returning to the stranger from that afternoon.at -

The heavy sound of the footsteps told her she was correct. It was not Jami coming up the stairs. She groped blindly under the bed until she latched onto the Louisville Slugger that had been her father's. She tiptoed to the door and listened as the footsteps got closer. They halted abruptly on the other side of the door.

The flight or fight reflex kicked in. She chose to fight. Grabbing the doorknob, she wailed a rebel yell. Pouncing through the door with the bat swinging Faith went on the offensive. The bat met flesh with a meaty trunk and a deep bass howl of pain.

"Damn it Faith! What the fuck!"

"Grey." Faith choked in recognition. "What are you doing outside my bedroom?"

"Getting the shit beat out of me obviously."

"Funny." She snapped. "Really, why are you here?"

"Jami sent me to check on you. She's been trying to get a hold of you all day." He grumbled.

Grey's handsome face, a masculine version of his sisters, was set in a scowl. The irritated look reminded Faith that she had just whacked him.

"You're hurt." she squealed.

"No shit. You just hit me with a freakin' bat. Give me that damned thing." He barked, grabbing the offensive weapon from her shaky grasp.

"Oh, hell Grey, I'm so sorry. Go sit on my bed and I'll get you some ice for your arm." Faith insisted as she turned on the light for him.

"Thanks." He grumbled.

Grey entered the room taking a seat on the sea of fluffy pink bedding. The decor gelled perfectly with the girl he knew, but she was a woman now. Though he couldn't remember the exact moment he noticed the change he could vividly recall the way it had affected him. Somehow, he had gone from his sister's giggly friend to a grown woman he couldn't seem to take his eyes off. He dated. He had even had one serious relationship. It didn't last. For him, no one else could measure up to Faith.

She returned with an ice pack. Grey banished the forbidden thoughts from his mind. He had grown accustomed to turning them off at will.

"Here we go." Faith spoke tenderly as she gently placed the ice pack to his bicep. "Do you think I broke the bone? Do you want to go to the emergency room?"

"I'm not a fucking pussy Faith. It's not broken. I'm just going to have a hell of a bruise."

Looking at her miserable face Grey silently chastised himself. He shouldn't have snapped at her like that. He tried to soften his words with a joke." Good thing for me you always sucked at baseball."

Faith burst into tears. Grey felt helpless. He took the bag of ice from her hand and wrapped an arm around her. "I'm sorry I snapped at you. Really, I'll be fine. No permanent damage was done."

His body went rigid when she laid her head on his chest. He had to force himself to relax and breathe. Resting his chin on the top of her head he inhaled the subtle fragrance of strawberry -scented shampoo. If being attacked brought her this close he wished she had beat the ever-loving shit out of him. Visions of him lying on her bed while she tended to his wounds floated through his mind. Cursing himself for his dirty man thoughts he wiped them from his mind continuing to hold her until her tears became soft snuffles.

"Forgive me. First I hit you now I'm trying to drown you." She sniffled.

"I'll dry."

"You're a great guy. You know that?"

"Yeah, That's me. Mr. Nice guy." Grey sighed. "Hey, look at me." He tipped her face up to his. Felling dense as he was, realized her tears were about more than just his sore arm. "Do you want to talk about it?"

"Nah, it's just been one of those days."

"You know you're not alone. I love you. All of us Archers love you. We're here if you need us." Grey couldn't believe how stupid he had been letting that "I love you." slip out. He caught a lucky break in that she didn't seem to catch his goof.

Faith kissed his cheek enjoying the clean male scent of him. A smile tugged at the corner of her mouth as she noticed him blushing. "I love you guys too. I promise the next time I need a shoulder to cry on you be the first one I call."

"I'm going to hold you to that." Grey reached over to grab a tissue and handed it to her.

"A little too late. I've ruined your shirt."

"Believe it or not I own more than one shirt." He teased.

"So anyway, uh, you said J sent you over because she was worried about me."

"She just said she couldn't reach you. She was having one of her feelings. She wanted to run home herself but I didn't want her out alone. She's probably losing her mind by now. I better get back and let her know you're okay."

"Thanks, Grey."

"No problem." He stood up and went to the door. "I almost forgot. I was ordered to tell you not to leave the house until Jami gets home and talks to you."

"Good grief. She can be so bossy."

"That's one way of putting it. Take care okay." He gave her a wink and left.

Faith listened until she heard the front door close and lock. Crawling back under her covers Faith knew it would be hours a while before she could sleep again that night.

Pacing in an alley across the street Magnus cursed his luck. Thwarted by a damn interfering human. He watched as the asshole jogged off down the street. He was reconsidering his decision about not killing the man. He had eavesdropped on the conversation. It was obvious the boy had feelings for his little victim. Better to use that. And he would find a way. The more pain he inflicted on Cain the sweeter the victory.

The quiet of the night was broken by the sound of someone approaching. In a movement so fast the recipient never saw it coming Magnus had his accomplice by the throat shaking him like a dog with a rat in its mouth." Where have you been maggot?" he snarled, releasing his hold. The demon fell to his knees.

Hissing as it got to its feet he croaked. "I didn't see him leave. I followed as soon as I saw he was gone."

Magnus balled his hand into a fist. He belted his conspirator in the side of the head relishing the snapping sound that accompanied violent act. "I was so close. Her innocence was offered up to me for the taking. That filthy human showed up and ruined everything."

"What's the rush? I thought you wanted to take your time? Enjoy the taste of her sweet flesh. Prolong the pleasure." He drugs his tongue across his lips, closing his eyes as he imagined taking her himself.

"You sorry excuse for a demon. Who are you to council me? Look at yourself. You have no control over your own perversions." Magnus snarled.

The demon shrugged. "It's one girl. What's the big deal?"

"This is about more than one girl idiot."

"You can't be serious about going after Cain. You know you can't kill him. Lucifer will have your balls in a basket. Then there's the Bloody Seven with their fucking swords of Solomon. They don't like you screwing with the order of the universe. I happen to like this head I'm wearing. I'm growing attached to it. You dragging us into a gang war between Heaven and Hell is not what I signed up for."

For an idiot, the lesser demon had a strong sense of self-preservation.

"Calm yourself. I have no intention of losing my head to an assassin's blade either. Just do as I say. Follow me and that body you've become so fond of will be yours for the keeping."

"I'm listening." The demon's eyes grew bright with anticipation.

"I'mWe're going to break the little bitch. I've got her on the edge. All we've got to do is give her a little nudge to push her over. When she's falling apart her Dream Man will be waiting to pick up the pieces."

"What's the plan?"

Magnus gave his ally a slow sinister grin. "I'm going to give you what you've been begging for. Do you think you can handle it without screwing up?"

The demon nodded eagerly to Magnus. "It will be my pleasure."

CHAPTER FIVE

"Damn it's been a long night," Jami grumbled to herself as she finished the night's receipts and locked up her mother's office.

After relieving her worries over Faith, Grey had spent the night behind the bar whining about his boo-boo. She was disappointed that she hadn't been there to watch Faith use her brother for batting practice. It served him right for being late and leaving her to pick up the slack. Then Micah had fallen behind in the kitchen. The horn dog had been too busy reeling in some newbie blonde who caught his eye. She loved them both but damn they could piss her off.

Cain had been watching her all night. She normally would have been thrilled with the attention but tonight he had been looking at her like he had never seen her before. Every time she caught him staring, he would quickly shift his attention back to Ennie.

There was something about Cain's friend. She was sweet and friendly every time they spoke. Even so the vibe Jami was getting from the woman was giving her a case of the heebie-jeebies.

Jami left the office. She found Grey doing a final wipe down of the bar. The neon lights advertising various brands of beer were unplugged for the night. Only the lights directly over the bar remained lit. Finally, it was time to walk out the door, go home, and have a talk with her roommate.

Grey and Micah shared an apartment over the bar. Since Jami only lived down the street, one of them always took the time to walk her home. They lived in a small town but didn't feel that any woman should be walking alone at four in the morning. Especially not their baby sister.

"You ready to go sis?" Grey asked.

"You're damaged. Why isn't Micah walking me? Did he take off without finishing the kitchen?"

"Uh, as far as I know, he's still getting busy in there," Grey explained, while trying to usher his sister toward the door.

Jami could tell when she was trying to be hurried along. She knew the two of them were up to something. Her sibling radar was beeping like a car alarm. The kitchen lights were turned off. She fixed her eyes on Grey. "Micah!" she shouted, looking around her brother who was determined to block her view.

Micah came stumbling out of the dark kitchen with the blonde girl. She was rookie drunk. Surprise, surprise. Her shirt had vanished at some point leaving her boobs to bobble freely as she tried to coil herself around Micah.

Jami's jaw dropped. Grey turned quickly so he wouldn't laugh in her face and make himself a target for her soon -to -be unleashed wrath.

"For shit's sake." She bellowed. "Couldn't you have at least waited until you got the tart upstairs?"

Micah went stone still. Jami's comment managed to get the tart's attention. She turned to face Jami. She put her hands on her hips. Her face looking ridiculously offended. Either she forgot she was topless or she just didn't care. "Who you callin' slut." She garbled drunkenly.

"If the pastry... oops.... pasty fits..." Jami snarked.

Grey could handle only so much. He erupted into whooping laughter. Earning him a blistering glare from his sister.

The outraged tart made a lunge for Jami. Micah grunted, grabbing his women for the night by the arm.

Grey held his gut. He was doubled over in unrestrained mirth as he tried to decide which was swinging faster the girl's fists or her tits.

"Bitch." The girl squealed. "I dare you to come over here and say that."

Micah whispered in the girl's ear. She was too far gone to care. "Come on J" Micah implored.

Her brother trying to save his tart only added fuel to Jami's fire. She started forward only to be impeded by Grey. She slugged him on his sore arm.

"Dammit J" He yowled, rubbing his aching arm. "That was a cheap shot."

"She called me a bitch." Jami seethed.

Deciding things had gone far enough Cain stepped out of the darkness.

"Excuse me, children." He interrupted. All four of the participants froze. "Amusing as this has been, I suggest you end it here before someone draws blood."

"You're in on this too." Jami gaped. "When did this become a strip club?"

"I was sitting quietly with a friend enjoying a drink and some conversation." He replied.

The blonde simmered down when she got a look at Cain. She was sizing him up and happy with what she was seeing. She was too drunk to realize she was further inciting Jami to violence.

Cain noticed Jami suddenly go ramrod stiff. She was ready to pounce. Cain moved closer taking her gently by the arm. "Grey, why don't you help your brother escort the young lady upstairs?"

"Young lady my ass." Jami snipped.

Micah opened his mouth to speak. A sharp look from Cain kept him silent.

Grey started toward the pair. The girl dismissed Cain as unattainable and turned her eyes to Grey. She smirked like a cat being gifted with two bowls of cream.

"Yeah, bro why don't you help. I'm sure it wouldn't be the first time."

Gray looked at his sister with disbelief.

"Go," Cain ordered him. "I'll get her home."

"Thanks, man." Grey nodded to Cain who was valiantly trying to keep an annoyed adult look on his face.

Grey rushed off not daring a backward glance. The door closed behind the three of them.

Jami looked to Cain. "Why am I my brother's keeper?" She groaned.

"I asked that same question myself once," Cain answered quietly.

Jami did a zombie walk to the bar muttering to herself as she went. "What else? What the hell else could possibly happen? This entire day has been surreal."

Ennie had been waiting in the shadows. Now she followed Cain over to the bar.

Jami automatically placed three shot glasses in front of them. Reaching to a shelf behind her she took down a bottle of Jack Daniels and poured. Nodding at Cain and Ennie she took her shot.

"Why do I have the feeling that the two of you are about to make my night even better?"

"ESP?" En quipped.

"Yeah oookay," Jami answered shooting En a wtf look.

"Come on J." Cain urged. "Chill. I want to introduce you to my friend."

"You already did." Jami frowned.

"Not officially," Cain said slyly. "I call her Ennie. Most people know her as W.O. Rodne."

En flashed a cheeky grin and waggled her fingers.

"No way." Jami gushed. "I love you. I've read all your books. No wonder I got weird vibes from you. I can't believe I didn't recognize you from the pictures on your books."

"I get that a lot."

"Pardon?"

"Never mind. It's just nice to meet a fan. Most people call me a crackpot."

"Seriously? I think you're amazing."

"DoSo, you believe in the paranormal?" En lightly prodded.

"I'm not sure but your books make me want to believe," Jami answered honestly.

"Excellent. That will make this so much easier."

"Pour us another round J we're going to need it," Cain advised.

"I knew it. Okay, spill." She ordered as she poured the shots.

"She's very blunt isn't she," Ennie said to Cain her voice laced with approval.

"Blunt, opinionated, feisty…" Cain rattled off.

"Enough." Jami silenced him. "You're stalling."

"Alright then." En plowed forward. "You're a witch."

Jami's mouth opened and closed. No words came out only a series of squeaks and grunts.

"No." En held her hand up before Jami could argue. "Don't sputter at me. It takes one to know one."

Cain watched amused as Jami's face underwent a series of comical contortions.

"So, what you're telling me is that you really are a witch. Your books are real." Jami got out when she, at last, remembered how to speak.

"I am, they are, and so are you." Ennie grabbed a cardboard coaster from a stack on the bar. "Do you have a pen?"

Jami reached under the bar and brought out a red sharpie then handed her a cardboard coaster.

Ennie took the marker. She wrote her pen name in all capital letters. She then turned the coaster to Jami so she would be reading it correctly.

"What do you see?" En asked, her fingertip pointing to the coaster.

"Your name."

En waved her hand above the coaster. "Now what do you see?"

Jami got goosebumps as the letters on the coaster started to shift and reform themselves before her eyes. When the letters aligned again, they read W.O. Endor.

"That did not just happen." Denied Jami, who did not want to believe what she had just witnessed.

Cain remained silent. He knew he could not influence her. Jami would have to make the decision to believe or not on her own.

Ennie knew she was going to argue. She looked at the whiskey bottle. The bottle floated into the air then proceeded to pour three perfect shots before returning to its place on the bar.

Jami watched the entire exhibition without blinking. She looked first to the glasses then to the bottle. "Fuck it." She picked up the bottle and tossed her head back. Thankfully there was a bar stool beside her. She planted herself on it.

En looked to Cain for help. He shrugged.

"W.O. Endor." Jami laughed. "Endor, what the Witch of Endor was your great grandma or something?"

"Cut it out. You know very well who I am. Just like you see the truth when you look at Cain." En demanded.

If Jami had not already been seated, she would have hit the floor. "How did you know?"

"Like recognizes like. You could shield yourself from Cain but the instant you let your shield slip I sensed you. I taught Cain magic but he wasn't born a witch like you and I. You also kept your power hidden. That's why he never caught on to you."

"This isn't real. Someone Roofied me. I am having a drug-induced hallucination. All I have to do is snap myself out of it." Jami began shaking her head. She closed her eyes and pinched herself on both arms. She told herself when she opened her eyes, she would be at home in bed laughing over her bizarre dream.

Very slowly Jami opened her eyes. "Aw shit. Your still here." She whined.

"You done?" Cain asked her, mildly amused by her antics.

"I'm thinking about it." She snapped, knocking back one of the magically poured shots.

Cain reached out and took her hand. She tried to pull away but he wouldn't allow it. He looked her in the eyes. "I've never known you to run from anything. More often than not you run headlong into trouble. We don't have time for denial. I need you to be the fearless woman I've always known you to be."

So much for staying out of it. He could tell she had accepted the truth she was just hell-bent on being stubborn and now was not the time.

Jami melted at his words of praise. She turned to Ennie determined to deal with this new reality.

"Do you agree you're a witch?" En demanded.

"I never considered it. Even after I read your books I thought, psychic maybe. I've always had these feelings, I guess you could call them. My parents called it overactive imagination. The older I got they started getting upset with me. I learned how to ignore it. Eventually, it just shut off completely."

"Okay, that's a start. You are way above the level of a psychic. You felt something from me all along didn't you? You just didn't understand what you were feeling."

"I did feel something. It gave me the willies."

"That would be the feeling." En laughed. "Most true born witches are solitary creatures. We don't care for other witches invading our space unless they are invited. Unless you're me of course. When I show up to the party arrive, everyone gets out of my way."

"Why?"

"I'm the oldest most powerful witch in existence. Nobody wants to screw with me."

Jami could believe that. "Alrighty." She gulped. "And Cain?"

Cain turned away. He had no desire to see her acceptance of him turn to fear.

Ennie understood her old friend. She spoke for him. "Come on girl. You went to Sunday school. You've known since you were a little girl. Cain Adamson."

"One Immortal maybe. Two is a little too much." Jami's voice dripped sarcasm.

Cain turned back to her. The truth was literally in his eyes.

"Of course. Cain Adamson. Living in Adamstown. You even named your house Eden." Jami's voice grew shrill. "I "I developed a cynical sense of humor over the millennia." He smirked.

"And your bff is the Witch of Endor."

"That about sums it up." He agreed.

"And I'm a witch."

"You are."

"I need another drink." Jami took another shot.

"Why don't we take this somewhere more comfortable? We've still got a lot to talk about." En suggested.

"Shit. I need to get home. We can all go there." Jami offered. She couldn't believe she forgot about Faith. With all the freaky shit she just got nailed with her best friend had slipped her mind. Guilt slumped her shoulders. How could she be such a shitty friend when Faith needed her?

"Cain will you grab my bags, please. They are over by the table." En asked.

Cain handed her the keys to his car. "You two get in the car. I'll grab the bags and lock up."

Jami handed him her keys.

"Let's go." En started for the door. "I'll explain how Faith fits into this on the way."

"What?" Jami yelped.

Grey fell asleep with his headphones on. The sound of Slash playing guitar never failed to drown out the sound of Micah's sessions that pounded through the walls.

He was dreaming about Faith. Not an unusual occurrence. When he woke up in the morning, he would feel guilty about it. For now, he was riding it out with a whole lot of Hell Yeah.

His sleeping mind had her laid out on the pink bed in her room. She reclined on the pillows bare-breasted. Her only covering a lacy white thong.

She ran her tongue along her full pink lips. One hand was behind her head while the other lightly stroke the delicate patch of skin just about her thong.

"I want you." She purred, giving him one hell of a cock throb.

Grey crawled onto the bed with her. She pulled him close sealing their lips in a hot kiss. Grey was crazy with lust as she twined her legs around his, rubbing her thinly covered crotch against his hip. He cupped a breast kneading the pliant flesh as he thumbed her hard nipple.

Grey released her mouth. She buried her hands in his hair pushing his head down. He began kissing his way to her breasts. Faith moaned wanting more. She reached between them taking his cock into her hand. She began to stroke him. Grey loved the way she was running the show. He was just as impatient as she was. Feeling his way down her silken skin he slipped his hand inside the tiny scrap of lace. His finger went right between her shaved lips rubbing until she was wet and ready.

Grey eagerly pulled her thong to one side. Faith guided his cock to where she was dying for him to go.

"Wake up!" A deep voice shouted in Grey's ear.

"Waaa..." Gray grunted.

"Wake up asshole." Blared through the headphones.

Grey's eyes snapped open.

He looked down. Holy shit. Micah's Ho was under him and he had been about to fuck her. Her drunk bloodshot eyes leered at him with hunger.

He jerked the headphones, throwing them off like they were on fire. Jumping up he grabbed his jeans from where he had thrown them on the floor and pulled them on to cover himself from her rapt gaze. Although now his hard -on was nothing more than a shriveled turtle.

"Out." He snarled. His hand raised with the thumb pointing to the door.

"But we were having fun." She whined. "Come back to bed. Let's finish what we started."

"I would rather do it myself. Now get the hell out."

The girl shot him a hostile look over her shoulder as she stumbled drunkenly out of the room. "Your loss." she sighed over her shoulder as she went through the open door.

Grey grabbed a towel he had thrown over a chair earlier in the day. As he headed for the shower, he noticed the headphones where they had landed on the floor.

"Nah." He mumbled to himself. There was no way his headphones woke him up in time to save him from a terrible mistake. It was just part of the dream, right?

CHAPTER SIX

This morning Faith kept on going as she sneaked past Jami's door. She felt like a rotten Judas about doing it this way. She would obediently take her lumps later when her friend gives her a well-deserved ass chewing. She tried to assuage her guilty conscience by leaving a note on the kitchen table for Jami to find when she stumbled down for her morning coffee.

These restless nights were draining her. She couldn't remember the last time she had a good night's sleep. She was dragging so bad that each step she took felt like a mile long-mile-long hike uphill.

Still, as tired as she was, she allowed herself only a single cup of coffee to get moving. According to her GPS she had a three -hour drive ahead of her. No way was she swilling coffee when her only bathroom option was a skeevy rest area along the turnpike.

Her destination was a community park. After reading the story in the newspaper she felt compelled to make this one last pilgrimage. According to what she had read a group of girls had brutally attacked a friend. She had been stabbed multiple times and rolled into a drainage ditch. An early morning jogger discovered the girl when he heard her weak cries. The Good Samaritan called 911 then remained with the girl until police and EMT's arrived. She was now in critical condition in the local hospital.

Faith was at a loss when she tried to imagine what could possibly incite a group of children twelve and thirteen-year-olds to do something so horribly cruel.

The police now had the six girls responsible in custody. Their explanation was beyond the boundaries of stupidity. They read a book of supposed magic spells. The girls lied to their parents telling them they were at a sleepover. They all went to the park and drew straws. The short straw was the victim. They believed if they all took a turn at stabbing their friend under the full moon, spoke a bunch of Mumbo jumbos, and left the victim alone they could return in the morning to find their friend completely healed. Obviously, they had been mistaken. More like deluded.

Faith had reached her destination. She let out a sigh of relief. Nothing was more mind -numbing than the Pennsylvania Turnpike. The parking area was nearly filled. The place looked like every other small town park Faith had ever seen. There were swings, monkey bars, and sliding boards mingling with picnic tables, benches, and a basketball court. The only visible sign of tragedy was a group of people clustered around an area cordoned off with yellow police issue crime scene tape.

As Faith approached several people gathered parted the way for her. A spot had been designated for gifts, flowers, or cards. Someone had also erected a stand filled with candles their wicks wavering in the soft breeze. Before hitting the park road, Faith had stopped and bought a teddy bear and a bouquet of daisies. She placed them with the gifts left by others. She lit a candle and offered a silent prayer for the poor girl's recovery. Faith turned to leave but was held back by a hushed, "Thank you."

Faith turned to stare into the red -rimmed eyes of a stout care-worn woman. The lady smiled weakly. Something about her made Faith think of homemade Toll House cookies and puppies adorned in hand -knitted sweaters. Her short grey hair resembled an unintentional Einstein do. Her pale face was puffy from crying. In her hand, she held a wad of damp tissues.

"No need to thank me." Faith responded. "Do you know her?"

"She's my niece. I'm Amy." She tucked the tissues into her pocket and held out her hand.

Faith took the hand she offered. "Nice to meet you, Amy. I'm Faith. I'm terribly sorry to hear about your niece. I'm sure she will come through this."

"She will." Amy agreed, her voice filled with conviction. "She's a strong girl."

The sharp sound of raised voices and slamming car doors drew their attention.

"That's Jessica Landry from the news." Amy squeaked.

A voluptuous brunette was standing beside a white SUV with the news channels logo emblazoned across the side. At her side, a cameraman stood pointing in their direction while he spoke with the anchorwoman. She shook her head in agreement with whatever it was he said then turned to check her makeup in the rear view mirror. Assured that she looked spectacular she turned on her spiked heels and began walking toward Faith and Amy.

"Your right. "Faith agreed. She would know that face anywhere. Jami was a news junkie. The Five was her favorite program. She dvr'd it every day so she could watch it while she had her morning coffee. Jami constantly criticized the local news anchor calling her a K.G. wannabe. She was certain Jessica Landry was on a mission to replace Kimberly Guilfoyle.

Amy began frantically trying to pull herself together. Faith was about to offer her a hairbrush when they were approached by a… cowboy.

Lancaster County Pennsylvania is a rural area. There is an abundance of Amish folk with their horse and buggies jamming up traffic. Farms were abundant in the area. Cowboys…not so much. Cowboys as hot as this one, hell no.

"Excuse me, ladies." He interrupted, whipping off a tan Stetson and revealing a head of white -blonde hair that women could only dream of achieving with a box of L'oreal. "Would either of you happen to be the owner of a blue Chevy Cavalier?"

"Me." Faith chirped. "I drive a blue Cavalier."

"I thought you might want to know your lights are on."

Faith's face flushed red with embarrassment. "Thank you."

"You're welcome." He smiled.

Faith felt her jaw drop. Her blush burned deeper. With a smile like that this guy should be doing toothpaste commercials. The man was just too good -looking to be believed.

"I better go." Faith told Amy. "I'll be thinking of you and your family."

Amy smiled wanly. Her attention was focused on the approaching newswoman and her cameraman.

Faith looked around for the cowboy. When she didn't see him, she assumed he disappeared into the crowd. She trotted off to her car hoping her battery wasn't dead.

Cain, Jami, and Ennie entered the girl's rental house on Main Street. At first glance, everything looked as it should be. Jami maneuvered her guests into the living room. The television was on as always. A local weatherman standing beside a big yellow sunshine was predicting sixty-nine degrees and sunny skies. Jami instructed Cain and Ennie to help themselves to whatever food and beverages they could find in the kitchen.

She rushed up the stairs barreling into Faith's room calling out for her to get her butt up. The bed was empty. She went down the hall to check the bathroom. No luck there. One last place. Her own bedroom. Jami did not really expect to find her there so she was not surprised when she found the room unoccupied. Panic took over. She tore down the stairs to tell the others that Faith was MIA.

Cain stepped out of the kitchen as Jami hit the bottom of the stairs. He held a bottle of Budweiser in one hand and a piece of paper in the other. He caught Jami just before she plowed into him.

"Slow down Flash." He warned.

"Faith's gone." She blurted.

"Yes, she is." He agreed. "I know where to find her."

"You do? Is that one of your superpowers? You know where to find people." Jami was in awe.

"No. I found a note on the kitchen table. Here." He handed her a scrap of paper.

Jami rolled her eyes at Cain and read the note. "She's out trying to save the world again. She must have left early. Damn, what do we do now?"

En walked up and plucked the note from Jami's fingers. "It says she's at a park. There will be people around. Magnus won't try anything there."

"Are you sure?"

"Pretty sure." En nodded.

"Gee En, the next time I need reassurance you're the first person I'll call."

"Nothing is ever certain. I do know this. He's an Incubus. He has got to be alone with her to take what he wants. He's got to feed off her to weaken her. He needs privacy for that. Only when Faith willingly sleeps with him can his evil completely corrupt her. After she goes to the dark side, all of the good she's destined to do will never come to pass. She will be ruined. He will kill her or have her kill herself then he will drag her to Hell as a prize for his Master."

"Uh, I'm just going to try to call her again." Jami dialed, as she paced the living room then redialed and paced some more. Cain and En sat down watching as her frustration grew.

"She has her phone on ignore. It keeps dumping me into voicemail. This is my fault. She's avoiding me so I don't raise hell with her again."

En decided a distraction was necessary. "Since you can't reach her, we may as well get busy around here. Cain, where is the salt?"

"In the kitchen. I put it on the table."

"I'll get it." Jami volunteered. She returned with three round blue canisters of Morton's Salt. "What's all the salt for? Are we going to make Margaritas and pray to Jimmy Buffet to scare away the Boogeyman?"

En grinned at Jami's smart mouth. "We are going to salt all of the doors and windows. Salt is pure. We use it to repel impure things. Demons cannot cross a salt line."

"Cool, but what about Cain? Is he pure or impure or what?"

Cain grinned roguishly "Or what."

Jami's heart skipped a beat. When he smiled, which was a rare sight, she swore he was so handsome her knees turned to jelly.

En ignored him. "He has been invited in. That gives him immunity." En explained. "Listen Jami, you need to be taking mental notes on all of this. As soon as we're done with the salting I plan to unlock the powers you've been suppressing. You're going to have to learn how to protect yourself and the people you care about."

"Yes, Ma'am."

They made quick work of the downstairs. Jami listened as En gave her a simple but informative lesson. She ended the speech with a warning that the salt line must not be broken.

Cain entered Faith's room first. He halted as he reached the bed. His eyes burned with rage.

Ennie followed him into the room. "Spirits save us!" She yelped. "I've gone blind."

Jami grabbed her arm. "What is it?"

"I've never seen this much pink in my life."

Oh," For pity's sake." Jami sighed.

"Excuse me." Cain snapped. "En, do you smell it?"

She nodded. "The brimstone. Yes, he's been here. More than once. The smell is strong."

"What do you mean he's been here?" Jami questioned. "What the hell is brimstone?"

En answered her second question first. "Brimstone is the Chanel No. 5 of Hell. It's only discernible to supernatural beings. Which you are. You should be able to smell it. Close your eyes and take a deep breath."

Jami did as she was told. "Ack." She wrinkled her nose. "I think I've got it. It's kind of like burning rubber that has been soaked in acid and put out with sulfur."

"That's the smell. Remember it. That is the scent of a demon. Recognizing it could save your life someday."

"I can't believe it's been here. In my house. I think I'm going to be sick."

"I'm going to work in another room," Cain spoke through clenched teeth. His anger was being held back by a single thin thread. The presence of Magnus in this house with the girls was inciting in him the need to do violence. The driving desire to tear the bastard apart for this violation made him furious with himself for not killing the demon earlier when he had the chance.

Ennie and Jami had only one window left to salt but neither one of them we're anxious to intrude on Cain. They had seen the look on his face. They could sense he needed some time to rein in his anger.

"Is the salt going to work if he has already been here?" Jami asked En.

"It will essentially revoke his invitation. Someone would have to break the salt line and renew the invitation."

"Do you think he has already gotten to her?" Jami's voice quivered with fear for her friend. "Are we too late?"

En rushed to hug her. "No baby I don't think she's gone dark. She went to do something good today. She wouldn't still care about people if her soul were completely compromised."

Jami slumped in En's arms. Relief washed through her as she considered the wisdom of En's words.

Cain poked his head in the door. He told them the rest of the upstairs was finished. With the salting done it was time for them to do the unlocking of Jami's powers.

Faith stepped into a time-worn Mom and Pop Diner. The stools around the counter were dulled metallic bases topped with red vinyl seats. She chose one at the end of the counter away from the few other customers. Faith took a seat at the chipped and scratched counter and waited for the waitress. Taking her phone out of her purse she tried to call Jami again. Shaking her head, she silently cursed her best friend. Jami once again must have forgotten to charge her phone.

A cheerful middle-aged waitress appeared. She wore the stereotypical pink polyester uniform and white apron. She placed a napkin with utensils rolled inside on the counter along with a glass of water sans ice then handed Faith a plastic-bound menu. Sally, according to her nametag, informed Faith she would be back to take her order.

True to her word Sally filled a few cups of coffee for waiting customers then made her way back to Faith. Faith ordered a club sandwich and a glass of iced tea. Sally bounced off to put in her order. While Faith waited for her food to arrive she took the opportunity to use the ladies' room.

Faith returned to find a seat next to her occupied. She glanced at the newcomer. He turned to her and said hello. Faith was chilled to her marrow. It was him again. He was flesh and blood and sitting right next to her with his male model looks and his designer clothes. Faith was certain he was not a regular at the diner. She wanted to dart but found herself immobile. Suddenly she had vivid images of him from her dream the night before playing in her head. She was positive he could see her thoughts written plainly on her face. She quickly lowered her eyes and prayed her face was not red as a can of coke from the blush she could feel creeping up her cheeks.

"You're very attractive when you blush." He complimented her.

"Um...I'm sorry. Do I know you?" She asked, daring to look back at him.

"Don't be sorry. I believe we've crossed paths a few times though we've never officially met. My name is Magnus."

"I'm Faith."

"I know. I've seen you at Archers." He confessed. "I asked about you."

Faith tensed once again ready to bolt. Her uneasiness growing at his admission.

Magnus picked up on her fear. He captured her eyes and held them. "Don't panic. I'm not a stalker." He could feel her tension vanish as he willed her fear away. "Any man who sees a beautiful woman and does not attempt to discover her identity isn't much of a man as far as I'm concerned. Not only are you physically beautiful but you seem to have a beautiful soul as well."

"Thank you." Faith acknowledged the compliment. "So, tell me about yourself."

"I work for my Father. I protect his interests and increase his holdings."

"Oh, you're one of those corporate hostile takeover guys."

"Exactly." He smirked in agreement. "What do you do when you're not at Archers?"

"I own a bookstore." Faith told him proudly.

"That sounds...er...interesting." He grimaced.

Faith laughed. "Too tame for you, right. It's more interesting than you might think. I enjoy it. I'm sure you enjoy the work you do. It must be exciting."

"Absolutely. I love to hand my Father a newly acquired prize."

Faith was beginning to feel uncomfortable again. She took the last bite of her sandwich and a sip of tea. She politely excused herself. "It was very nice meeting you, Magnus. I need to get back to my store now. Maybe we will run into each other again sometime."

"I'm counting on it." He responded.

Faith laid the money for her check and a nice tip on the counter and left the diner without a backward glance.

CHAPTER SEVEN

They were gathered in Jami's bedroom. Cain scanned the interior. He was having difficulty reconciling the sassy tough girl he knew with all the lavender and frou-frou that covered the room. There was even a wall of shelves filled with a doll collection. He noticed something off and walked over to take a closer look at the baby dolls. None of them were babies. He recognized Elvira Mistress of the Dark, Bela Lugosi as Dracula, The Wicked Witch from the Wizard of Oz, Frankenstein's Monster and his Bride, and many more Horror Characters. That was more like the Jami he knew.

When Cain salted the room, he had not paid attention to the decor. Now his curiosity was peaked. Upon further inspection, he found the pictures on the wall above the dresser, not family photos. They were autographed pictures of Horror Icons. Represented among them were Vincent Price, Frank Langella, Boris Karloff, Robert Englund, and Lon Chaney. The kicker to the Horror Fetish collection had to be the Bates Motel night light.

Jami got a glimpse of the Holy Shit looks on Cain's face. She stared him down. "What?" She snapped. "You got a problem with that? You don't think a female can get a little freaky?"

"I'm just shocked there are no pictures of Hannity or Gutfeld." He chuckled.

"They're in the office at the bar. Their Moms." She shot back.

Cain loved her sass. He took in her five-foot five form. Those jeans she was wearing showed off a very nice ass. She was thin but not anorexically so. Her breasts were the nicest set of B cups ever to grace a tee shirt. Pouty pink lips and ash blonde hair set off a pair of baby blues that were now glaring at him. All in all, a very nicely put-together package.

"What?" She demanded, feeling unsettled by his stare.

"To answer your question about freaky females. I would love to see you get your freak on."

Instead of getting indignant over his blatant sexual innuendo, she gave him a lusty smile. "Any time you feel up to it." She left no doubt in his mind of what she wanted.

En coughed into her hand to hide a chuckle. It wasn't often Cain was at a loss for words. It was going to be highly entertaining to watch these two. No need for her to tell Cain "I told you so". As much as she was enjoying Cain's awkward moment, she had to break it up and move on to more important things.

"It's time to get started. Ennie insisted.

Cain and Jami turned to En looking at her like they had forgotten she was still in the room with them.

"We will do the ritual here. This is your personal space. It holds the essence of who you are."

"Is this going to hurt?" Jami asked.

"No. When it's finished your senses will feel sharper, crisper, but the ritual itself will not be painful for you."

"But you will be drained." Cain admonished En. "This might not be the right time for this. We can't afford to have your powers down."

"I am the strongest Witch in creation. I am never powerless. We need her now. She is full of untapped power. We don't have the luxury of waiting."

"I know you're right but that doesn't mean I have to like it." He grunted.

"Sit please and stay out of my way." En requested of Cain. To Jami she directed. "I need four candles, the salt, and a bowl please."

Jami handed her the salt she had brought into the room with her. "I'll be right back with the rest."

With Jami out of the room, En turned to Cain. "I know you better than anyone. The good, the bad, and the ugly. Get over yourself. It is what it is. You can deal with your guilt when this is over. No, I take that back. You can wallow in it just like you've done since the dawn of time. Right now, were in a fight. Do not hold her back. She needs the strength her powers will bring her."

Cain's eyes blazed but En wasn't backing down. "If you cause her to question me or herself, she will be hurt."

"You're a bitch." Cain seethed.

"I'm a lot worse than that."

Jami returned with her arms filled with candles and a ceramic bowl dangling precariously from her fingertips. She felt the tension when she entered the room. Cain's eyes flashed from twin licks of fire to dull red. Being a smart woman she decided not to ask. She stood quietly awaiting instruction.

En looked at the load Jami carried. Her almond eyes grew big as saucers. Her mouth fell open.

"What?" Jami wondered. "Did I forget something?"

"Jar candles? That's all you have?" En questioned aghast.

"Well yeah," Jami replied. She flapped the bowl at En who grabbed it before it hit the floor. "We're always misplacing flashlights. Mom bought us a case of these in case the power ever goes out. Their Pina Colada flavor. They smell really good."

Cain was doubled over in his chair laughing. He couldn't decide what was funnier - En's disgust with the inferior candles or Jami's innocent lack of understanding as to why En was unhappy with them.

En threw up her hands. "Spirits save me." She moaned. "Put them on the floor over here."

Jami obeyed still not understanding what En was so worked up about.

En turned the bowl over in her hands. "This is beautiful." The bowl showed age. There was crazing in several spots. It had been exquisitely hand-painted. It must have been a special piece at one time.

Cain was out of the chair and snatching the bowl from En's hand in an instant. In a low gravelly voice, he informed them. "This was Caroline's. Levi gave this to her as an anniversary gift. She cherished it. She only used it for special occasions."

"Levi and Caroline Archer?" Jami questioned in awe. "The Levi and Caroline Archer who built the Inn. The first Archers. You knew them?"

"They were my friends. That's a story for another time." Cain reverently handed the bowl to Jami. "She would be happy that it survived and you have it now."

"You chose perfectly for the ritual. This is part of who you are and where you come from." En praised her.

Jami gulped misty-eyed. "I never knew."

"On some level you did. That's why you brought it now." En placed her hand on Jami's shoulder. "Come now. We need to begin."

Jami followed En clutching the bowl to her chest.

En began by enclosing them in a circle of salt warning Jami once again not to break the circle. She set the candles at the four compass points. The candles seemingly lit themselves. Jami jumped and let out a squeak.

"Cain, would you please get the lights?" Requested En.

Cain doused the room in darkness and returned to his seat.

"Jami sit down and set your bowl in the center of the circle."

Ennie sat across from Jami mirroring her position. She reaches into her pocket and pulled out a cloth bag of herbs. She poured the contents into the bowl. In her palm, she held a silver sewing needle. "Hold out your hand."

Jami held out her hand palm up. En punctured her index finger. She held it over the bowl squeezing it until three drops fell. En repeated the process on her own finger. As the third drop of En's blood hit the mixture in the bowl an orange flame rose up between them. Jami yelped causing En to raise her eyebrows. The fire dissipated leaving behind a fine cloud of smoke with a lavender fragrance.

En took both of Jami's hands in her own lacing their fingers together. She began a smooth mellow chant. The mesmerizing tone of her voice wrapped around Jami like a warm breeze comforting and relaxing her. Jami felt her eyes grow heavy and begin to close.

Jami grew dizzy from the barrage of the ancient wisdom Ennie carried within her. It spilled into her like a cooling waterfall filling her veins, her heart, and her mind. The missing part of herself had come home. For the first time since she was a child who believed in magic, Jami felt complete.

The two of them sat ensconced in a sphere of crystal blue light. Jami had no idea how long they sat there or when En's hypnotic chant went silent. When she came back to awareness, she blinked like she was waking from a long deep sleep.

En leaned over. She kissed Jami on the forehead. "Sister." She whispered with a loving smile. She released Jami's hands. En's eyes rolled back in her head as she slumped onto the floor unconscious.

"Cain!" Jami screamed. "Help me."

He was by her side before his name finished falling from her lips. Gently he picked up En's limp body cradling her in his arms.

"Wake up," Cain demanded. "Wake up you old hag. If you were lying to me, I'll kill you with my bare hands."

En's eyes fluttered. "Screw you. You big bully." She grunted.

"She's fine." He told Jami. "If she can smart mouth me, she's going to be okay."

Jami noticed however that he was not putting her down. She asked En. "How are you feeling?"

"Weak and tired." She answered. "What can I do?" Jami asked wanting desperately to help.

"Feed me. I'm famished. I need to recharge my energy."

Jami looked to Cain. "I could eat." He agreed.

"I hope scrambled eggs and toast are okay. That's about all I've got at the moment."

"Yum." En smacked her lips.

"Sounds like a banquet to me," Cain added.

"Great. Would you mind carrying our fainting lady downstairs?" She asked. "Breakfast is coming up."

Cain tucked En up on the living room couch then went into the kitchen to give Jami a hand. He found her energetically scrambling eggs with a wire whisk.

"How is she doing?" Jami inquired. "She scared me when she collapsed like that."

"She will be alright. She just needs food and some sleep to get her strength back, how are you doing?"

"Great." She assured him, pulling a skillet out from a lower cabinet. "I feel really...great. It's like when you have the flu and after days of being flat on your back you feel healthy again and ready to take on the world."

"What can I do to help?" He offered. "How about toast? I do pretty well with toast. Where's the toaster?"

Jami chuckled at his eagerness to toast some bread. "Bottom cabinet to the left." She directed him.

"Cain got the toaster and plugged it in. The bread was already lying on the counter. He slid two slices in then reached for the butter dish. He located a butter knife. Jami handed him a plate and a glass jar of homemade raspberry jelly.

"You're taking all of this really well." He complimented her. "I wouldn't have blamed you if you had bolted."

"I wasn't given much of a choice."

"I can't tell you how sorry I am that you and Faith were drug into all of this shit. I'm the one Magnus is after. The last thing I ever wanted was for any of you to get hurt."

"I know that. Don't worry about it. Faith and I are big girls. We can handle ourselves."

"You don't understand what we're up against. You can't imagine the ugliness you will witness until this is over. This is not an adventure or something you've seen in a movie. It's the real deal and people will get hurt."

"No Archer has ever run from a fight. The men in my family have fought in every war and conflict since the Revolution. The women in my family stayed home and kept things running while raising their children. All any of them had were swords, knives, and guns. I have the great and mighty Cain and the badass Witch of Endor fighting with me. I think I can deal with," Jami paused. "Umm, by the way. Do you have any superpowers?"

"Cain's tanned face paled. His bloody eyes were the only visible mark. The curse went much deeper. Would she still be so accepting when she knew all his secrets? It looked like he was about to find out.

"I kill." He spoke softly, absentmindedly slathering the toast with butter and jelly.

"Come again?"

Cain slid two more pieces of bread into the toaster. "I kill." He repeated. He was to blame for putting her in this position. The least he could do was give her the unvarnished truth. "It's not a superpower it's a curse. Jami, I am, the original killer. I was cursed for murdering my brother. My own blood. I was condemned to wander the earth eternally. Never to have a true home, a family, or love. Always alone. Forever killing. I've got more blood on my hands than you could possibly imagine."

Standing beside Jami in the brightly lit kitchen Cain revealed the beast within himself. His eyes glowed crimson fire, his incisors elongated into sharply pointed fangs, and his hands turned into Raptor-like claws. All the tools he had been given to help ensure his continued survival. His continued misery.

Jami couldn't move. Her legs jellied under her as she fought to stay upright. She maintained a white-knuckled grip on the counter.

What have I done Cain thought to himself as he watched her inner struggle? Shame and despair gnawed at his gut. He caged his beast returning to his normal form and turned to walk away.

"Holy Shit" Jami exploded. "We are so going to whoop-ass."

"What?" He demanded, unable to believe his ears. He turned back to face her.

"Look, I don't know Cain the son of Adam. I do know Cain Adamson. He's a good man. I mean if Satan can be good and turn bad can't you be bad and turn good?"

"If only it were that simple. You mean I don't repulse you?"

"No way." She waved a hand blowing off his self-recriminations. "What else can you do?"

"I'm stronger than a mortal. I'm faster. I have a trigger to warn me when something supernatural is close. Essentially I'm equipped to defend myself so my curse carries on forever."

"Wow." Jami whistled. "We're gonna kick their butts. We're gonna kick their butts." She sang.

"You are incredible."

"You are correct." She replied smugly.

Then she did the most unexpected thing. She kissed him. Slowly she ran her tongue over his lips tasting them. As the kiss heated up, she melded their mouths together. Cain growled low in his throat pulling her softness up against him.

"Is anyone going to feed me?" Ennie shouted from the living room. "My stomach's growling louder than the Hounds of Hell."

Cain reluctantly pulled back from Jami. "Witch." He groaned.

"I think we better feed her before she starts chewing my sofa." Turning her back to Cain she started making a plate for En doing her best to hide the shit-eating grin on her face.

They ate sitting around the coffee table. Jami made two additional trips for more jelly toast and milk for En. She ate like a man. Jami had no idea where the tiny woman put it.

Replete and exhausted En announced her intention of getting some sleep which she proceeded to do. It didn't take long before her snores vibrated through the room. They served as a lullaby dragging both Cain and Jami into sleep along with her.

CHAPTER EIGHT

Katie sat perched on a high wooden stool behind the counter of Martins Books. It was a slow morning but she didn't mind. She was enjoying reading. Her elbows rested on the glass countertop. She cupped her chin in her palms. Hazel's eyes sped back and forth across the printed page. She was so engrossed in the adventure that played out before her reality ceased to exist. Someday, she knew, she would have an adventure of her own.

The tinkling of the door chimes jolted her back to the real world alerting her that a customer had entered the store.

The man who walked in had the looks of an angel. His head haloed by the shafts of sunlight from the picture window held her captivated. He was the living breathing compilation of every male hero she had ever read about. Tousled blonde hair hung just past his shoulders. Stormy grey eyes appeared to look straight into her deepest thoughts. Dimples that would look silly on any other man combined with a smile that left her believing he had a naughty secret he wanted to share only with her.

"Hi." Katie greeted him shyly. "Faith isn't here can I help you with something?"

"I'm looking for a self-help book." He explained. "Something about helping you talk to a girl you're attracted to."

Katie gasped. "You can't be serious?"

"I am. You see I'm attracted to this lady but I'm nervous about approaching her."

"I really don't think you need a book for that."

"Maybe you can help me. What do you look for in a man?"

"I... umm..." Nervously Katie pushed her glasses higher up on her freckled nose.

"Come on Katie." He prodded. "What can I do to get you to notice me?"

"Me?" Katie was struck dumb. Men this gorgeous did not flirt with girls like her. There was no way this was happening. It had to be another of her daydreams.

He gave her that naughty smile. Her stomach fluttered and her palms became sweaty. She was afraid she was going to have a panic attack. She had to tell herself to exhale before she began to hyperventilate.

"Don't tell me you haven't noticed the way I'm always looking at you."

Truthfully, she had noticed his eyes following lately when they crossed paths around town. She had told herself it was wishful thinking. "I did wonder a few times."

He edged closer to her coming around behind the counter. She was skittish. It gave him a perverse thrill. With his index finger, he teased the carroty curls around her flushed face. "I know I've caught you looking at me."

"Well, you're nice to look at." Katie blurted artlessly.

He barked a throaty laugh. "I'm glad you think so. Tell me, why don't you ever talk to me when you see me?"

"I didn't think you would be interested in a girl like me."

"You're wrong. I'm very interested." He corrected her. "Is it bothering you, my touching your hair? It feels so soft."

"No." She shivered. "It doesn't bother me."

"Would it bother you if I kissed you?" He asked her, his voice erotically husky.

Katie briefly considered pinching herself. "I think I would like that." She sighed.

He deftly removed her glasses. Bending down he teased her with a feathery kiss then pulled back. Katie looked up blinking. What happened? Why had he stopped?

His grey eyes were dilated with lust. He tipped her head back for easier access to her sweet mouth. The kisses were now hot and drugging. Katie stood up off the stool easing into him wanting to feel him closer. The kisses became hungry. Katie went limp in his arms. He held her up pulling her as close as he could. She trembled as he ran the pink tip of his tongue along the straining blue veins in her neck then trailed wet sucking kisses along the damp path his tongue made. At some point, the line between passion and pain was crossed.

"Please stop." Katie gasped. "You're hurting me."

He withdrew instantly. "I would never hurt you, Katie. I promise it will be painless."

Wondering at the odd statement she forced her eyes to focus without her glasses. Her piercing scream echoed through the isles of books as she got a good look at his face. What she was seeing couldn't possibly be real. Her eyes had to be playing tricks on her. She opened her mouth to scream again but closed it in shock as he began to speak as calmly as if this were an everyday conversation between two friends.

"Calm down. Isn't this the adventure you've been longing for?"

"Your...you're..."

"Not human." He finished for her.

His eyes were milky white. Katie struggled trying to break free. She twisted her arms and pummeled him with her fists. When that had no effect, she dug her fingernails into his arms until she drew blood. He groaned. The deranged smile on his face suggested he was enjoying her struggles.

"Katie my sweet girl. Let me love you. Till death do us part. Isn't that what your daddy used to say every time he laid hands on that bitch you called Mother?"

Scalding tears had been flowing from her eyes. If he meant those words to keep her pliant and afraid it had not worked. The tears were born of raw anger. Glaring up into his now twisted inhuman face she spat. "Get the hell away from me."

He laughed at her. Katie groped in her pocket for her cell phone. Never breaking eye contact he seized the hand that held the phone and squeezed. Katie whimpered as the fragile bones in her hand did the snap, crackle, pop. He released her hand. Throbbing pain shot from her fingertips to her shoulder. Her right arm was numb and useless.

"That's it, Katie. Keep fighting me. I like it when you fight me."

He purred. "Get me hot. We'll both enjoy it more that way." He ground his erection hard against her hip.

Katie went still. Unable to stop herself she looked down and saw his cock straining behind the fly of his jeans. She gagged as bile rose up in her throat. He ran his tongue over his fangs in anticipation.

"You sick bastard. "She choked. "I won't let you turn me into some bloodsucking vamp. You'll have to kill me first."

"Don't be a fool. There are no such creatures as Vampires. You read too many fairy tales. I have no intention of turning you into anything. I will be killing you. You did get that much correct."

Katie's mind reeled as he made his declaration of her impending death. With nothing to lose, she decided to go with the one method that had worked for women down through the ages. He oof'd as her knee made contact with his balls.

He had no choice but to release her. With her good hand, Katie grabbed a pair of scissors from under the counter shoving them into the front waistband of her jeans. His body blocked her way to the front door. She ran for the back exit. As she gripped the door handle, she felt herself being jerked backward by her hair.

She allowed herself to be spun around. She pulled the scissors and stabbed him in his upper chest with all the strength she could muster. The scissors barely broke his skin. He laughed at her pathetic attempt.

Out of options Katie started to scream. Maybe she would get lucky and someone passing by would hear her and call for help.

He whispered in her ear. "Scream, scream, scream. I so wanted to prolong this I had hoped to be buried deep inside you when you breathe your last. Unfortunately, I've been at it too long already. Can't have someone popping in on us. It would ruin the mood."

Katie fought against her fear. The feisty heroines in her books would never go out like helpless victims. Digging deep she called upon her inner bitch, sucked it up, and pulled out a little tude.

"Fuck you." She snarled. "I'll see you in Hell."

"Yes. You will." He agreed. "Goodbye, my love."

He roughly pulled her hair exposing her throat. Taking a deep breath filling his nose with the scent of her fear he bent his head.

Slowly he punctured her skin savoring the spurt of blood as it flowed into his mouth then shook his head viciously ripping out her throat.

Like a lover, he tenderly put his bloody lips to her cooling lips. With one hand he removed her shirt then carelessly allowed her body to drop to the floor. He used her tee-shirt to wipe the blood from his face. He wished he'd had time for more than a kiss but her screams may have alerted someone and he couldn't take the chance of being caught. If he ruined Magnus' plans the Incubus would kill him. Ah, well, he had enjoyed himself. Stepping over Katie's body he walked to the door closing it behind him as he casually made his way to the exit.

Dust bunnies disturbed the air above Katie's lifeless body as two beings materialized. Both wore hats, one a tan Stetson, the other a straw Fedora. In appearance, they were opposites until you looked into their eyes. Both were an identical frosty blue.

The one removed his Fedora. He knelt beside Katie. Reaching out he reverently closed her unseeing eyes. "Such a waste of life." He mourned.

"It always is Esiasch." The cowboy declared using the Enochian word for brother. His face set in a mask of stoney resolve.

"We have very little time before the soul departs from her body." Lo returned the hat to his head as he stood and spoke to Sully. "We will have to act quickly, we're going to do this."

Sully didn't look at his brother in arms. His eyes stayed locked on the dead girl at his feet. "How do you justify this? Why the hell do we continue to allow it? She was just a kid for fuck sake."

"We do what is necessary. Sometimes there are innocent casualties. We do what we must and save those we can." Lo reminded him.

"Fuck necessary." Sully rasped. "I'm sick to death of that word. It's a fucking game we play. This child was nothing more than an innocent pawn. Cannon fodder."

"And so, it has been since even before our time." Lo reminded him.

"Why do we allow it to continue? We have the power to stop this senseless slaughter. Why don't we use it?"

"We were created for one purpose. To guard the key." Lo reminded him.

"Assassins is what we are. Created to kill." Sully countered.

"Only those who are a threat to the key. We assure you the Gates of Hell are never compromised. We save billions of innocents every day by making sure the Key is secure. That is what we were created for."

"Fuuuck!" Anger and frustration exploded from Sully. Glass rattled in the window panes. Books fell from shelves as walls shook.

"Enough," Lo demanded. "Your temper does not change what is."

Sully reigned himself in. Lo was correct, but that didn't make this right. They were under orders and they would obey. Humanity hinged on their actions.

"What are our orders?"

"One of us will have to travel with her to the Affa and hold her there until contact is made. The other will stay here and hold off those who come for her."

"I need a good fight." Sully's hand went to the hilt of his sword. "I'll stay.

"You will have to deal with Reapers from above and below," Lo warned him.

"Let em' bring it. I'd rather fight all four Horsemen than go to that hole of spooks." Sully shivered at the thought of the Affa.

A barely audible shhh arose from the floor. A luminous outline rose up between them.

"Enjoy your fight," Lo said, nodding. He reached out to the soul. Both vanished.

Sully listened intently for the thundering to begin. He felt the vibrations before he heard the rumble. He pulled his sword. The gleam from the blade left a prism of colors trailing in its wake.

"Come and get it, boys. Ima spanks your ass and leave you crying like a bitch." He smiled expectantly. This was something he could understand. This was a real battle where all the combatants knew the rules and were prepared to accept the consequences.

"No way." Faith groaned. She pounded her first off the steering wheel. "This is so not happening."

She turned the key for the third time while insistently pumping the gas pedal. Still nothing. Not even the wah, wah, wah, sound telling her the car was a least trying to start. It was dead and now she had probably flooded the damn thing. Faith spooked at an unexpected tap on the window. She looked out and saw Magnus. Faith hurried to roll down the window.

"You look like you could use some help." He offered, peering through the half-open window at her flushed face.

"Yeah, it doesn't want to start."

"Pop the hood and I'll take a look."

"Thanks."

Magnus went around to the front of the car. Faith pulled the hood release. Her view of him was obscured as he lifted the hood.

"Try it again," Magnus instructed.

Faith turned the key again only to get the same result…nothing. She slid out of the car and went to join Magnus. "I can't believe this. I just had it inspected two weeks ago. It was running great."

Magnus made noises of commiseration pretending to understand her ordeal. It was so easy for him to mess with these technology dependent mortals. It only cost him a thought to drain a battery or render a cell phone useless.

"Can you see what's wrong?" Faith asked hopefully. She looked at the car engine. It may as well be an alien spacecraft for all she understood about cars.

"Ah, I have a confession to make," Magnus spoke gravely.

Faith sucked in her breath. Had this been a trick? Was he stalking her?

Magnus grimaced. "I am a complete idiot when it comes to cars."

Faith burst into bubbly laughter at what she thought was a manly embarrassment. "Why did you look at the engine then?"

"I was hoping some secret male knowledge would spark in my brain and tell me what to do."

"Didn't happen huh?" She grinned, shaking her head.

"No lightning bolts. Not even static." He admitted. "So now that you know my shameful secret will you let me give you a ride?"

"I don't want to inconvenience you. I'll just call my mechanic." Faith walked a few paces away to make her phone call.

"Alright." Magnus waited patiently reclining against her car. He was not worried about missing an opportunity. He knew the outcome of her call would end in his favor.

She returned to tell him, "No answer. Maybe he's out to lunch."

"Looks like you're stuck with me. Come on. I'm parked over here."

"Are you sure you don't mind? It's a long drive." She wondered what she could possibly come up with to discuss with this man while they were closed in a car for the next three hours.

"Not at all. It will give me a chance to get to know you better." His borrowed body thrilled with excitement. His plan was working perfectly. By night's end, her body would belong to him and her soul would belong to Lucifer.

"Stop crying!" Ennie shrilled. "For the love of all the spirits stop crying!"

Cain woke instantly. He rushed to kneel in front of En. She was sitting with her knees drawn up and her hands covering her ears. Jami groggy from sleep and half hungover was struggling to comprehend the scene in front of her.

En continued to cry out. It was clear she was in pain. She was rocking back and forth tears streaming down her cheeks. Cain sat rooted to the floor at a loss as to how to help her.

Comprehension finally cleared Jami's befuddled head. She went to kneel next to Cain. "Help her." She pleaded. "Why are you just sitting there?"

"I can't." Cain snapped. "I'm afraid if I touch her, I might shock her into some kind of trauma. I've never seen her affected like this before."

"What's wrong with her?" Demanded a terrified Jami.

"Some kind of spirit has latched onto her."

"Well, why is she freaking? I thought she talks about these things all the time. I mean that is what she does right?"

"Yes, but something is wrong this time. Usually, she can turn the voices on and off. It appears this one doesn't want to go. She should be able to stop it. It must be one hell of a determined soul. She's in pain. It's hurting her."

"We've got to do something. We can't leave her like this. I'm a witch too. Isn't there something I can do to help her?"

"I don't know," Cain answered honestly. "You can try. Your right we've got to do something."

Jami sat facing En. Her friend's face was soaked with tears. Her hair was drenched with sweat yet she shivered as if she were freezing cold. She whimpered now unable to attempt to fight back.

"Ennie, it's me, sister," Jami spoke soothingly. She held out a hand mentally willing En to take it.

En senses, though fragile at the moment, felt the pull and made the connection. She grasped Jami's hand in a fierce grip. Her other hand reached out blindly. Jami took it becoming En's anchor. If she did not have such a firm grip on En the force of the spirits would have knocked Jami on her ass as it flew from Ennie's body into her own.

Cain watched as the air current around them began to pop and sizzle. The walls of the house started to pound. A squalling wind churned up around the women. Strands of Jami's ash blonde hair tangled with En's chestnut waves until Cain could no longer see their faces.

Framed pictures fell from walls. Lamps turned over their bulbs flashing and popping as they crashed to the floor. Glass figurines flew through the air smashing against the walls.

Amidst the chaos, Cain managed to discern a vaguely familiar voice. Unable to see the girl's faces he was unable to distinguish whose voice it was speaking through. Where it had been screaming in En's head earlier it now came through as timid and frightened.

"Help me." The voice trembled. "Please help."

"Who are you?" En demanded, helping Cain ascertain the spirit was speaking through Jami.

The only answer En received was another plaintive cry for help.

Cain paced behind the couch. The fractured voice tore at his insides. He growled despising the fact that he had to stand impotently on the sidelines and wait for whatever was coming.

"If you want my help you must calm down. We want to help you. Can you tell me your name?"

"K-K-Katie." The voice stammered.

Fuck. Cain knew of only one Katie who could have been drawn into this. His fury rose as he realized she was gone. She had not even begun to live yet and the bastard had made sure she never would. She was so young to become the first casualty in Magnus' bloody game for vengeance. Another lost soul to add to the list of the dead he was responsible for.

"Very good Katie." En praised her. "What do you want to tell us?"

"It's dark here. I'm scared."

"I know you're scared. I'm going to help you out of the dark. First, you need to tell me why you came to me."

"He hurt me." The voice sobbed. "I loved him and he hurt me."

"Who is he, Katie? Who hurt you? Tell me his name."

"Jami?"

"Jami is here Katie. It's okay. Jami is safe. Tell me who hurt you."

"Blood" Katie cried. "Tell Jami about the blood."

"What does Jami need to know about the blood?"

"The blood is hers. It's Jami's blood." Katie cried wailed frantically.

En knew she would not be able to get anything more from the girl. "Okay, Katie." She soothed. "It's over. Can you see the light? Look for the light. Katie? Katie? Awk. She's gone. We've lost her damn it."

Cain vaulted over the couch in time to catch the girls. They were both trembling. He grabbed a quilt from the back of the couch and wrapped it tightly around them both. It seemed to take him a lifetime before he managed to untangle their hair enough that he could see their faces. They were both white as chalk from shock.

Jami was the first to recover enough to speak. "This witch stuff is not as much fun as I thought it would be."

Cain just gawked.

"I need a drink," En informed him.

"I'm on it." He stood to go to the kitchen. As he reached for the refrigerator door, he heard Jami cry out. She must have just realized what she had heard. Cain felt a lump form in his throat knowing that he would have to go back into the living room and help Jami handle the fact that she had just lost a friend.

In Enochian, the language of the Angels, it is called Salman Affa Zizop. House of the Empty Vessels. Within all human beings there resides a soul. Every soul is enshrined in a pliable membrane. When nurtured by the light this membrane grows, thrives, and expands filling the body it resides in. In contrast, a soul contaminated by darkness stagnates, blackens, and withers.

Upon death, a soul is either escorted to Paradise by a Reaper of Light or pulled screaming, and clawing to Hell by a host of Dark Reapers. These souls suffer the torments of Hell until Lucifer is done with them.

Once a damned soul is emptied it is sent to the Affa as a mindless predator. They know only that they are empty and need a soul to fill them.

It is these soul-starved vessels that inhabit the Salman Affa Zizop. There these creatures are locked in constant battle. The strongest feeding off the weakest. The most perverse and twisted growing as they feed.

This unholy place is where Lo chose to hide Katie. After the demon claimed her soul for his Master it became a prize to be won. Reapers from both sides would fight to claim her. Lo took her to the one place it would be unlikely he would be followed. No one willingly chose to go to the Affa.

Lo kept himself hidden as he fought to keep the soul eaters away from Katie and himself. The light inside her drew them to her. The low-frequency hum of his sword sent the weaker ones skittering away. Those who dared to close in on them were dust the instant they met his blade.

Katie's battered soul screamed for help. Lo forced himself to endure her cries. It served as penance that he should choke on her fear. No matter the importance of his mission it was wrong for him to bring her to this vile place. Something so pure should never have to come in contact with something so loathsome.

Damn Sully for voicing that which he dares not. If Lo allowed himself to think about his actions he would become as broken as another of their brother in arms. Philadelphia could no longer fulfill his duties to the Order. His mind had shattered centuries ago. He had never been able to walk in the grey in between. For Phil, it had always come down to the black and white. The right and wrong.

When Lo and his six brothers had been chosen to be soldiers in the Order of the Key aka The Bloody Seven, he had felt humbled. To be a guardian to the Key to the Gates of Hell was a noble calling. Now he was jaded, weary, and filled with self-loathing.

After what seemed like an eternity Katie's cries were answered. By the time contact had been made Lo was doubtful they understood the message he instructed Katie to send. It had been a calculated risk.

After the message had been sent Lo went to her. He held her in his arms murmuring words of comfort. A wave of his hand produced a brilliant blaze of light so bright in the darkness the creatures of the Affa ran in fear. The light held a doorway. The crystal door knob creating a spectacular prism of color.

Lo's icy blue eyes studied her sweet face. He knew her confused eyes and terrified face would be forever engraved in his mind. Lo turned her around in his arms facing her toward the shimmering kaleidoscope of light.

"It's time to go home." He spoke softly to Katie.

"Home?" She asked, puzzled.

"Your job here is done. You were very brave. You have the heart of a warrior." Lo chastely kissed the top of her head.

Katie took a tentative step toward the light. Then another. She places her hand on the crystal knob. In a heartbeat, she was gone. She never looked back. For that Lo was grateful.

CHAPTER NINE

Blue and red lights swirled from the roofs of three Borough police vehicles. They were parked in the middle of the street along with one ambulance from Ephrata Hospital. There were no flashing lights on the ambulance.

The sidewalk directly in front of Martins Books was closed off by sawhorse barricades. Outside of the barriers the sidewalk and street were choked with groups of nosy neighbors, curiosity seekers, and reporters. There would be plenty to talk about around the town's dinner tables tonight.

A block away Faith recklessly lept from Magnus' car before the Lexus rolled to a stop. She hit the ground running shoving her way through the crowd only to be stalled out at the door of her store. Officer Roberts stood between her and the interior an impenetrable wall of blue.

"Let me in. Where is Katie? What's happening?" Faith demanded.

Officer Roberts was a bear of a man. Faith had known him since she was a child. He coached the soccer team his daughter, Faith, and Jami played on. As he looked at Faith's worried face and knew what awaited her on the other side of the door it took everything in him not to wrap her in his arms and drag her away. Instead, he did his job as distasteful as it might be.

"Faith I want you to wait right here. I'm going to let the Chief know you're here." He informed her.

Faith nodded dumbly. Why wasn't she just allowed to go inside? It was her store. What the hell happened in there?

Faith felt eyes boring into her back. She saw people she knew. People she considered friends staring at her and talking behind their hands. Newspeople called out to her. She couldn't hear the blood rushing through her head. A feeling of dread washed over her. Everything was moving in slow motion. She inched closer to the door.

Magnus came up behind her. He had left the car he had stolen down the street with its engine still running. "Do as he ask Faith."

"I need to get in there," she argued.

"He said he would be right back. I'm sure they will want to speak with you." Magnus spoke reasonably.

Magnus stood behind her, keeping his hands on her shoulders to hold her in place.

Officer Roberts returned. He took her by the arm. He didn't say a word as he led her inside. He also didn't see Magnus who followed them inside. The demon was skillfully cloaking himself. He would be visible only to Faith.

Once inside the store Faith gasped. She covered her mouth with her hands to hold back a scream. Laid out before her was the ruination of her dreams. Broken glass, splintered wood, and the worst of it… the books. Scattered and forlorn, ripped and disemboweled, their pages covered every available surface but one.

Faith swayed on her feet. Behind the counter, a long black bag with a zipper down the front laid on the floor. Faith had seen enough television to know what that black bag meant. Someone was dead. Faith looked to the two EMT's standing by the bag waiting patiently to put the body on the waiting gurney. This time her scream could not be contained. "Nooo." She wailed. "Not Katie. Please not Katie."

Magnus put both hands around her waist to keep her on her feet.

"I told you to detain her." The Chief bellowed at Roberts.

"Do it yourself." Roberts shot back. "She hasn't done anything to warrant cuffing her."

"Then you take responsibility for her if she decides to run."

"I'd be happy to." Roberts declared.

The Chief stalked over to Faith. "Before we can go any further, I'm going to have to ask you to make an identification." He cold-bloodedly demanded.

"I… is it Katie?" Faith gulped in great draws of air as fought back the urge to vomit.

"That's who we believe it to be. She has no family left around this area. That leaves the I.D. up to you." The Chief nodded to the EMT's letting them know to unzip the bag. He drew Faith closer.

They got as far as Katie's chest when Faith shook her head affirmatively. "It's her." She choked. Faith could barely recognize her friend whose face was now battered and crusted with blood. Her shirt was missing so that Faith could see the sensible white bra she wore was stained brown with drying blood. If it had not been for the carrotty color of her hair Faith would have found it difficult to make any identification at all.

No longer able to hold back Faith turned to the side. She vomited the club sandwich she had for lunch onto the cluttered floor.

"Do you need to use the restroom?" The Chief asked, reaching to help her.

"I can get there on my own." Faith snapped.

She was not really on her own. Magnus helped her through the detritus. He waited outside of the bathroom. From what little he saw of the body it appeared his minion had enjoyed his assignment. The rest of the store though…something else had happened here. Something had left this place in ruin. But what? And why?

Cain, Jami, and Ennie lounged precariously amid the destruction of the living room. None of them had the ambition to take on the laborious task of cleaning the mess. They were all up in their own heads trying to make sense of Katie's words and the fact that she was gone.

Cain's cell phone started vibrating in his pocket. The caller's number was not one he recognized. With everything that was going on he decided it was best to answer. It turned out to be a smart decision. The caller was Officer Roberts. After he ended the call, he found two sets of eyes looking at him expectantly.

"Before I say a word, I want you to keep your mouths shut and let me get it all out." He looked pointedly at Jami. "No running off halfcocked."

"Alright." En agreed.

"Okay, sure, no cock here."

Cain frowned at her. "Katie is gone, obviously. That call was from Officer Roberts. She was found at the store."

"Faith." Jami blurted. She knew this was going to hit her friend hard. She had to be there for her.

"She's safe." Cain assured her.

"Why do I feel like there is a but coming?" En questioned him.

"Because there is. But...they are holding her there questioning her. It seems the Chief wants to know not only about Katie but also about the death of Myrtle Moyer."

"That cocksucking weasel." Jami cursed. She and Ennie were putting on their shoes getting ready to go running down the street to Faith.

"We've gotta get down there. Jami demanded." Faith needs me. She's going to be a mess."

"I'm ready." En announced. She had quickly run a hairbrush through her hair and slipped on her shoes. She handed the brush to Jami who then managed to slide on shoes and brush her hair simultaneously.

"Let's go." Cain directed. "We'll walk. It will be faster."

Jami made it to the front porch steps when she heard the sound of leaves rustling like a storm was coming. No, that couldn't be right, there was no wind. "What is that? Oh shit. No fucking way."

Cain and Ennie were right on her heels. Jami began moving back until she was stopped by the hard wall of Cains chest. They were all looking up to the source of the sound.

"Shit!" Cain grabbed them both by an arm in an attempt to get them indoors.

"Let me go." En demanded. "I got this." En threw out a shield to protect the three of them.

The sky before them was a writhing black mass. What looked like every crow in the state of Pennsylvania was in rabid flight. The three of them were the bullseye. The sound they heard was not the rustling of leaves but the manic flapping of wings.

Jami tried to jump back as the ugly birds thwacked against Ens shield. She only got as far as stepping on Cains foot. He cursed her as they watched the bloody gore splatter while the frenzied birds broke their necks against the shield then fall to the porch in tangled piles. Jami couldn't stand to see anymore she buried her face in Cain's chest.

En held the shield while as a group they moved backward toward the door. When they were far enough inside En dropped the shield while Cain threw the door shut.

"I'm gonna hurl." Jami groaned, still hanging onto Cain. Her face was visibly green and she clapped a hand over her mouth as her stomach lurched.

Cain quickly set her away from him. She threw him an indignant glare. Her need to vomit vanishing with her irritation.

"Sorry, I don't do puke." He readily admitted.

"My hero." She snipped.

"Someone doesn't want us to leave." En stated the obvious.

"You think?" Cain snarked.

The sound of meaty thunks beat against the door. Jami vaguely wondered how she was going to explain the mess then her mind snapped back to the fact that she had to get to Faith. She hurriedly redirected them. "Basement door. Follow me."

Jami led them through the kitchen. Throwing open the basement door she was hit by the damp musty smell mingling with the perfumed scent of laundry soap and fabric softener. Jami was always creeped out when she had to go down to do the laundry but not this time. She thundered down the steps.

The house was old enough to still have a coal room. The girls never went in there since the house had been converted to electric heat before they signed a lease. The door to the coal room was weathered and dry rot had broken it apart around the edges leaving gaps around the frame. The owners had left the ancient cast iron slide bar handle in place. The handle rattled as the door shook nearly off its rusted hinges. Around the gaping frame hundreds of brown recluse spiders spilled through the cracks in waves flooding into the outer room. The cement floor now resembling an undulating brown shag carpet.

Jami screeched. She lunged onto the top of the washing machine. Ennie followed her lead and vaulted onto the dryer leaving Cain to stomp the scuttling arachnids as they made their way across the floor.

As soon as Ennie deemed herself out of harm's way she held out her palm toward the spiders. Balls of fire flew from her hands leaving charcoal and scorch marks on the cement floor. Jami bounced up and down from her perch yelling and pointing as she supervised her friends. Finally, Cain backed up onto the stairs so En could finish them off.

With the invaders now charbroiled they all stopped to take a breath. Jami and En came down from their appliances and Cain returned from the stairs.

"Bad things come in threes." Warned Jami.

"Knock wood." Cain ordered.

Not wanting to go near the coal door En rapped on Jami's head three times.

"Smart ass." Jami drawled, rubbing the spot where En's knuckles came into contact with her head.

"Always." En replied. "Is this the best he's got?"

"He's trying to distract us. Nothing he's done could really hurt us. He wants us alive for his end game. Right now, he's just trying to stall us. He needs to keep us from getting to Faith."

"Whatever. All I'm sure of right now is that we will get to Faith and I won't be doing any laundry for a while." Jami added.

Cain shook his head at her. He opened the outside door only to slam it shut again. "Who made the crack about bad things coming in threes?" Cain snapped.

Ennie pointed to Jami. "I guess her head isn't made of wood after all. Congratulations Pinocchio you are a real girl."

"Funny." Jami stuck her tongue out at her.

"Cut it out." Cain snarled. He reached over and grabbed a handy shovel. "Get back up where you were."

They didn't question his orders. Both of the girls hopped right back up where they had been.

"Close your eyes." He demanded. They instantly obeyed.

Cain raised his right hand holding the shovel. With his left hand he went for the door handle. He had approximately three seconds to react as the white eyed snarling Rottweiler sprang at him.

"I've got a migraine." Cain muttered to himself. "The first one in a thousand years."

They stood in the backyard. An unconscious dog lying at their feet. En and Jami were bitching him out about cruelty to animals.

"That's the Purcell's dog. They love that dog." Jami was ranting.

"Enough." Cain growled. "All I did was knock it out. I could have ripped its throat out. Then you really would have something to bitch about."

The girls had the grace to look shamefaced. What else could he have done under the circumstances?

"The dog will wake up. The demon will take off. That's it, period." He scolded. "Now let's go get Faith."

The townies congregated on Main Street rivaled the turn out for the Fourth of July Parade. Cain led the way leaving the spectators to move out of the way or get mowed down. They wound their way to the store without any more trouble until they reached an Officer standing guard at a barricade.

"Let us through Tom." Jami ordered the young Deputy.

"Sorry Jami." He smirked. "The Chief says no one gets in."

"Tell Roberts Cain is here."

"Umm… I'm sorry Mr. Adamson. Really." The kid genuflected at Cain's scowling face. "Officer Roberts got no say sir. I've got my orders direct from the Chief. I'm not to let anyone in. No exceptions."

Cain kept a leash on his temper. But damn he wanted to smack the kid. He had to remind himself the little shit was only doing his job.

Jami was not so thoughtful. "You weasley little butt munch. You were a snothead in high school and you're still a snothead." She taunted him. "I'll bet even with that badge you still can't get laid."

The Deputy turned beet red. He kept angry eyes on Jami. "And you were always a bitch."

"Gah." En groaned. She shoved Jami behind her before she could do any more damage. "You have got to learn some tact. Let me handle this."

"Hello Officer." En voice was silky as she batted her lashes and flashed a smile. "Please excuse Jami she's just worried for her friend. You understand of course. She does not realize what a tremendous responsibility you carry trying to uphold the law."

"It's a responsibility I take very seriously." He pronounced. En's flattery was working. The color was fading from his cheeks. He was entranced by the exotic beauty speaking to him.

"I can see that you do. Jami was wrong about that badge. Personally, I think it gives you an air of strength and authority. If I Jami hadn't called you by name, I would have thought you were the Chief."

He puffed out his scrawny chest. The praise fueling his self-importance.

"You have piercing eyes. Such a deep shade of brown." En complimented him as she moved in closer.

He was enthralled. En captured him with her eyes. "Your orders were to allow us entry,"

In a daze he moved the barricade allowing them to pass. When they safely behind the Deputy En looked at Jami. "If you mention the force, I'll smack you."

Jam's eyes went wide. That's exactly what had been on the tip of her tongue. She stumbled as she passed by the stores picture window. She could see Faith inside. She was speaking to the Chief.

Cain and En stopped to see what held her attention.

"Does she look awkward to you?" Cain asked, staring through the window his eyebrows scrunched together in concentration.

"She's being interrogated for shit sake. Of course, she looks awkward." Jami snapped.

"No look." En explained. "She's leaning backward like she is reclining on thin air."

"She's right." Cain agreed.

En exhaled deeply onto the window glass. Using her fingertips, she drew a smudge across the glass.

Jami watched curiously. "What are you doing?"

En answered. "If I'm right. Which I always am. Magnus is standing behind Faith. He's altered perception to cloak himself. I'm countering it by distorting perception on our side. Yup, I was right. Take a gander."

Jami squinted through the glass streaks. "Is that him? The bastard is in there with Faith right now."

"That's him." Cain grunted.

"I'm going to kill him." Jami stated flatly. "Let's go. Let's finish the bastard."

Cain stepped in front of her. "Not you." He gave her a hard look.

"Screw you." Jami snapped defiantly.

"Magnus could snap her neck before you could blink. He would do it too. Do you think he gives a fuck that there are cops in there? You can't fight him."

Jami knew she had no defense against the truth. She stood silently seething.

"What's the plan?" En asked.

"I go in. You wait here. Now that I know he's there he can't block me."

Both women stared at him with identical expressions of ire. He ignored them and walked to the door.

"What took you so long?" Roberts demanded. "I called you thirty minutes ago."

"Ran into some trouble." Cain answered.

"More trouble than this?" Roberts demanded.

Cain shrugged. "Little bit."

"Okay I won't ask." Roberts wisely decided. He turned and led Cain into the store.

Cain entered the ruins of the store. His eyes locked with Magnus. The demons face appeared shocked as he clued into the fact that Cain could see him. He subtly moved his hand from Faiths shoulder to her neck. Long fingers wrapped around her throat to begin a slow massage. Faith believed he was attempting to calm her. Cain knew the asshole was baiting him.

Cain sent him a silent message. "Try it."

Magnus leered flashing his fangs. He responded silently back to Cain. "How fast are you, old man?"

"Let's find out." Cain strutted forward his eyes never leaving Magnus. He was intentionally provoking him. If Magnus was going to snap her neck, he would have done it the second he realized Cain could see him.

Faith was the first to notice him. "Cain?" Faith asked, relief reflected on her pale face at the sight of him.

"I'm here." He told her, letting her know that he had come to offer his assistance.

The Chief whirled around. "Adamson, what the hell are you doing here? This is a crime scene."

"I'm not leaving Faith alone while you question her."

"I'm not…" Faith began. Magnus put his lips to her ear and shushed her.

"What the hell does it matter to you?" The Chief called him out. "You've got no stake in this."

"Preacher appointed me Faiths guardian." Cain informed him. "It's a responsibility I take seriously."

"She's over twenty-one." The Chief pointed out, "You have no legal say in this situation."

"It's a moral obligation." Cain explained, his jaw set.

"Moral obligations don't mean shit to me. Just because your family founded this town doesn't mean you run it. You have no right to be at my crime scene."

"You know what? Your right." Cain looked to Faith. "How long has the good Chief been questioning you? Did he read you your rights?"

"I don't know. It's been a while. Maybe an hour or so and no he did not read me my rights." Faith answered wearily.

Cain pulled his cell phone from his pocket. "You are so right, Chief. I'm not in charge here. I'll just call the Mayor and let him know you have been holding Faith here for over an hour questioning her without a lawyer and with zero evidence. You don't have any evidence, do you?"

When the Chief only sputtered Cain went on.

"I'm sure Mayor Shafer will want to come on down and personally check things out."

"You think you scare me? This girl is a suspect in two murders."

"I'm dialing." Cain warned him.

The Chief looked like the top of his bald head was going to blow off. Cain had him over a barrel and he knew it. "Fine, take her. I was done with her anyway. Stay close to home young lady."

Cain took a card out of his wallet. He thrust it at the Chief. "You want to talk to her again. Call her lawyer."

"This is the Mayor's number." the Chief barked.

"Yes, it is." Cain smiled smugly. "He is also my lawyer."

Magnus whispered something in Faiths ear. She nodded then he vanished.

Cain raged inside that the demon slipped through his fingers. He knew there would be another opportunity but he sure as hell wanted to put an end to this before someone else got hurt. It was obvious how deeply he had managed to get into Faith's head. They had to break the link and as soon as possible.

Faith threw herself into his arms. He held her tight keeping her close so she couldn't see her friends' body being lifted to the gurney and rolled out of the store. He had accomplished something positive. They had Faith back where they could keep her safe. For that he was supremely grateful.

Cain emerged with Faith at his side. Jami swooped in to wrap Faith in a suffocating bear hug. Cain nudged them to get moving but it was too late.

"Miss Martin! Miss Martin!" A feminine voice rose above all the others.

A microphone was thrust into their faces. "Miss Martin is it true you're the prime suspect in the murders of Myrtle Moyer and Katie Shepard?"

If it were possible Faith's face went even paler. Jami had always been protective of Faith. Now even more so. Cain watched as Jami's eyes went from sympathy for her friend to squinting with rage in a flash.

Jami rushed the Reporter snatching the offensive microphone from her expensively manicured hand. She threw it to the pavement and stomped on it.

"Listen very carefully you half assed K.G. wannabee. Kimberly may have run off with Trumpy Jr. but your still a small time joke. You will never make it to the big leagues." She rasped through the boiling anger she just found an outlet for. "Now, you speak to Faith again and I'll knock those pearly white caps down your throat and throw a party while you choke on them."

"Insult me if it makes you feel better. But people have the right to the truth." Jessica Landry demanded. "You won't silence me."

"Bitch you wouldn't know the truth if it bit you in the ass." Jami used both hands and gave her a hard shove. The stunned reporters' eyes grew round as half dollars as she squealed tottering on her stilettos. Unable to stop the freefall her well rounded derriere hit the asphalt.

Cain hauled Jami back before she could kick the reporter while she was down.

Jessica Landry screeched up at her cameraman. "Did you get that? She assaulted me. I'm going to press charges."

Ennie smiled down at her. "The Chief of police is right inside that door. Knock yourself out."

Magnus watched from the crowd. The young witch had one hell of a temper. He enjoyed the entertainment she provided. Anger would burn off her energy leaving her weakened. She would not be thinking clearly. All the better for him. The young ones could always count on for allowing themselves to be ruled by their emotions.

They were walking back to the girl's house now. Faith clung pathetically to the Archer witch. His plan had worked. She was broken now. At her weakest and most vulnerable. More importantly she trusted him. He had been the one to stand beside her in her darkest hour. She trusted him and would come to him the next time without fear. Things were falling into place just as he had planned.

Soon Faith would be his. A beautiful prize for the Master. He would take her right from under Cain's nose. Magnus smirked as he considered his own cleverness.

CHAPTER TEN

Cain walked ahead of the girls. They would have to take Faith in the house through the basement to avoid the bird splatter. He also wanted to make sure the demon dog had returned to its owner and was not lying-in wait for their return. What he had not been expecting was to find not a single feather or even splat of bird shit remained from the airborne attack. Since it was all clear he waited on the steps until he saw them approach and waved them to the front door.

Jami and En looked at him in surprise but didn't comment. Jami opened the door to usher Faith inside. As Faith reached the threshold, she raised her hands to her head and cringed in pain.

"Ahhh." She groaned, jerking back from the doorway.

"Go inside Faith." Cain prompted, silently hoping she would be able to cross the threshold.

"Ahhh." She cried again, grabbing her head in her hands as Cain urged her across the line of salt. Cain felt a barrier. It was like trying to push through a sheer wall of gelatin. He sighed in relief as Faith managed to walk through. If she had been truly turned, she would have essentially bounced back unable to cross.

"What's wrong?" Jami questioned Faith. Jami did not understand the contamination in Faith was what was causing the pain.

"Nothing. I had a sharp pain but it's gone now."

Jami took Faith into the living room. Cain and En hung back.

"She's infected." En looked to Cain with worry clouding her face. "She did manage to cross the salt line though."

"I think she's hanging on by her fingernails. We got her back just in time. You should have seen her with him. Another day and we might have been too late."

They all gathered in the living room which was still in sorry shape. Faith was in no condition to even notice the mess. Jami had introduced her to Ennie on the walk home. Now En was handing a glass of whiskey to Jami urging her to get Faith to drink.

Jami sat on the couch with Faith. She bundled her into a fleece blanket yet Faith's teeth continued to chatter from shock. Jami relentlessly bullied her to sip at the amber liquid she pushed at her lips. Faith, too weary to argue, allowed herself to be bullied not even aware of the taste of the alcohol burning its way down her throat.

Ennie took it upon herself to start the job of cleaning. Trash bag in hand she roamed the living room ridding it of glass, wood splinters, and broken bric a brac. Cain's head spun as he watched her bounce busily around.

"Damn it En. Stop!" Cain barked. "You're making me edgy."

Jami and Faith both jumped spooked by the deep timber of his growling voice.

"Don't you dare try to play boss man with me." She snapped back. "Someone needs to do it and I can't sit still right now."

"Her throat was ripped out." A small quiet voice intervened." Her shirt was gone. What happened to her? What did she go through? Did she have time to be scared or was it over quickly?"

Cain and En quit their bickering and turned toward the girls. It was the first words Faith had spoken since leaving the crime scene.

"Oh sweetie." Jami cried, throwing her arms around her friend.

Faith shrugged out of Jamis embrace. "Why?" She demanded, her voice rising. "What kind of animal would do something like that? No money was taken. Nothing of value was missing. The police found her purse undisturbed. Some sick bastard just walked in and murdered a sweet innocent girl. Why?"

I know you don't want to hear this but sometimes it's just evil for evil's sake honey." Cain tried to give her an answer. "Sometimes there is no reason. At least none that we can understand."

Time was of the essence but they were unwilling to put Faith's mental health in jeopardy. They had agreed she needed some rest before hearing the awful truth of what was really happening and how she was involved.

"I called one of the girls to cover for me tonight." Jami told Faith. "I'm not leaving you. I think you could use a nap. You're exhausted. Why don't you let me take you upstairs and tuck you in?"

Jami put out her hand. Faith listlessly put her own into it. She followed Jami up the stairs like a sleepwalker.

"I'll be up in a minute." En called after them.

The door to Faith's room squeaked open. They could hear Jami getting Faith settled into her bed like a child being tucked in for the night.

En asked Cain. "What do you think? You know her better than I do. Is she going to be able to handle the truth?"

"She's stronger than she looks. We will get her through this. We have to."

"Okay then. I trust your judgement. I'm going to make sure she sleeps. I put a little something in her drink but I think this needs a bit more of a personal touch."

"I'm headed to Archers. I want to see if I can catch any useful gossip. Maybe I can find out if Magnus has shown his face lately. I need you to watch over them."

"Don't worry about us. I can handle anyone or anything that comes along. You watch your back." She warned.

"I always do." He smirked.

Ennie went into Faith's room. Jami had the poor girl wedged in with multiple pillows in various shades of pink. Faith was oblivious. Her eyes were already heavy from En's sleepy time potion. Still, she fought sleep. Jami sat beside her talking softly. En went around to the other side of the bed. She put a finger up to her lips to quiet Jami.

Ennie took a seat. She relaxed into one of the many pillows. In the experienced way of mothers, she brushed Faiths hair from her face. A lilting lullabye whispered from her lips. She caressed Faith's forehead then with feathery strokes traced her eyebrows. At last Faith's eyelids fluttered closed as she drifted into a much-needed restoring sleep.

"Geez, how did you do that? Jami amazed. "You made it look so easy."

"It was my mom magic. Sometimes just feeling safe and cared for is a kind of magic." En explained, looking down tenderly at Faith's sleeping face.

"Your so... I don't know... wise."

"I hope I picked up a few things over the centuries."

"You told Cain you would teach me."

"I will. Witchcraft is in your blood just as it is in mine. Control is the key. Well, that and common sense. You pull the power through yourself. Focus it. Use it. The hardest part is knowing if and when you should use it.'

"Sounds like a piece of cake." Jami dripped sarcasm.

"I'll be right by your side. I'm certain you're of my blood line I felt it when we unlock your powers. You will remain under my protection until I decide you can handle yourself. You truly are my little sister."

"I feel the same way. It's like I've known you my whole life."

"Well now that we've got some time to ourselves, aren't you going to ask me?"

"Ask you what?" Jami wondered.

"About Cain of course."

"Can you read minds?" Jami would not have been surprised at all if En had answered yes.

"I can read yours little sister." En answered shrewdly.

"Okay." Jami demanded. "Tell me about Cain."

Cain decided to walk to Archers. He needed the time alone to put things into perspective. Rolling his neck, the subtle pop and crack sounded abnormally loud in the still quiet of the night. The crisp evening air was doing its job admirably. It swept away the cobwebs from his mind bringing his woolley senses back online. It felt good to be out walking in the dark silence of the evening.

A few steps away from the entrance of Archers Cain felt the stabbing pain seared into the back of his skull. "Shit." he groaned, something nasty was very close.

The whomping thwack of crunching metal along with a bellowing shout drew his attention to the rear parking lot. He hurried toward the commotion and there it was, the source of the clamor.

Silhouetted in the sharp glare of a single floodlight were two figures. One figure appeared to be out cold. The unmoving body slumped ass over elbow up against the side of a green industrial sized dumpster.

Cain's eyes, better suited to darkness, identified the lump as one of the Miller boys. A harmless enough local who was a regular at the bar. The kid was usually accompanied by his buddy Eric. Cain looked around the lot and was not surprised to discover Eric was the second participant in the smackdown.

"What the hell is going on out here?" Cain railed at the one still standing.

Eric turned toward Cain. His movements were stiff and jerky. He didn't respond to Cain's question. The white eyes and demented cackle were answer enough. Here was the source of the evil he felt.

"Of course." Cain sighed in annoyance. His body began to shift. Fangs and claws appeared along with his boiling red eyes.

"If you attack Master Murderer you will damage this body I'm inhabiting." The demon hissed.

"Then I guess it sucks to be him today. If it sends you back to the pit I'm down with the violence."

Cain called his bluff. This was an old worn-out routine with demons. Cain wondered, not for the first time if they would ever come up with a new threat. Demons were such predictable assholes.

Cain moved so fast the demon never saw him coming. Before he knew what hit him Cain had a clawed hand wrapped around his throat. He threw one leg around the demons. Hooking his foot, he gave a shove with his free hand. Throwing the demon off balance he rode it to the gravel. Cain sat on the thing's chest pinning its arms with his knees.

"Gotcha."

Cain reached into the inside pocket of his leather jacket pulling out a syringe. "It's 2017 asshole. I'm guessing you haven't been in there for more than a few hours." He waved the syringe in its face. "This should do the trick. No need to hurt the kid you riding."

Uncapping the syringe with his teeth Cain hammered the needle into the demon's neck and pushed in the plunger.

The possessed body stopped squirming and began convulsing. A shrill squeal howled through the night. Windows in the cars of unlucky bar patrons shattered like rows of dominoes littering the gravel with pea sized pieces of broken glass.

"Holy Water asshole." Cain spat, as he jumped off the writhing body.

Cain watched as the body went still. The stench of brimstone grew stronger as the demon gave up the fight. A gelatinous oily smoke rose up undulating above the abandoned body. Cain stood his ground squaring off with the inky mass.

"Go back and tell your Master the next time he sends something after me he should make sure it can at least give me a good fight."

"I was sent only to observe." The darkness hissed.

"All you managed to observe was me giving you an ass whooping. I hope your boss isn't too disappointed. Give Lucy my regards. I banish you back to Hell."

The darkness began to waver forming into a funnel. It was quickly swallowed into the ground returning to the Hell that spawned it.

Cain roused the unconscious boys. He admonished them sternly about the evils of alcohol and arguing over which one of them had the hottest wife. Shamefaced they apologized to each other, swore never to bring the subject up again, and lit out for home.

Jami borrowed some blankets from Faith's closet. She and En nestled themselves at the foot of the bed so their conversation would not disturb Faith.

"Come on." Jami urged. "Tell, tell."

"Patience, it's a longish story." En took a quick glance to be sure Faith was sleeping soundly before beginning.

"Then you should get started." Jami pressed En.

Ennie chuckled at her antics and began. "I met Cain in Jerusalem. I was High Priestess to the Queen of Sheba."

"No fucking way." Jami interrupted wide eyed.

"Yes way. Now hush."

"King Solomon had requested my Queens presence. Each afternoon the King and my Queen would shut themselves up alone together and talk for hours. I would cover myself and wander the city. It was a wondrous spectacle. The dusty streets, the marketplace, the never-ending stream of people and the bright array of colors. I miss it." En sighed wistfully. "Ah well, you can't go back and in all honesty, I don't really want to. I much prefer modern day conveniences. So, we had been there about six months when I noticed that a stranger was following me each day as I left the palace."

"Hold on. Stop, wait a second." Jami stopped her.

"What now." En sighed.

"Sorry, but damn, I gotta ask." Jami began overflowing with questions. "You were there. I gotta know. Did you see the Ark of the Covenant? Did it look like it does in the movies? Where is it now?"

"I should have expected this."

"Well yeah, you should have." Jami looked at her friend with an expression like that said, duh.

"Ethiopia. The Ark is in Ethiopia. Solomon was as brilliant as the stories say. He knew what a prize the Ark was. I was there when his son Menelik arrived with it. Solomon sent priests to care for it. No, I never set eyes on it. I had no desire to become a pile of smoldering ash. I may be immortal but the Ark would have ended me."

"How did you know it was the true Ark?" Questioned Jami.

"The power. You could feel the power it contained. I've never felt anything else like it."

"Whoa."

"Yes. Now let's get back to the story."

"Right."

"So, I confronted my stalker. I pulled his head cover off and demanded an explanation. It was then that I saw his eyes. I knew he was the cursed one. I recoiled in fear."

"Ennie!" Jami squealed. "How could you be so mean to Cain?"

"Cain wasn't always as you know him. Stories were told of his unbridled butchery. He was a killer of innocents long before he became the man you know him as today. Don't romanticize who he was."

"But he changed." Jami argued.

"That's what I've been trying to tell you." En replied exasperated." He begged my forgiveness for frightening me then started to walk away. I was stunned. I called him back. He explained that he knew my identity. He was concerned about the demon presence in Jerusalem. He worried about how long Solomon would be able to control them. He asked me if I would consider teaching him magic. I told him to find me the next day and I would give him my answer." En paused for breath.

"Well obviously you taught him."

"That's right. That night I called the spirits and questioned them. I was blown away by what I learned. Cain had been killing demons. He loathed doing it because it also killed the human host. He wanted to learn magic to see if a demon could be expelled without harming the host. The next day I went out into the city. Cain was waiting. I agreed to teach him."

"Each evening Makeda, my Queen, would relate to me that she had learned from the King about demons. With this knowledge Cain and I fought the demons that escaped Solomon's control. Cain is not a witch of the blood. His magic is limited. Without his curse he would have no magic at all. "En explained. "Do you know of the Testament of Solomon?"

"Faith mentioned it once. She said Solomon had a ring that gave him control over demons. He used demons to build the Temple. She said it was a bunch of bullshit." Jami answered.

"It's not. I own one of the original copies of the Testament. We will go into it in depth when your training begins."

"Sounds like a good time. You never said there would be bookwork." Jami grumbled.

En ignored the sarcasm. "We fought the demons. I taught Cain. We were together until I left with my Queen."

"Explain together?"

"We worked together and yes we were lovers. We were never, however, in love. I know you understand the difference."

"Yes, actually, I do."

"When the Temple was destroyed more demons were released. The fallout was cataclysmic. Fissures were created across the earth. They are what are now referred to as Hellmouths."

"Like Buffy and Sunnydale?"

"You are going to be my greatest challenge." Dore grumbled, rubbing her temples.

"Centralia." Jami thought aloud. "It's so close."

"That's what drew Cain to this area. The distance between Hell and the surface is very close there. It is an easy passage for demons."

"So, demons are popping out of a Hellmouth that's only twenty minutes from here?"

"Yup."

"Well that just fills me with joy. So, what happened with you and Cain?"

"I stayed with the Queen and later I served her son. It was two hundred years until I saw Cain again."

"That's it? End of story? You have got to be kidding me."

"That's it" En confirmed.

"But, well uh, you know…when you bump into each other do you still…uh…bump into each other?"

"Not since our first separation. We love each other deeply but not like that."

"I've got to ask. Is he?"

"Now we get down to it. What do you think little sister? The man is hot and there is nothing average about him. Let me tell you, immortality, is just another word for longevity."

"Oof. No ten seconds to love, huh?"

"More like he shook me all night long."

"Yikes."

Jami's mind was running rampant until a scream from the other end of the bed had both her and Ennie jumping to their feet.

CHAPTER ELEVEN

Grey noticed Cain as soon as he walked in the door. He had been on the lookout all evening in hopes that Cain would show. As soon as Cain eased himself onto his regular barstool Grey placed a frosty mug in front of him.

"How is she?" Grey asked worriedly. He could not imagine how shook-up Faith must be. Katie was like a little sister to her. She would drag her into the bar once or twice a week to make sure she had something decent to eat and to force the shy girl to socialize.

"She was resting when I left." Cain informed him. "She tough. She will pull through this."

Cain took a long pull on his beer. He could tell Grey had more to say so he patiently waited for him to spit it out.

"The Chief was here." Grey finally spilled.

"Really?" Cain's right eyebrow arched. "What did he want?"

"He said he had a few questions for me and Micah. He heard this was the one place Katie was known to frequent. Then he asked us, and I quote, "Just how well did we know her?""

"Oh, for shit sake." Snapped Cain. "Please tell me lover boy kept it in his pants."

"Micah didn't really know her. She wasn't exactly his type."

"You mean she had more brains than boobs?"

"Exactly." Grey agreed. "So, what do you think the Chief was getting at?"

"He was fishing. I heard Katie was in love with someone. No one seems to know who the guy was. The Chief must be looking for her secret lover."

"For the record it wasn't me." Grey blurted. He popped the cap off a bottle of Bud and passed it to the guy two stools over.

"Calm down kid. I didn't think it was you. You don't lead girls on. Your heart belongs to a little blondie."

Grey's mouth dropped open. "How did you know? Am I that obvious? Crap, does everybody know?" Grey was freaking.

"Nah, I'm just that observant. Don't worry your secret's safe with me." Cain assured him. "Why don't you nut up and tell the girl how you feel?"

"I'm a lowly bartender who lives above his parents bar. I've got nothing to offer her."

"How about yourself?" Argued Cain. "You're a good kid. You're nice looking. Loyal to a fault. You work your ass off. Don't think I don't know about the backdoor action either."

Grey feigned ignorance. "I don't know what you're talking about."

"You give lunches to the Amish children who can't afford it every morning when they pass by on their way to school."

"Is there anything you don't know?"

"Yeah, why a guy like you thinks so little of himself."

"Well, the way you talk, I feel like a Saint. You want to write a letter of recommendation?"

"Don't need to. She already knows all that. Spend some time with her. Let her know what's up. I think she will surprise you. Right now, I think you would be good for her."

"I'll think about that. Thanks."

"Anytime." Cain said, realizing he really meant it. "Now get me another beer."

As Cain took a swallow of his freshie he sputtered and nearly choked on the damn thing. The air around him sizzled. He heard a pop that was inaudible to humans. They empty seat beside him was now occupied.

Seated next to Cain was a being he did his level best to avoid at all costs. Outward appearance pegged the guy at about twenty years old. His eyes twinkled ice blue. He was outfitted in current hipster fashion. Which just made him all the more irritating in Cain's estimation. Looking at the way he did, he was as out of place at Archers as a turd in a punchbowl at a Junior League luncheon. This…was one of the ten most powerful beings in creation. He was also one of the few immortals who scared the shit out of Cain although it would be a cold day in Hell that Cain let him know it.

"Don't worry they think I've been sitting here all evening." He said with a dazzling smile.

"Hello Ladocia." Cain ground out, a cheesy fake grin plastered on his face.

"Cain my old friend. Always in the middle of a mess. Speaking of which, I tidied up that little bit of destruction you left in the parking lot. No sense in letting the kiddies be accused of random acts of vandalism."

"Aren't you just Mr. Helpful tonight? If you were out there watching why didn't you just cast out the damn demon and save me the annoyance."

"I enjoy watching someone else do the dirty work. Besides, that was a cakewalk for you."

"Thanks." Cain grumbled irritably. "I'm glad you liked the show. You didn't come here just to watch me fight. You want to tell me what you're doing in my town?"

Lo snickered. "Right now, I would like one of those drinks with an umbrella in it."

"Only if you take off that ridiculous hat. I don't want people thinking my boyfriend."

"What?" Lo dripped sarcasm. "Too much?"

"Ya think?'

Lo snapped his fingers and the hat vanished.

Grey sat a drink with an umbrella in front of Lo and a fresh beer in front of Cain. He walked off to take care of other customers since it was obvious the guy wanted to talk with Cain privately.

Lo took his time sipping his drink through a swizzle straw while twirling his tiny umbrella. He behaved as though he had all the time in the world, which he did. Cain knew when he was being screwed with. He also knew Lo would get to the point when he damn well felt like it.

"This is really quite refreshing." Lo informed Cain.

"Glad you're enjoying it." Cain played along.

"Can't you guess why I am here?"

"Let me think. Your precious Key must be in jeopardy again. Why can't the seven of you manage to keep track of one damn key? Especially when it's the Key to the fucking Gates of Hell. I would like to believe something like that would be a high priority."

"If only you knew. Unfortunately, the Key cannot be easily contained. Occasionally it eludes us."

"That makes about as much sense as anything else you ever say."

Abruptly everything in the bar froze but the two of them. Lo locked his eyes onto Cains. Lo's crystal blues no longer twinkled. Instead, they showed the pain of a being who had witnessed the rise and fall of civilizations and carried the weight of those worlds with him. Cain understood. He carried that same weight within himself. "This little drama you've got going is just the tip of a shitstorm that heading your way. Protect the ones you care about. Don't let your guard down for an instant."

"Okay Great Gazoo. If you're so worried, why don't you give me something to work with? A little info on this shitstorm would be helpful."

"All you have to do is follow your nose."

"What the hell is that supposed to mean?"

Cain never got his answer. Lo was gone. The bar patrons were again moving around and speaking completely unaware anything supernatural had just taken place. The jukebox resumed playing and pool balls cracked. All was back to normal.

"Shit." Cain grunted. The evasive little fucker had done it to him again.

"What the hell?" Jami squalled.

Faiths face was twisted in pain. She cried out unintelligent gibberish. En lunged. Faith's flailing fists missed giving her a shiner by mere millimeters. En straddled her fighting to pin her arms down.

A hollow disembodied voice ricochet through the room. Magnus taunted them while he played with Faiths mind. The chilling sound raised gooseflesh on the two witches as they scrambled to protect the charge.

"I thought he couldn't get in." Jami accused. "What the hell Ennie."

"He's not in the house. He shouldn't be able to get through at all. I underestimated him."

"Don't leave me." Faith wailed. "Please don't go."

Jami stood horrified next to the bed. She leaned over to reassure Faith. "Were here. We're not going to leave you."

"She's not speaking to us." En corrected her. "She's talking to him. He's in her head."

"Fuck!' Jami cursed. "Can't you stop him?"

"Working on it."

"Magnus waits." Faith carried on clawing at the bedcovers. En was pitched around as Faith fought to get up and leave the bed. "Magnus."

Malevolent laughter continued to whip around the room. Jami fought not to scream out in frustration and fear. Then En called for her help.

"Take my place. Hold her down. Try not to let her hurt herself."

It seemed to take forever for them to alternate positions while trying to keep Faith pinned to the bed. Throughout the exhausting process Faith continued to call out to her demon lover. Jami felt hot tears roll down her cheeks. She was terrified she was going to lose her best friend.

"Faith listen to me." Jami demanded. "You're not alone. Do you hear me? We all love you. You are not alone."

"Keep talking to her. She needs to hear your voice not his."

Jami longed to cover her ears and shut out the ceaseless laughter. She knew she couldn't. She dug down pulling on some core of inner strength and she bullied her friend to fight. She kept up a litany of demands that Faith fight Magnus and come back to the people who love her.

Ennie reached into her pocket. Earlier she had put a vial of Holy Water inside just in case. There was no time to be gentle. She pulled the stopper and splashed the water onto Faiths face. All it accomplished was a scream. En reached around her neck. She removed a silver crucifix suspended on a long silver chain.

"I can't hold on much longer." Jami shouted.

"You won't have to." En yelled. She jumped onto the bed. Grabbing Faiths head she put the chain around her neck. Holding the crucifix up between the three of them she called out using the demon's true name.

"La Mech I command you to leave this place. You are not welcome here." En shouted, the force of her will carrying her demand to the incubus.

The demon weakened. The wicked peals of laughter melted away. Faith calmed instantly. The only sounds in the room were the ragged breaths coming from Jami and En.

"He's gone for now." En told Jami.

"Is she okay?"

"She will be." En vowed, her voice hard as steel. "She will be."

Magnus stood in an alley. He had been watching the shadowy commotion going on through the bedroom window. "It's so easy." He congratulated himself.

An unknown demon was approaching him. He could smell it. A waist high set of pearlescent eyes loped toward him. The stocky Rottweiler halted before him baring its teeth. A low steady growl rising from its chest.

"Who are you?" Magnus demanded of the beast. It was the same animal he had sent after Cain and the women earlier. Something else was using it now. He was amused that Cain had allowed the beast to live.

A voice emerged from the nightmarish canine though its mouth now wore a toothy smile. "I'm not stupid enough to give you my name La Mech." It answered. By using his true name, he had shown Magnus who had the upper hand.

"What do you want?" Magnus seethed.

Unnaturally still the dog responded. "I was sent to give you a message."

"Then deliver it and leave me."

"You're being watched. Ladocia has eyes on you. You would be wise to end this quickly. You're playing games with the wrong beings. Finish this before they finish you."

"Who sent you?" Magnus hissed, his eyes spitting fire at the creature's insolence.

"You need to stop worrying so much about WHO and take care of the business at hand."

A cloud of demon smog rose from the dog. It swirled around Magnus' legs then drilled into the ground at his feet.

The now harmless pet sensed the evil in Magnus. With a piercing yalp the animal ran off into the night.

Before leaving archers, Cain stopped by the kitchen. Micah fixed him up a care package. Knowing Ennie's appetite if he returned without sustenance, she might not let him back in the house. He was also hoping Faith would eat a little something. She looked like she had lost a lot of weight since he had seen her last and, in his opinion, she was too thin to begin with.

Micah had asked how the girls were doing. Cain filled him. He was surprised when Micah asked him about Katie. He had apparently spoken to her a few times and thought she was a sweet kid. Most of all he was pissed that the Chief had questioned him and Grey. He told Cain to let the girls know he would come help if they needed anything. Cain sometimes forgot that underneath the horn dog image Micah really was a good kid.

Hitting the night air, it struck him the stench of brimstone was lodged in his nose. His tussle with the demon had saturated his clothes with the nasty stink. He didn't want to risk the time it would take to go home to shower and put on some fresh clothes. Worry for the girls would not allow it. He could only imagine the mischief they had gotten in during his absence.

As Cain walked back through his conversation with Lo something clicked in his head. "Follow my nose. Very funny Lo. Why didn't you just tell me I reek asshole?"

Ennie was in the kitchen when she heard the front door rattle. Since the bad guys rarely bothered to knock, she ran to answer it.

"It's about time you got back." She scolded Cain before he could get in the house. "Ewww, you stink."

"Good to see you too. Is that anyway to greet someone who brought you food?" He taunted her, waving the bags at her eye level.

Momentarily sidelined by the hunger pangs rolling through her belly she snatched the bags Cain was holding in front of her face. She waved him inside and hustled back to the kitchen with her bags of goodies. Cain chuckled when her tummy let out a fierce growl.

"I humbly apologize. You're my hero. You still stink though." En raised an eyebrow in question.

"I'll fill you in later." He evaded. "How are the girls?"

Cain followed waiting for an answer. She opened the first of two bags inhaling appreciatively. "Ummm meatball subs. You really are my hero."

"I'm thrilled that your tummy is doing the happy dance. Now what are you NOT telling me?"

En located paper plates and napkins. While she fixed plates for everyone, she filled Cain in on what went down during his absence. "He's in her head." She finished, then pulled four bottles of Bud from the fridge. She handed them to Cain to uncap.

"We already suspected as much."

"Well, dammit. Watching that sweet child crying for him was just…ahhh…repellant." En rubbed her tired eyes forcing back the tears that threatened to erupt.

Cain pulled her into his arms. "We'll get them through this."

En shook herself as if she could shake off the despair. "I need to feed them. Will you help me take this up?"

"No. Bring it into the living room. I'll carry her down. I refuse to eat inside that day glow pink room."

"It's fuschia." En corrected him.

Cain headed for the stairs with a martyred sigh.

Ennie had managed to finish cleaning up the living room after they sent Magnus packing. Jami and Faith sat on one side of the freshly polished coffee table. Cain and Ennie sat opposite them.

"Eat." En commanded the girls. "You need the energy."

The room fell silent as appetites were satisfied. Each one of them were lost in their own thoughts. Faith only nibbled at her food. No one pushed her. They were all grateful to see her eat anything at all. The color was at last returning to her face although the dark circles under her eyes remained.

"I swear." En grumbled, setting her empty beer bottle on the table. "If this goes on much longer, I'm going to turn into a lush."

"Cheers." Jami said, tipping her beer toward En then polishing it off." I need another. Anyone else?"

Everyone nodded.

Jami returned with four cold ones. She passed them around and plopped back onto the floor.

Faith caught Jami's eyes. "Here's to us."

"Here's to love." Jami continued.

"All the times that we fucked up." They finished in unison. Jami was a big Halestorm fan. This was their drinking song. A way to remember the good times.

"I fucked up. Didn't I?" Faith asked.

"No." Jami insisted. "You did nothing wrong."

Cain and En chimed in. All three of them talking over each other assuring her that none of what was going on was her fault.

"Okay stop." Faith got them quiet. "I need to know what the hell is going on."

Cain, En, and Jami all looked to each other waiting for someone to find the balls to volunteer.

"Jami, you wanna take this one?" Cain offered her up like a sacrificial lamb.

"Sure." She assured him, giving him the hairy eyeball.

CHAPTER TWELVE

Jami took a deep breath and before starting. She looked Faith in the eyes then let her have it. "Okie Dokie." Jami began. She ping ponged her eyes between Cain and Ennie before settling back on Faith. She squared her shoulders and dove in. "Magnus is a demon. An Incubus to be exact. He's been draining you in your sleep. That's why you have been so run down lately. He wants to corrupt you soul and deliver you to his Master. Your destiny is to do good things in the world. He wants to make sure that never happens."

Jami paused. Faith seemed to be taking it well so far. The looks she got from Cain and En were encouraging her to go on.

"Our old friend Cain is reeely old. Like Old Testament old. In fact, he is the original Cain, as in Cain and Abel. Except now he's on the side of the good guys. Ennie here." She waved a hand in En direction. En waggled her fingers at Faith. "She's the Witch of Endor. She's a good guy too."

"We met earlier." En reminded Faith. "You were pretty out of it."

"W.O. Rodne?" Faith questioned.

"Yes. How did you know?"

"I have…had your books at the store. I recognized you from your pictures."

"Of course. I should have realized."

"Okay." Jami interrupted, not wanting Faith to be thinking about the store. "Last but not least. Dum, Dum, Dum." She rumbled for dramatic effect. "I'm a Witch."

Three sets of eyes focused on Faith waiting for a reaction. When it came it was the last thing Cain, the only male in the room, expected.

"No way." Faith gaped. Her green eyes opened wide as she attempted to read the truth from her friend's face.

"Way." Jami confirmed.

"For real?"

"Yup." Jami shook her head up and down vigorously.

"Bullshit."

"No shit."

"Day-um."

"Uh huh."

"Stop!" Cain bellowed. Mick Jagger was singing in his head. "It's just my nineteenth nervous breakdown. Here it comes…Here it comes…" He shook his head to clear the Stones out.

"What language are you speaking?" *I need a damn female to English dictionary. Is it possible to get a migraine twice in the same day?"*

Cain's man tirade set En off. She burst into hysterical laughter. It turned into a full-fledged giggle fit. She flopped onto her side holding her stomach gasping for breath between bouts. Her laughter infected Jami. She added her bubbling peals of giggles to En's. The two of them rolled around on the floor crazed with mirth.

Faith watched them in wonder. She looked to Cain as if asking if this was a normal thing or had they lost their minds.

Cain smiled. He knew they needed an emotional release even if it was at his expense. Laughter was always better than tears. Better they get it out of their systems now then fall apart when it really mattered.

"I guess that's why they call it Happy Hour." Faith remarked.

Jami crawled over and sat by Faith's feet with her back against the sofa while she tried to catch her breath.

Ennie fueled by food jumped up. She actively began collecting paper plates and empty bottles.

Jami called out. "Wait up En. I'll give you a hand."

"That's okay. You sit with Faith." She threw Cain a pointed stare. "Cain will help me."

"Sure thing." He volunteered. Cain began picking up empty bottles En's hands were too full to carry. They disappeared into the kitchen.

"What's up?" Cain asked when they were alone. He took the empties and disposed of them in one of the two bins under the sink.

"Time to spill. You want to tell me why you smell like demon funk?"

"Probably from the demon I met up with in the parking lot of Archers."

"And?"

"And… It was just a lower-level piece of shit. I took care of it with some Holy Water."

"Okay." En stood with her hands on her hips. "Now tell me the rest of it." She took a seat at the kitchen table.

"The rest of what?" Cain asked trying to look innocent.

En gave him the look.

"Fuck me." Cain grumbled, even an immortal man can't help but be quelled by The Look.

En smirked. "Not for centuries. Spit it out already will ya."

"Ladocia is here." He dropped the bomb.

"Just Ladocia?"

"Isn't he enough?"

"You know as well as I do if one of the Bloody Seven is here the others aren't far behind. Why the hell would they be interested in an Incubus? A powerful Incubus, but it hardly seems worth their time."

Cain went to the fridge and got another beer.

"Grab me one please."

He twisted the top off the one in his hand and passed it to her then reached back inside to get another for himself.

"I don't have a clue what their up to. Lo and the rest only show themselves when there is a threat to their fucking Key. He insinuated there is a bigger picture here. He said that this is only the beginning."

"Then why don't they do something about it?" En bitched.

"I have a feeling whoever is yanking Lo's chain is keeping him leashed until they see how our little drama plays out."

"Well, that is truly frightening. I can't imagine anyone having the balls to yank Lo's chain."

"Whoever it is must have the biggest balls of them all."

The vote was unanimous. Everyone wanted a shower and a change of clothes. They were all feeling grubby and in need of refreshing.

Faith got first shot at the bathroom followed by Ennie. While they got dressed and blow dried in Faiths bedroom Cain got his chance to wash off the demon stank. Jami had opted for last shower not wanting to be rushed by others waiting their turn.

Instead of rummaging through dresser drawers for something to wear Jami sat on her bed blankly staring at the wall. "He's in my shower." She whispered to herself. "He's naked in my shower."

This was a fantasy that had been playing out in her head for years. Only in her fantasy she was in the shower with him. Her hands would be slick with soap as she ran them down his muscular chest to his washboard abs then around to his firm ass. Her pale body pressing against his caramel skin while she licked the dripping water off his collar bone, ahhh, just the thought made her mouth water.

"Ack!" She squealed. "I'm acting like a twitter pated teenager."

Hoisting herself off the bed she was resolved to bring her fantasies to reality. She would march right into that bathroom, strip, and join him in the steamy confines of the shower. It was time to make fantasy reality.

She stood rooted like a stump. Her legs refusing to propel her forward.

"Come on girl, move." She ordered herself.

The unexpected bleating of her cell phone made her jump. She glared at the phone. "Not now." The phone ignored her, continuing its annoying hum. Angrily resigned she snatched it from the bed.

"What?" She snapped at the unknown caller.

"Jami Archer?"

"Yeah. Who is this?"

"My name is Magnus. I'm sure Faith has mentioned me."

"Yeah, she said you have a little pecker." Jami may have sounded like a smartass but she could feel herself begin to tremble.

"Very amusing." His tone of voice said he really wasn't finding it amusing at all. In fact, he sounded downright prissy.

"I've got nothing to say to a cocksucking sick fuck like you."

"Shut up bitch." He snarled.

"Fuck you." Jami pushed the end button. She was raging as well as pants pissing scared. Her hand was trembling so badly that when her phone went off again her fingers stumbled across the smooth surface. When she put the phone to her ear she didn't speak. She couldn't. Screams were blaring in her ear. She clapped a hand over her mouth to cut off the screams that threatened to tear from her own mouth.

"Jami…help me…Jami." There was a loud crash then a second of silence.

"I have your brothers."

"Grey?" Jami squeaked. "Micah?"

"They are alive for now. Are you ready to listen or should I change their present status?"

Jami choked on the threat. Knowing that the demon would have no problem killing her brothers as he had Katie. Jami wisely kept her comments to herself and did as Magnus asked. "I'll listen."

"Good choice. You will come to me. If you tell Cain or his pet Witch or they follow you, I will kill your brothers. Do you understand?"

"Yes." She ground out through clenched teeth.

"Excellent." He purred, giving her goosebumps.

"Where?" Jami asked. Her voice sounded strange in her ears as if it were someone else speaking.

"Your bar. You have ten minutes. If I even suspect you are not alone, I will paint the walls with their blood."

He ended the call. Jami's ass hit the bed. The phone fell from her hand to land soundlessly on the carpet.

Jami bowed her head. "God help me." She whispered.

Jami crept down the hallway. Peeking in Faiths room she was grateful to find her alone. She knew she could bullshit Faith but she could never pull it off with Ennie. So far luck was on her side.

She fought to keep her voice casual as she lied. "Hey girl. Cain asked me to run out to his place and grab him some clothes. I won't be long."

"Do you want me to go with you?" Faith offered. "I don't think they would want you to be alone."

"Nah, you stay here. You've had enough today. I'm a Witch remember? I can handle myself. You know Cain wouldn't let me go if he didn't think it was safe." Jami lied like a champ.

"Your guess you're right. Just be careful and hurry."

"I'll be quick."

Jami slunk down the stairs. She could hear Ennie mumbling to herself as she plowed through her suitcase in the living room. Some guiding hand must surely be leading her. She was going to get out of the house without anyone trying to stop her or tag along.

As quietly as possible she cracked open the front door just enough to shimmy through then gingerly closed it behind her.

Jami hit the sidewalk running. She didn't notice the chill in the night air. Her bare feet flew across the rough pavement. She had no plan. There was nothing on her mind but her sibling's safety. She just ran.

Cain leaned back against the shower wall. The hot water pounded his chest. He turned to wet his hair. Shit, but the shower thrumming into his tense muscles felt good. He did a thorough once over with a bar of Dove. His hair still stank. All he could find was some pomegranate scented shampoo. The smell reminded him of Jami. It conjured images of her. Vividly erotic images. Closing his eyes, he allowed himself to enjoy a moment of healthy lust.

He visualized her on her knees in front of him. Her ash blonde hair darkened by the water. He fisted his hands in her wet hair. She stared up at him, keeping eye contact while her mouth moved up and down his cock in a slow torturous rhythm.

Cain growled. He knew his eyes would be glowing red with lust. He slid his hands down his ripped abs easing his way down to his throbbing hard on.

Instead of grabbing his dick he grabbed the faucet and turned the water on ice cold. "Fuuuck."

What the hell was he thinking? He was too damn old for this shit. She was so young. She had yet to see the true ugliness of his world. She still had a great big world to explore and a lifetime to explore it. When this was over, she would leave with Ennie. All he had to offer her was a few nights of really great sex. And he knew it would be fucking terrific. But he didn't want to get involved with her. She might just be the one who could make him feel something. That thought terrified him more than going up against a horde of demons.

Cain stood in the frigid water until any sexual thoughts were impossible. Teeth chattering and goose fleshed he turned the tap off. Jerking back the shower curtain he grabbed a towel and roughly dried himself. He wrapped the towel around his hips then inspected the clothes Jami had left for him. She had been careful to explain the items had belonged to Grey.

He spied a pair of tightly whites. No fucking way. He would go commando before squeezing his boys into those nut crushers. There was a pair of basic gray sweatpants that didn't look like they would be too awfully short and the inevitable black Archers tee shirt, extra-large. The shirt would be snug but it would have to do. He got himself dressed, ran a brush through his hair, and made use of the toothbrush Jami left him. It was still in the wrapper. Mom Archer must keep them stocked in toothbrushes as well as jar candles.

He went in Jami's room in search of socks. She wasn't there so he went to Faith's room in search of Jami. There he found Faith and Ennie sitting on the bed with their heads bent over piles of white cotton bags tied at the top with string. Cain knew these bundles to be Ennie's herbs.

He had to smile at the picture they presented. Both were dressed in workout clothes and had their hair pulled back into ponytails. They looked like two teenage girls getting together to discuss boys and fashions, or whatever it was girls discussed when they got together.

"What are you lovely ladies working at?" Cain asked with a genuine smile.

Faith looked up with a smile. Ennie was the one who answered. She held up a bag of herbs and waved it at him. "Taking stock of our supplies." En looked again tilting her head. "Why are your lips blue?"

Cain gave her a sour look.

"Heh, heh, heh." En chortled.

"Where's Jami? It's her turn in the shower and I could use some socks."

"Your socks should be here any time. Jami went to your house for clothes." Faith spoke innocently.

"Why would her clothes be at my house?" Cain asked joking.

"Ugh, Cain your jokes suck. If you're going to use Faith as your straight man you need to pay her. A lot"

En teased.

Faith looked confused as she looked at Cain. He got a lump in the pit of his stomach. Ennie looked at both of them and realized she was missing something.

Stating the obvious Faith said, "You already have clean clothes on."

"Why would you think that she went to my place?"

"She came in here when you were in the shower and told me you asked her to go get you some clothes. She lied to me." Faith groaned at the fact she had been duped.

"Uh oh." En whistled.

"Damn that girl." Cain cursed. "How long has she been gone?"

"Fifteen, twenty minutes at the most."

"Where would she go that she wouldn't want us to know?" En asked.

"I saw her phone on the floor of her room. I should have known something was up. She wouldn't have left it behind." Cain started to simmer.

"Maybe she got an emergency call?" Faith suggested.

"Why would she lie about something like that?" En wondered. "If something was wrong, she would have told us."

"I'll go grab her phone." Faith offered, hurrying out of the room.

"Stay calm. It won't do any good to lose your temper." En ordered Cain. "You need to think straight not angry."

"Right."

"It says the last call was from an unknown caller fifteen minutes ago." Faith said as she returned.

"There's only one place I can think of that she would go." Cain surmised. "Lo told me to follow my nose."

"Well, that makes sense. Care to elaborate?" En drawled.

"Actually, it does. I stank like brimstone from fighting that demon at Archers." Cain explained.

"Are you sure about this?"

"It's all I've got. I need to get to the bar. That's where she is."

"What if it's a trap?" Faith worried.

"Of course, it's a trap." Cain confirmed. "I've still got to go."

Cain looked pointedly at En. "You two stay put. Be ready for anything."

"What's your plan?"

"Dunno. I'm gonna wing it." Cain grinned dangerously. "Could one of you ladies please find me some socks?"

CHAPTER THIRTEEN

Jami skidded to a halt at the door of Archers. She bent over with her hands on her knees gasping for breath. All of her life this place had been as much her home as the house next door where they lived. A welcoming place full of friends and laughter. Not so tonight. As she stood before the entry she was nauseated from fear. The familiar stones of the building now seemed an unfamiliar menacing facade.

The keys she held in numbed fingers stabbed in the direction of the keyhole. After several fumbling attempts sheer luck brought her to her goal. She threw open the heavy oak door so hard it bounced back and nearly knocked her over.

Anorexic streams of moonlight offered small reprive to the lightless vacant interior. Jami squinted searching for any sign of movement. She moved silently. Her ears were perked as she listened for any signs of life.

"Jami?" A weak voice cracked.

"Micah, are you okay? Did they hurt you? Where's Grey?"

"They have him upstairs. Quick untie me before they come back."

Jami walked toward the sound of her brother's voice. Feeling her way through the tables she located him in the far corner. His head hung limp. He sat unmoving with his hands tied behind his back.

"Did they hurt you?" She whispered as she moved to untie him. "Micah what?"

He stood in one fluid motion. The loose rope dropped to the floor. "Surprise."

"What the shit? This isn't funny. What's going on?" She railed. Then she got a good look at his face. His eyes were white.

"Micah went bye-bye." The demon hissed.

"Nooo." Jami moaned in denial. She did not want to believe what was right before her eyes. Her baby brother was a puppet for a demon.

A multitude of thoughts bounced spastically through her head. What was happening to Gray? Should she try to make a run for it? If she ran would the demon kill one or both of her brothers? Was Grey already dead? How could she be so stupid?

He saw the indecision on her face and took action before she could bolt. He swung his fist making contact with her temple then grabbed her around the waist before she could hit the floor. Placing her in the chair he had just vacated he tied her arms behind her back. Uncertain of her powers as a witch he had carved a dampening spell under the seat of the chair to drain her. He wanted her helpless. She was the real bait.

He had been instructed to contact Magnus when Cain arrived. He would eventually turn up searching for her. A spell had been carved around the threshold. Cain would be denied entry. When they lifted the spell the first thing Cain would see would be Magnus killing the young Witch.

At the house Faith and Ennie were hastily assembling a demon fighting arsenal.

"Have you got a small duffel bag or backpack?" En asked.

"Sure, I'll get it." Faith went to the closet and returned with a black leather backpack. She handed it to Ennie.

Ennie took the pack. She looked confused. "It's black."

"Yes."

"But…it's not pink." Ennie gasped in mock surprise.

"Ha. Ha." Faith played. "You're just jealous because you don't have my style."

En laughed at her snark. Most individuals would be a gibbering mess. Faith was handling things a lot better than any of them had expected. En had taken an immediate liking to the sweet girl with a big heart. If nothing else came out of this fucking nightmare she would be thankful for her new relationships with Jami and Faith.

"May I ask you something?" Faith tentatively inquired.

"Anything."

"I heard you call Jami little sister. Is that a Witch thing?"

"More of a blood thing. I'm certain Jami is from my bloodline. True Witches, the strongest ones, are born to it. It's passed down through the blood."

"That means you have children."

Leave it to Faith to ask about children En thought. "Yes, I had three beautiful daughters. Two were mortal one was a witch. My mortal daughters lived happy lives. They married and had children. My bloodline is scattered across the earth. I occasionally stumble onto one as I did Jami. When I do it's always the one with the gift of Witchcraft."

"What happened to your third daughter?"

"She was taken from me a very long time ago."

"I'm so sorry." Faith couldn't miss the flash of pain on En's face. She felt terrible that she had brought up something that hurt her.

"No matter the time span the pain of losing a child does not diminish. That is why I stay away from my descendants as much as I can. Knowing who I am puts them in danger. I would never have revealed myself to Jami had she not already been in danger."

"I'm sorry I brought up bad memories."

"Sweet child." Ennie laid a palm on her cheek. "Don't upset yourself about it. If I didn't want you to know about it, I never would have told you."

Faith was choking up. "Thank you."

Jami regained consciousness. She kept her eyes closed fearful of what she would find if she opened them. She thought it was best to just play opossum. It seemed her luck had run out. Her captor had been watching and knew the instant she came around.

"I know you're awake."

Jami opened her eyes and glared at him. "You've already killed Grey, haven't you?"

"He's alive and sleeping like a baby." The demon admitted. "Magnus has plans for him. It's your life you should be worrying about."

"Oooh… is the part where the part where the evil villain tells his helpless victim all about his dastardly scheme?"

"May as well. I've got some time to kill." He shrugged. The demon inside Micah pulled out a chair. He turned it backward straddling it to sit. His blank stare was a reminder to Jami that Micah may already be lost. She refused to allow herself to think that way. They would save Micah from this monster. They had to. "Let's see, where to begin. Ah, I know. Let's start with you. Cain will come running to your rescue. Magnus will slit your throat and leave me on the brink of death. Magnus will poof out to safety and make an anonymous call to the police revealing the name of the real killer."

"Cain is innocent. The police will never be able to prove he killed anyone."

"Of course, your right. When they find Grey upstairs covered in our blood it will be Grey who they arrest for murder. I'll pull through so it will only be attempted murder for me."

"No one will ever believe Grey would hurt us."

"They will when it comes out that we discovered Grey's secret."

"What secret?" Jami snapped, her fear mounting.

"He's the one that murdered poor Katie. At least that's what the police will think after they search. I made sure I wore one of Grey's dirty shirts when I killed her. Trust me when I say there was more than enough of her blood on it when I finished with her. That shirt is now laying under the corner of Grey's bed where it can easily be spotted."

"He had no motive to kill Katie."

"Yes, he did. Grey is in love with Faith. The police knew Katie had an obsession with someone. It turns out she was stalking Grey. He was afraid her relentless perusal would ruin any chance he had with Faith. I discovered what he had done to Katie. I confided in you. We confronted him. Begged him to turn himself in to the police. He went mad and attacked us. I will, of course, confirm all of this from my hospital bed. So, you see. Cain will be busy trying to keep your brother from frying. Magnus will get to Faith and the Witch. When

Cain has lost everyone, it will be easy for Magnus to kill him. Hell, he won't even put up a fight."

"You're a dick."

"That's all you have to say?"

"What, you want me to tell you how clever you are? Sorry asshole but there's a major flaw in your plan."

"This plan is foolproof." He hissed.

"You seem to think Faith is the weak link in the chain. That is your mistake. She knows what Magnus is now. She will fight him so will Ennie."

"The Witch is nothing. The girl is already too far under Magnus' control."

"Don't underestimate the Witch of Endor. She will fight for Faith. So will Cain. Magnus could never kill him. You are both delusional."

"With you dead Faith will beg Magnus to take her. They won't be able to stop it." He smirked.

Jami was afraid he may be right. Faith lost too much. If they were to take her from Faith she might not recover. She might give up and go to Magnus willingly.

"So, what do you get out of this? I can't believe you're helping Magnus out of the kindness of your little demon heart."

"I get to keep this attractive young body. Maybe when things die down, I'll find a rich widow to support me while I fuck every hot piece of ass who catches my attention. I could become the next great serial killer."

"Everyone needs a goal." Jami snorted.

"Right." The demon agreed.

"You're missing one thing?"

"Oh really. What's that?"

"Me asshole." A masculine voice came from behind him. The demon didn't have time to turn around and defend himself before Grey attacked. Hefting an industrial sized baking sheet above them he brought it down on Micah's head with all his strength. The demon fell to the floor with a satisfying thud.

"It's about time Bro. Could you have waited a little longer?"

"Talk about ungrateful." Grey groused. "And to think you're the sibling who doesn't try to frame me for murder."

"Could you untie me please?" Jami grumbled.

"Yes, sister dear."

The solid old door of Archers threatened to be ripped from its hinges. The door shook the walls so hard beer signs were shaking threatening to fall from their anchors and crash to the floor.

"It's Cain." Jami surmised as the front of the building shook. "Let him in before we owe Mom and Pop a new door."

Grey jogged to the abused oak panel. Jami stayed where she was rubbing her wrists to restore the circulation. The pins and needles from having her wrists bound were painful. As Grey grabbed for the handle, she was hit with the thought that she probably should have been the one to open the door.

"Hey Bro…"

Oops, too late. Grey stood rooted to the floor. Cain was trying to get in the door only to bounce off the invisible barrier of the demon's wards.

Grey just goggled at the sight before him. His mouth hung lax as his brain fought to assimilate what he was seeing. His rational mind insisted it couldn't be real and yet here he stood. Cain was a fucking Vampire.

"Invite me in." Cain roared.

"Screw you!" Grey shouted back. He heard the slapping of bare feet behind him and knew Jami was approaching.

"Jami, stay back." He ordered, pushing his sister to keep her safely behind him.

"Grey, stop." She argued, squirming. "You don't understand."

"Jami…" He argued, exasperated at her lack of cooperation.

At last, she squirmed free of her brothers hold. "Cain, I invite you in."

Cain burst through the barrier. His curse remained in control. His eyes spitting flames, fangs bared, he rushed at Jami. Grabbing her tightly he held her close then just as quickly shoved her away. His eyes swept over her inspecting from head to toe for any injuries.

"Are you hurt?" He demanded.

"I'm fine, really."

Cain kissed her with desperation born of relief. Reacting on instinct at the thought that he could have lost her. Jami returned the kiss with a fierceness of her own.

Grey was back to gaping. He stood stupidly watching as his little sister accepted the tongue of an undead bloodsucker into her mouth. Wtf? This had to be the weirdest night of his life.

"Yo J." He ranted. "You're smooching up on a fucking vampire."

Jami pulled her lips off Cain. "No, I'm not."

"Then you are either blind or in denial." Grey argued as he tugged at his sister's arm.

Cain turned to face Grey. All signs of his curse were gone. He once again looked like the man Grey had always known.

It was too much for Grey. His legs gave way and he sank to the floor. He shook his head trying to rattle his mind back on track.

Jami took pity on her brother. "Grey I would like to introduce you to Cain. Son of Adam." She looked up to Cain. "Cain you already know my brother the goofball."

Cain reached down giving Grey his hand and pulling him to his feet. "Come on kid. Buy me a drink and I'll explain everything."

Magnus loitered in the local Turkey Hill Mini Market. He was killing time until his lackey alerted him to Cain's arrival. He found these small shopping spaces fascinating. He stood now leisurely enjoying a Red Bull. Shortly after arriving in the mortal realm he had discovered the beverage and was now addicted to them. He browsed the headlines of the tabloids smirking over the outlandish things mortals chose to believe. Magnus much more enjoyed the glossy magazines with the busty supermodels gracing their covers.

He was the only customer at this early hour. They young human behind the counter sipped his coffee while keeping his eyes on Magnus wondering if he was planning to steal any of the merchandise, he was responsible for.

Magnus picked up the newest issue of Cosmo glancing through the pages in the hope of discovering what precisely the elusive G-spot was and why it was so important for a man to locate.

A snap stung inside his head causing him to drop the magazine. The psychic link between him and his partner had been severed. Something must have befallen the worthless demon.

That could only mean one thing for Magnus. His carefully laid plan had failed.

Magnus' rage was a thundering storm through the small store. Cans of soda popped their tops, bags of chips exploded like colorful confetti flying through the air, all manner of paper goods blew through the racks.

The shocked clerk shouted. "Hey dude, stop that shit. You're tearing the place up. You gonna pay for this mess or what?"

Magnus stomped through the wreckage towards the clerk who stood staring at the man coming toward him like a deer caught in headlights. Magnus thrust out a hand taking the stunned clerk by the throat. The clerk lost control of his bladder. A warm stream of urine flowed down his leg and onto the linoleum floor.

Magnus looked with disgust at the yellowish puddle. "Whatever." He sneered. It was more than likely best not to leave a body behind. The boy was scared enough no one would believe his fantastic story anyway. He released him. The clerk huddled down behind the counter shaking. Magnus just walked out of the store into the cool night breeze.

All was not lost. He could still bring pain to Cain before sunrise.

Magnus flashed himself to Faiths backyard. Through the curtains he could see two female figures moving around the room. He knew it was Faith and the witch.

Excellent, Cain would return to find their bodies waiting for him.

"I would like you to do something for me." Ennie prompted Faith.

"Of course, anything." Faith readily agreed.

En went to where they had laid out their arsenal on the fuschia comforter. She reached down and plucked out a small silver dagger the size of her palm.

"If we mingle our blood you will always be able to call out to me. I will hear your voice even if I am on the other side of the world.

All you will need to do is think of me. Call my name. I will hear you and I will come. We will have a psychic link."

"I would love to be able to have that connection with you." Faith said, putting her hand to her heart.

En struck quickly. She grabbed Faith's hand slicing across the palm with her dagger. En repeated the action on her own palm. She laced the fingers of their bleeding hands together effectively mingling their blood.

"Repeat this with me three times." En instructed.

"My blood into your blood…Your blood into mine…Binding us together…Forever ours to find."

Faith and En repeated the chant three times.

Faith felt her hand tingle and grow pleasantly warm. En unclasped their hands. Faith looked at her palm in awe. There was not a trace of blood. The cut was completely healed.

The kinship Faith felt was unexpectedly brought to an end. A bolt of lightning flashed through the room leaving behind a black scorch mark on the pink wall. Faith cried out. En grabbed the girl and shoved her back. "Stay behind me." She insisted.

The air shimmered slowing taking on the shape of a man. Neither one of the girls had a question as to who the shape would become. The room quivered with a sickening feeling of dread.

En pulled on her power making ready to square off against Magnus.

He stood by the window. The look he threw at En told her she was nothing more to him than a minor irritant. As if he thought the infamous Witch of Endor nothing more than a fly to be absently swatted away.

"How did you get in here? I banished you?" En demanded.

"Simple really. Just like your bit of blood magic before I popped in. I bound Faith to me. I fed her a few drops of my blood while she slept."

Faith stood immobile. She was sickened by the thought that she had come into contact with his evil blood. She wished there were a way to purge herself. A bleaching of the soul.

"So Witch, you can't banish me. I'll keep coming back. With the blood bond in place I no longer need an invitation. Only Faith can expel me and she won't do that. Will you love?"

That voice, those eyes, they held Faith under their spell. She was unable to find her voice to speak. He held her as surely as a wild animal held its prey.

En turned and taking her by the shoulders gave her a good shaking. "Faith snap out of it."

Faith continued as she was, entranced.

CHAPTER FOURTEEN

Explanations had to be delayed until more practical matters were attended to.

Cain attended to their captive. This time there would be no surprise escape from his restraints. Grey went to switch on a few lights so he and Jami could quit tripping and stumbling around in the dark bar. Jami went to check the door for damages and relock it before someone saw the lights, thought they were open, and stumbled inside looking for a drink.

They reconvened at the bar. Cain straddled his usual barstool, Jami took a seat beside him, and Grey took his place behind the bar. They had done this hundreds of times after closing. This could have been any one of a hundred different nights, but it wasn't.

Grey pulled up the stool he kept behind the bar sitting across from them. He set out three squat glasses as well as a bottle of Jack. Under the hazy bar lights, he poured the whiskey and goaded the Immortal. "You got some splanin' to do."

Jami stifled a laugh behind her hand.

Cain leveled a frown at the pair of them sighing in resignation. The more people who knew the truth the greater the danger. Unfortunately, Grey had seen too much. Saving his sister had earned him the truth.

"I'm not a vampire. I'm an Immortal. I was cursed to wander the earth until the end of days."

"Uh huh." Grey digested that bit of info. "I realize I'm a little slow but I can put a few things together. Cain Adamson huh. Son of the first dude, ever right? Adams-son. Wow you're as old as dirt."

"Not quite, but close." Cain grimaced.

Grey looked to his sister. She nodded the affirmative. "It's true Bro."

Grey raked his hands through his hair. He expelled his breath in a long burst.

"Grey..." Jami started.

He held up a hand for her to stop. "Whoa Sis, just chill a sec and let me take this in okay."

Cain put a hand on her back the look on his face telling her to have a little patience. She clamped her mouth shut. Her brother was such a down to earth level headed person she should have known it would be more difficult for him to accept than it had been for her.

After several minutes of silence Grey spoke up. "So, what the hell are you doing here? I mean why would an immortal being hang out in Podunk Pennsylvania?"

"What better place for me than Adamstown? "He quipped." This is the Antiques capital of the U.S.A. I'm as antique as they come."

Jami snickered. "Seriously."

"This is the closest I've ever come to a home. I was cursed to wander. I can only stay so long before I put myself at risk. I'm always drawn back here though."

Cain rubbed his chin. Jami noticed his eyes seemed distant. His mind was somewhere else. He was thinking of a different place, a different time.

"The truth is I'm honoring a promise I made a long time ago. I vowed I would protect this family."

"Do Mom and Pop know about you?" Grey asked.

"Yeah, anyway." Jami added, wondering why she had not thought to ask that question herself.

"No, you kids are the first to know since Levi and Caroline Archer."

"Shit." Blurted Gey. "Did you hear that? He's talking about our freaking ancestors."

"What don't you understand about immortal?"

"Don't get snarky with me brat." Gray snapped at his sister. "This is some freaky shit."

"Hold up you two." Cain stopped the bickering before it escalated. "Grey I'm still the same man you've always known. The only difference is I've occasionally got fangs and claws. Oh yeah, and as you so nicely put it, I'm as old as dirt."

"Right, sure, no big deal." Grey looked at him like he thought he was full of shit.

"I would never harm any of you." Cain spoke seriously.

"I know that man, I do. Even when you were al grrrr'ed out, I was more shocked than afraid. I didn't think you would hurt us. I was just bugging that's all."

"We good?" Cain asked, holding out his hand.

Grey clasped the hand Cain offered and shook it. "We good."

The Witch of Endor was on the battlefield. She fearlessly faced down Magnus from across the room. A twisting stream of white and blue energy danced between her outstretched palms. En corralled the energy in one hand. She sent it toward Magnus. It flew like a lightning flash straight at the center of his chest. The blast never met its mark. Instead, it was consumed by a wall of flame Magnus used to shield himself. En pulled her power and twice more sent the balls of energy flying at her enemy only to have the same disappointing results. She could not even put a dent in his shield.

Magnus swiped at the chest of his black Ralph Lauren button down. "Not even singed. You're lucky. I love this shirt. Now, it's my turn." He taunted her.

Magnus made a fist. He gave his wrist a sharp twist. En fell to the carpet landing flat on her stomach. She fought to push herself upright. Her limbs would not respond. They were dead weights keeping her pinned in place. She was paralyzed from the shoulders down only able to move her head. Of course, he allowed that movement he wanted her to be able to see him take full possession of Faith. Ennie glared at him from her awkward position on the floor. Magnus smiled greasily back at her.

"I need to be sure you have a good view of what's going to happen. Make sure you tell Cain how easily I took her and how much she enjoyed it."

"Ennie!" Faith screamed. She backed up until the backs of her legs came in contact with the bed. Faith clutched at the bed behind her using it as an anchor.

Faith's head throbbed. Her tongue was pasted to the roof of her mouth. Her heart pounded so hard she was certain it could be heard at the opposite end of town.

How strong was he? She wondered. After what En had thrown at him and he didn't so much as flinch. They were going to die. Faith had no idea how to fight him.

He began to speak to her. Her body stilled again. Everything began to move in slow motion.

"It's time for us Faith. There's nothing left for you here. The Archers are finished. Grey killed Katie and Micah. He killed the young witch too. He will spend the rest of his life in prison. You will never see any of them again. Come with me now. Leave the pain and betrayal behind."

Drawn to him Faith began inching closer. Her eyes unblinking. Her face a mask of complacency.

"Faith, no." En pleaded. "He's a demon. He lies. They are not dead. Listen to me. He can't take your pain. He does not have that kind of power. He will only make it worse. He will bring you a new unimaginable pain. A never-ending pain."

Faith never took her eyes off Magnus. She didn't listen to En's pleas. Magnus held his hand out. His handsome face smiling at her drawing her to him. His voice smooth and compelling. "She doesn't want you to be happy. She's jealous of us. She's the one lying to you. Witches are evil. You know the truth." He continued. "Isn't it written Thou shalt not suffer a Witch to live?"

Faith continued on her course like a sleepwalker. As she passed where En lay plastered to the floor she urged her friend with the hand she held behind her back to stop her cries.

Ennie refused to give up. "Faith, stop. Don't go any closer." She begged.

Faith did stop. She looked down. "Shut up En. I've made my choice. Magnus has given me so much. It's time for me to give back. Can't you see? This is how it was meant to end."

"I knew you would make the right choice." He gloated.

Faith looked at Magnus. How had she not seen it before? Evil seeped from his pores. The face she thought beautiful was truly ugly twisted by hate. The stench of his evil clung to him like a rancid cologne.

"Magnus." She sighed.

"Yes, my love."

"This is gonna hurt." She spoke smoothly.

"What?" He looked confused.

Faith whipped a pink plastic pistol filled with Holy Water from behind her back. She shot him point blank between the eyes. Her heart thrummed with satisfaction at the look of surprise on his face.

"I sever our connection. You no longer have any power here. I banish you from this place. I uninvited your nasty demon ass." It was Magnus himself quoting scripture that told her how she needed to fight.

"Bitch." Magnus hissed. He covered his face with his hands. The Holy Water bubbled and blistered the skin of his face. "This is not over." Magnus managed the last threat before he smoked out and vanished.

Faith looked down at En. Waving the plastic gun in her hand she told En simply, "It's fuschia." Then she sagged to the floor.

The banishment of Magnus released the hold on Ennie. Free from the paralysis En scrooched over to where Faith sat. "That was some damn fine shooting Tex."

"Thanks." Faith smiled. She had just freed herself from Magnus. She felt giddy.

"You had me worried for about half a second."

"Fool me once shame on you. Fool me twice shame on me." Faith quotes. "I'm not that gullible.

"Good to know."

"I'll admit it. I was scared shitless. I thought we were going to die. When I backed up and felt that water gun, I thought what the hell, may as well give it a shot."

"Puns? You're giving me puns? "En chuckled. "And to think, you gave me a hard time when I asked you to fill those guns."

"My bad. "Faith owned it. "So, what now? Do you think he's… Jami and the boys?"

"No. I honestly believe their fine. Demons excel at lying. Cain would never allow them to be harmed. I'm sure he got to them in time."

"You really think so?"

"I'm certain of it." She declared as she looked her in the eyes and braced her hands on her shoulders.

As soon as the words were out of her mouth her cell phone chirped. En listened for a minute. "Okay" She said, ending the call.

"That was Jami." She informed the worried girl. "They are fine. They need us at the bar. She wants us to bring her phone."

"Is it safe to go out?"

"Now is the best time. Magnus will be holed up licking his wounds."

"Well then." Faith said. "What are we waiting for?"

Magnus paced the dank length of his lair. He despised the musty smell of the old beaten earth he trod upon. His status demanded so much more than this vermin infested hole. Even now he could hear the scratching of rats as they sensed his evil and fled his arrival.

That idiot apprentice of his ruined everything by being abducted by the enemy. The Archers were still breathing. Faith was lost to him. The comfortable home he had appropriated upon arriving in this provincial town was no longer secure. He was sure the idiot had revealed its location. This filthy hole was the last place that remained secure. The entire situation was unacceptable.

His body thrummed with rage. The very foundation he took cover in began to quake. The old stones cracking from his fury. Loose mortar crumble to powder dusting a dirty coating onto his pristine Gucci loafers.

Magnus was ready to end this. In his mind they were all now guilty of crimes against him. He envisioned killing them in all manner of creative ways. One by one, forcing those waiting to watch their loved ones die slowly. Cain he would save for last. Magnus revealed at the thought of Cain's anguish. The time had come at last.

Magnus attempted to flash himself to Archers. Nothing happened. His powers were gone.

The ground under him began to shudder. His internal organs vibrated while his bones loosened themselves to rattle together. The air around him grew thick with the stench of brimstone. Fissures split the ground under him. Scorching heat blasted upward melting the soles of his shoes. His blood heated close to boiling. Magnus felt his corporeal form dissipate. A guttural rumble rose up from below. His vaporous form was pulled downward. Magnus was being called home.

Now that Cain had fessed up, he was ready to hear what the kiddies had to say for themselves. He did not doubt whatever it was would be cringe worthy.

"Who is volunteering to fill me in on what happened tonight?" He asked.

Jami and Grey cast fearful glances at each other neither one of them wanting to spill their guts. Cain swiveled his barstool toward Jami. "Go." He ordered.

"I got a phone call from Magnus. He told me he was holding the boys here. He gave me ten minutes and told me to come alone. He said if I brought you or you followed me all I would find were their dead bodies."

"So, you walked right into a trap. Way to use your head." He snapped at her. Cain tried to ignore the tightening in his gut as his mind played out scenarios of the many different ways things could have ended.

"That's not fair. They are my brothers. What was I supposed to do leave them to die?"

"I'm sorry I'm not being FAIR. I thought I was treating you like an adult."

Jami's face bloomed crimson with a combination of embarrassment and anger.

Cain wasn't finished with her. "You're in this game now. You've got to lead with your head, not your emotions. If you don't you won't be playing very long. You will be dead."

"You're an asshole." She blurted angrily.

"What's your point?"

"Ack." Jami gurgled, her anger making it impossible to make a coherent statement. "Gah. Whatever."

Cain turned his focus to Grey who had remained silent through his and Jami's exchange.

"Now that she's got that out of her system." He smirked. "You're up. Tell me the rest of it."

Grey having played the hero in the story unabashedly took up the narrative.

"Here's what happened." He began. "We closed up and went upstairs. Micha's been acting weird for a while now. Think about it. That stuff with the girl the other night. The kid is a dog but he never would have pulled such blatant shit even with Mom and Pop gone. He keeps his conquests under wraps. He doesn't want any of them finding out about each other. And any girl who would pop their mouth at his sister like that would have been out the door no matter how hot she was."

Grey stopped to check his audience to see if his point had been made. It had. Both Cain and Jami were nodding in the affirmative while murmuring words of agreement. Gratified to see they were all on the same page he continued.

"I just sat down on my bed. I put some P. Roach on Pandora getting ready to chill. Micah waltzes in and hands me a beer. Right away my radar goes off. The kids never that thoughtful. He kept looking at the beer then looking at me like he was waiting for me to toss my head back. It creeped me out. I thought he wanted me drunk so he could put the moves on some secret honey. I told him to get out so I could sleep. I don't know why I did it but I poured the beer out the window. I got in bed without taking my clothes off. I was wide the fuck awake. I pretended to sleep while I listened to him moving around the living room."

"I can't believe you wasted a beer." Jami busted on him. Grey just ignored the smart crack.

"Something about the way he was acting made my skin crawl. I can't explain it. It was almost like a voice in the back of my mind was warning me."

"Good instincts." Cain recognized.

"No shit." Grey agreed. "I guess it was about fifteen minutes later I heard my door open. He came in and went straight for the empty to make sure I drank it. Then he whispered my name. I didn't answer. He put his hand on my shoulder and shook me. I moaned a little and played like I was asleep. He must have believed it because he left."

Grey paused for breath. He poured himself a shot, downed it, and began again.

"I heard him going down to the bar. I waited, then I followed the little butt munch. I stayed on the stairway with the door cracked so I could keep an eye on him. I nearly pissed myself when I saw Jami show up. I snuck to the kitchen. That's when I saw him jump up, sucker punch J, and tie her to a chair. I waited, trying to figure out what the hell was going on and what I should do about it. Then she woke up and I managed to catch her attention. J kept him distracted. I got behind him and bashed him in the melon with the baking sheet." He finished. Then added a question. "That's not my brother is it?"

"No, it's not." Cain answered.

"Didn't think so." Grey shook his head a look of misery on his face.

"I gotta ask. "Cain wondered, not quite ready to follow up on the whole possession thing. "I know I'm going to pay for my curiosity but what the hell made you use a baking sheet? There's a kitchen full of knives, rolling pins, a bar full of bottles."

Grey hesitated looking sheepish. "I wanted to see if his head would make a dent. You know, like in the cartoons."

"Grey!" Jami screeched. "What the shit."

"That's as good a reason as any. Did it?" Cain held back his mirth as Jami's eyes shot daggers.

"What? Leave a dent?"

"Yeah."

"Nah." Grey pouted, not at all ashamed for his behavior.

"I've heard some dumbass conversations in this bar but this has got to be the dumbest." Jami declared, shaking her head.

"Okay folks. Now I've got a few questions. I need to know what we're dealing with so we can get Micah back." Cain shut down the jokes and got serious. "Take your time and think before you answer."

"Shoot."

"You said he's been acting weird. How long has that been going on?"

"A few weeks. I thought it was a chick thing at first. Then he started getting really bad headaches."

"That's right." Jami chimed in. "I remember him asking me for some aspirin. I sent him upstairs a few times to rest. He was really hurting. I tried to get him to the doctor but he wouldn't listen."

"After the headaches he would seem like a different person. A real asshole." Grey added. "I thought it was the pain ragging him out."

"When did the headaches stop?" Cain questioned.

"Maybe a week or two ago?"

"Anything else you can think of?"

"He would disappear at really odd times and…" Grey stopped, uncertain about saying more.

Cain needed to hear it all if they were going to have any chance of separating Micah from the demon. "Even if it seems stupid or insignificant, I need you to tell me."

"He smells funny, okay. At first, I blew it off. As he got worse so did the smell."

"A burnt acid smell?" Cain described.

"Yes, exactly."

"That would be brimstone."

"How would Grey be able to smell it?" Jami asked, "I thought only a supernatural being could smell brimstone?"

"They live together. When it gets strong enough a mortal can pick up the smell."

"So, all of that demon talk between Jami and Micah was real? My brother is possessed."

"Yeah."

"Well, we can fix him, right?" Grey asked Cain hopefully.

"Yeah, I refuse to believe otherwise."

Lo and Sully stood amidst the wreckage of what had been Martins Bookstore.

Sully determinedly averted his eyes from the one space on the floor devoid of debris. The place where Katie's body had been. He pushed his Stetson back on his head and rubbed his face with his palm as he waited for Lo to speak.

Lo kicked at the books littering the floor. "That was too fucking close."

"Calm down. I got to the kid in time." Sully reminded him. "I'll be damn lucky if I get to keep my balls after I fucked with the whole free will gig. That's twice now I've had to stop the kid from doing something stupid. The son of a bitch needs a full time Guardian Angel."

"If you hadn't been in his head warning him about his brother things would have had a very different outcome. Magnus would be celebrating with his Master instead of hiding like a bitch and The Key would be out of our hands again."

"The Key is still under wraps. I did my job and managed to save a few humans in the process."

"Magnus will be back." Lo predicted. "You can bet your ass that son of a bitch has something else up his sleeve. He won't let this end until he gets what he came for, Cain."

Sully watched as Lo bent down and retrieved something from the debris. It was a pair of glasses. The lenses were cracked but still intact. He folded in the earpieces then carefully placed them in the inside breast pocket of his jacket. Damn, Sully wondered, had something at last penetrated the layer of self-containment his brother kept tightly wound around himself? About fucking time.

As Lo felt the small piece of Katie resting against his chest he prayed for Magnus' return. He wanted to be the one to have the final confrontation with the demon. He craved the sound of his sword ringing out as it cleaved Magnus' head from his shoulders.

Lo thought his brother must be reading his mind when he saw Sully reach for the hilt of his sword.

"My girl is hungry for some demon flesh." Sully growled, baring his teeth.

"She's going to have to wait. I went to the Boss. Do not engage the Incubus."

"This is bullshit." Sully snarled.

"We're to continue to monitor the situation."

"Monitor the situation. What? In other words, we sit on our asses and wait for another innocent to die. I don't fucking think so."

"Don't get your dick in a twist. He never said exactly how long to monitor the situation before we step in." Lo smirked.

"A loophole. I like loopholes." Sully grinned broadly, flashing his pearly whites.

CHAPTER FIFTEEN

The cavernous chamber was carved from a vast deposit of Fire Opal. A circular staircase led to a platform the size of a basketball court. Outstanding in the middle of the platform sat an unrivaled work of art carved by the hands of Fallen Angels. The throne was sculpted from black diamonds into the shape of the Warrior Angel who occupied it. The beautifully cold face depicted the bloodlust of battle. Its wingspan ranged twenty feet wide. A spear clutched in its left fist. A sword gripped in its right. The Warriors massive body was dressed out in full battle armor.

Lucifer, once favored above all Angels, lounged carelessly upon the throne carved in his likeness. He was seven feet of masculine perfection. His body long, lean, and muscular with silken skin of a creamy unblemished gold. Black leather pants clung to taut thighs. His chest was bear with the exception of a solid gold Etruscan Cross encrusted with black diamonds that hung from a heavy gold chain.

The Fallen Angels body paled in comparison when looking upon his painfully exquisite face. He was, simply put, temptation. Spirals of hair the color of spun gold framed a face sculpted by Creation itself and hung carelessly to the small of his back. Almond shaped amethyst eyes were surrounded by thick dark eyelashes. His straight nose sat above full lips the color of a dewy pink rosebud. It should have been too feminine a face but its maker had allowed a square chiseled jawline leaving no doubt that he was pure male.

A petite caramel skinned female draped herself fluidly around his body. Her hands seemed child sized as she languorously massages his broad chest. The look on her face said that just the feel of his skin brought her untold pleasure.

Curled up at the right side of the throne rested a beastie made from nightmares. The shape of a lion, its body and legs were covered in burgundy scales. Only the enormous head and tail covered in the fur of a male lion erupting into a glorious orange mane.

The floor along the walls and behind the throne held pockets carved at random belching fire toward the vaulted ceiling. The light from the fires refracting off the black diamond of the throne casting a constant kaleidoscope of color against the opal walls.

Magnus knelt in supplication at the foot of the stairs. He had no recollection of how long he had been back in this realm or how long he had been kneeling before his Master. It could have been minutes or it could have been years. His bowed head throbbed in pain. His neck and back were now fused into their current position. Attempting to move was not an option.

A pair of black alligator skin boots their toes tipped in silver came into his field of vision. One of the boots caught him under the chin raising his head.

"La Mech, what am I supposed to do with you? I gave you one simple task and you fucked it up." The voice that spoke washed over the kneeling demon with was of power resembling electric shocks.

Magnus kept his mouth shut. He knew if he uttered one single syllable, he would get another close up of Lucifer's boot. The next time would be quite a bit more painful.

Lucifer called out to his female companion. "Cyndahl."

"Yes, my Prince." She answered obediently. The gold fishnet bodysuit she wore fought to hold her attributes in place as she wriggled like an excited puppy.

Lucifer smirked at her eagerness. "My lovely one. I have need of you."

"Anything my Prince." She licked her ruby lips in anticipation.

Lucifer laughed lustily at her antics. "Later."

Cyndahl pouted with disappointment.

"Find Tearzahn for me. Bring him directly to me. No stopping to play."

"Anything for you my most perfect Prince." She fawned, then hurried off to do his bidding.

"Stand up and face me." Lucifer commanded Magnus. His rumbling voice sent flames bursting throughout the chamber waking the sleeping demon lying by the throne.

Though moving would be painful Magnus did not dare to show it. He got to his feet. The creature descended. It's crocodile like claws clicking down the stairs. The demon was surprisingly fleet of foot and soon stood at Lucifer's side.

The Dark Lord smiled down at his brother. "Beelzebub you've come out of your coma." The demon shook its mane, releasing a fearsome roar showing twin rows of jagged teeth.

Magnus dropped his jaw at the mention of the demon's name. Could it be possible? This thing was surely not the Fallen Angel who was known to be Lucifer's right hand.

"Close your mouth. You look ridiculous." Beelzebub spoke.

Lucifer lost it, laughing his ass off at the look on Magnus' face. Magnus snapped his mouth shut and glared at the pair.

"You really gonna shoot daggers at me and my brother? What? Don't we measure up to your high standards?" Lucifer scoffed.

Magnus changed his attitude. "Never Master. You are perfection. I am and have always been your loyal servant."

"Then where is my fucking soul? I sent you for a soul. Where is it?" He looked down at his brother. "B, you see a soul?"

The demon let out another roar.

"I beg your pardon my Lord. There have been difficulties." Magnus pleaded.

"You should beg." Lucifer agreed. "And don't whine to me about Cain and the Witch. Of course, he's in your face. I sent you after that girl to fuck with him. Are you telling me you can't handle seducing this bitch out from under Cain's nose? Maybe we need to change your status as an Incubus? Perhaps you should spend some time with the lesser demons. That would cure you of your feelings of superiority."

"My Prince I could never feel superior to you. I exist only to serve. She's within my reach." Magnus dared." I beg of you. Give me twenty-four hours and you shall have your soul as well as Cain's misery. We both want the same things Master."

"You've almost got it right. You see I'm changing your orders. I'm raising the stakes." Lucifer paused listening. "Enter."

Cyndahl approached. A flame haired Warrior followed her. Both bowed.

Lucifer bade them, "Arise." He looked first to Cyndahl. "Go to my private rooms and wait."

"Oh yes." She oozed seductively, then scampered off like a child who had been given long desired gift.

Tearzahn gave Lucifer a throaty chuckle. "You just can't keep away from the women."

"They have always been my downfall." Lucifer replied in mock shame. They both laughed pulling into an embrace.

Magnus looked on. His gut filled with worry. Tearzahn was Lucifer's enforcer. He was not joking when he said he was raising the stakes. Magnus had never seen the deadly legend before but he had heard the stories of Tearzahn's brutality.

"It's been awhile brother." Tear spoke.

"Too long or not long enough?"

"A bit of both." Tear laughed.

Tear was fire to Lucifer's sun. His hair was the red of a ruby hanging just past his shoulders in a straight fall of silk. Large eyes the color of amber missed nothing. His face carried a youthful glow. The look of wide-eyed innocence at odds with his bloodthirsty character.

"I have a job for you brother. Finish it in the next forty-eight hours and you get a bonus."

"A bonus beyond killing. What is better than bloodshed?"

"Since I know your love of pussy is nearly as great as mine… how about three months above? Will that satisfy your lust?"

"Not hardly. It sounds too good to be true. You're either jerking my chain or it's a shit assignment."

"Would I do that to you?" Lucifer asked. His looked of wide-eyed innocence rivaling that of a child.

"Absolutely."

"Your right. I would." Lucifer readily agreed.

"So, what's the job?"

"La Mech here." Lucifer inclined his head. "Is in need of some supervision."

"You want me to babysit. No wonder your offer is so good."

"It involves Cain."

"Son of a bitch esiasch. Is this shit never going to end?"

"I'm working on it, but as you know time is irrelevant on so many levels. This however needs to reach its conclusion. I've waited long enough. Things above are ripe for the kind of change only I can offer."

"If it wasn't for you and it wasn't about him, I would tell you to shove it up your ass."

Beelzebub bared his teeth at Tear angered by the disrespect he was showing their brother.

"Shove it B. Who do you think I am to shiver in fear of you? Why don't you nut up and do something instead of hiding behind our brothers skirts like a frightened child? By the way nice tail. Keep it tucked between your legs. Do you even remember a time when you weren't a coward?" Tear taunted his brother.

With a snarl and his claws outstretched Beelzebub launched himself at Tear. Lucifer froze the attacking demon in midair.

"You coddle him." Tear accused, unfazed by the attempted attack.

"You're correct. I will continue to do so for as long as I choose. I rule here."

"Yes, my Lord." Tear replied dripping sarcasm.

Irritated with both Tear and B Lucifer growled. "Take your charge and return him above at once. I'm bored to tears by all of you. Go, the clocks ticking." Lucifer snapped his fingers. Tear and Magnus vanished. Beelzebub fell to the floor with a snarl and a yelp.

Grey held the door open for Faith. She rushed in with Ennie hot on her heels. Grey watched amused as En bounced backward with a curse.

"Dammit." She screeched. "They warded the door."

"Can you remove the wards?" Faith asked.

"Not until I've been invited in."

"Come in." Faith invited her.

"Sorry sweetie but it has to be a member of the family." En stared pointedly at Grey.

"You must be Ennie." Grey surmised. "I've heard a lot about you. I'm Grey."

"Nice to meet you Grey. Would you mind inviting me in or would you just like to continue this conversation across the threshold?"

"Grey grinned. "I would never leave a lady standing outside." Which is exactly what he had been doing. "Please come in." He waved her gallantly inside.

Ennie walked inside. She gave Grey an aggravated look. "Another smartass around here. Imagine my surprise."

"Sorry I couldn't resist." He apologized.

"Can you remove the wards now?" Faith asked.

"With Grey's consent."

"Ennie I would like it if you would remove the wards." Grey supplied.

"I would be happy to."

Ennie winked at Faith ready to put on a show for Grey. She held out her right-hand palm up. For dramatic effect she blew onto her palm. A ball of energy took form. En raised her fingers over the energy ball then waggled them. She pointed to the wards etched around the door frame. The energy passed through her fingertips. The wards began to glow then vanish.

Grey watched dumbfounded. Faith struggled not to laugh at him. The energy trickled into a frizzle. En began to sway on her feet. Grey snapped out of it and made a grab for her wrapping his arms around her waist.

"You don't look so good."

"I just ran out of juice. I'll be okay." She assured him.

"Let's sit you down." Faith suggested. They made their way to where Cain and Jami sat deep in conversation.

Faith got En settled then pulled Jami into a bear hug.

En caught her breath as she listened to Faith scold Jami. Jami for once was smart enough to stay quiet and accept the well-deserved reprimand.

"Can I get you anything?" Grey offered En.

Ennie propped her chin on her hands to help her keep her head up. "You know what sounds good if it's not too much trouble. A hot cup of tea with cream and sugar."

"No trouble. Anything else?"

"Food?" En perked up."

"Roast beef sandwich, pickles, chips?"

Ennies stomach growled loud enough for Grey to hear. She would have been embarrassed if she weren't ready to chew on the bar. "Oh, yes." She moaned. "I've finally found the perfect man. Will you marry me?"

"Sorry but my hearts spoken for."

"Crushed again." En sighed.

Cain sensed the demon was awake and eavesdropping. He needed to corral his crew and get them focused. He did not want the damn thing to over hear something it could use against them.

"En, I hate to interrupt your flirting. Unless you two are leaving to pick out rings we need to decide a few things."

En stuck her tongue out at him. "Hold your horses' big guy. I need to get something in my stomach before I pass out."

Cain was about to ask why she had depleted her energy to the point of passing out when Grey arrived with a tray of food. He laid the feast out in front of her. She eagerly slurped down half a cup of tea. The look of pure pleasure on her face was comical as she bit into the sandwich. She smiled in thanks when she saw Grey had thought to add a large glass of orange juice.

En reached across the bar and grabbed his hand. "Whoever she is she's a lucky girl."

Grey's eyes darted to Faith. Ennie gave him a cheeky wink. "Good choice."

"Considering the way you're inhaling that food I'm guessing something happened at the house." Cain probed.

En frowned at him. "Faith will you please fill them in while I finish eating."

"Sure." Faith described their encounter with Magnus. She downplayed her part of the confrontation. When she finished Grey gave them the Cliffs Notes version of his adventure then Jami had her turn. It wasn't long before everyone was up to speed.

"Looks like the kids won this round." Cain grumbled to En.

"Were becoming old and obsolete." En sniffed dramatically. "Maybe we should retire and let the kiddies fight the evil nasties."

"No way." Jami disagreed. "Your old fogies need to stick around and train up us youngsters."

"I can't win." En threw up her hands in defeat.

A slew of filthy curses interrupted their teasing. Cain was the only one who did not seem surprised by the outburst.

"Damn things got a foul mouth." Grey stated the obvious.

"Ennie can you do something to shut him up?" Jami asked.

"Sorry honey, until I get some sleep and recharge my batteries I'm out of commission."

"Aw hell looks like I'll have to do it my way." Cain muttered stalking toward the demon.

The demon saw Cain approaching and knew he had best get his licks in before he got knocked out again. "Faith, Katie wanted me to give you a message. It's all your fault. She cursed you until I ripped out her throat. Ahhh she tasted sooo sweet."

His vicious tirade of bullshit was cut short as Cain's fist connected with his jaw knocking him cold. He immediately felt guilty for his reaction. It was Micah's face he hit. When he saw the look on Faiths face all guilt vanished.

Faith's face was drained of color. She dropped her head. Jami put an arm around her shoulders. "Don't listen. It's lying."

"About what?' Faith lashed out. "That he killed her or that it's my fault? It sounds like the truth to me."

"Enough." Bellowed Cain, making the four of them jump. "You will not give some piece of shit demon the satisfaction getting to you. The blame for this damn mess lies solely on me and I'm damn sure I've got the shoulders to bear the weight."

Four sets of eyes stared.

"Everyone upstairs. Get some sleep. We're having an exorcism this afternoon. The bar will be closed tonight. I will wake you all at two o'clock."

"What about you?" Jami asked.

"I don't need to sleep. Someone has got to watch our boy. No go on. You're all exhausted."

No one dared to argue. They trooped toward the stairs. Faith hung back. Jami tried to push her along but she shook her head and looked toward Cain. Jami understood Faith's need to speak to him alone. She had not had the chance since she was told the truth about their situation. Jami went on her way allowing Faith her privacy.

Faith screwed up her courage and bravery approached the irascible immortal. "May I speak to you a moment?"

The look on her haunted face broke Cain down. The anger boiling inside his gut melted away. He held his arms open and Faith flew into them. She buried her face in his broad chest taking solace in the strong arms that held her snug.

"I'm so sorry baby girl. So damn sorry you got caught up in all this." He held on as she trembled. He worried he would crush her she felt so tiny and fragile in his arms.

"I'll end this. I promise you." He swore.

Faith pulled back enough to look at him. Cain decided then looking into her dry eyes that she was not as fragile as she looked. She had an inner core of strength that he should have recognized before now.

"She trusted me." Faith choked out. "I was all she had and I let her down. I should have been there for her. Instead, I was out worrying about strangers."

"This is not your fault. You were all used as pawns to draw me into a sick twisted game. You do not take the blame on yourself."

"I've got to make arrangements for Katie." She spoke with a steadier voice. "I have no idea how to find her mother."

"That is my problem. I'll take care of it."

Faith blinked rapidly as the truth dawned on her. She could not believe she had not put it together before now. "It was you. I always wondered how Katie's mother escaped that abusive bastard."

Cain neither confirmed nor denied her assumption. He continued with the problem at hand. "I'll take care of the arrangements. You've had enough."

"Thank you." She accepted gratefully. "It's nice to have someone to lean on again."

"I'm a poor substitute for your father. He was an exceptional man. I could never replace him. I wouldn't even try. I want you to know I will always be here for you. Big problems or small worries I'm right here if you need me."

Faith swiped at her eye before a tear that threatened to fall escaped. "I think that you would make a wonderful second father. I believe dad would be happy to know you're looking after me."

Cain's mind flashed to his own doomed children. That she would feel that way shook him. He had to clear his throat before he could speak. When he did it was to make a vow. "I vow from this day forward I will care for you as my own." He took her slender hand, kissed her palm, and placed it over his heart.

For the first time since she lost her father Faith didn't feel adrift in the world. She felt like she once again had an anchor and thought that maybe he might just feel the same.

"You know there is someone else right up those stairs who wants to take care of you."

"Jami's my sister. En now too. I'm grateful for both of them."

"I'm not talking about the girls."

Faith considered that. Cain could almost see the light bulb go on over her head. Bingo. A silly grin spread across her face.

"I see that thought crossed your mind." He was not surprised.

"He's not interested in a girl like me. He's Grey. He's Jami's cool older brother. He's like… Grey."

"Well hell you two were made for each other. You're as goofy for him as he is for you."

Her eyes lit up. It was a nice change. "He's goofy for me?" She demanded.

"Hell yes."

"OMG." Faith bubbled.

"I have no idea what that means." Cain chuckled. "Now my girl it's time for you to go upstairs and get some rest."

"Yes, sir Pops." Standing up on tip toes she planted a smacking kiss on his scruffy cheek. "Goodnight." She smiled, then turned and hurried up the stairs.

Not comfortable at all with the softer emotions Cain grumbled. "Now I'm Pops. I wish I could grill the kid and tell him he's not good enough for my girl. Unfortunately, they will be great together. I just have to make sure they get the chance."

CHAPTER SIXTEEN

Cain flipped the wall switch. The office light buzzed as it stubbornly flickered to life. The fluorescent bulb casts a sickly glow over the tidy room.

He located a yellow legal pad on the desktop. Foraging in the middle drawer he came across a fat black Sharpie and, hot damn, a roll of Scotch tape. In bold letters he wrote the word closed across the paper. Ripping his makeshift sign free of the tablet Cain took it and the tape to the front entrance. Opening the door, he taped the closed sign over the entrance window then retreated back into the office.

Cain pulled out the rolling desk chair and dropped his weary load on the seat. He closed his eyes and concentrated on his rising anger. His talk with Faith had quelled it momentarily. Walking through the bar and seeing Micah tied to the chair brought it rising back to the surface. Everyone he cared for had narrowly escaped Magnus' last plot and he had not been there to stop it. He had been as useless as an infant.

His relationship with Micah and the Archers was the only thing stopping him from rushing into the barroom and ripping the demon in the kid to bloody bits. He had not sacrificed a host since the days when in his ignorance he had known no other way. The thought that he could even think of it now when someone he cared about was inside there crying out for help sickened him. He had to calm himself before he tried to question the damn thing or risk falling back into the all-consuming rage that had cursed him.

A familiar voice spoke to Cain from the doorway. "Don't you dare go dark side on me now. After all of these centuries are you really going to throw it all away?"

Lo reclined against the doorframe. His arms folded across his chest his legs crossed at the ankles he looked completely at ease. No longer dressed in the current fashion instead he was dressed like the assassin he truly was. Brown leather pants, tan tee shirt, and worn steel toe work boots. While common enough, on Lo looked menacing. Even his boyish looks came off more aggressive. The tight fit of his clothes giving definition to his true size and stature. He may have been lounging casually but his countenance…wickedly pissed.

Cain's head was not in a good place to take any shit from the Immortal Assassin. "If you're not here to help get the fuck out. I don't have the patience for your head games."

Lo ignored the venom in Cain's voice. "You have never needed to keep your anger at bay more than now. Stop feeling sorry for yourself."

Cain exploded from the chair throwing it into a backward spin. He pounded his fists into the desktop. "Fuuck yoou."

"You curse too much." Lo antagonized Cain. "Considering how long you have been alive I would expect you to have a larger vocabulary."

"Grrr." Cain flew at his antagonist like a wild beast unleashed. His claws raked Lo's throat leaving bloody trails behind. Lo vanished. He reappeared behind Cain tapping him on the shoulder with his index finger. Cain spun grabbed Lo around the waist and bulldozed him into the wall. The sound of breaking ribs was evident.

This time Cain turned to find Lo seated calmly behind the desk. Any evidence of violence committed upon his person vanished. His elbows were planted on the desktop with his fingers steepled under his chin. A look of unending patience adorned his face.

"Done yet?"

The snarky comment only incensed Cain more. He gave the desk a mighty heave hoping it would land on the asshole. The heavy metal desk levitated five feet into the air and hung there.

Lo looked under the desk at Cain. "This is pointless you know. I'm glad you blew off some steam. Now why don't you sit down and we will have a civilized chat."

"If I catch you, I will kill you."

"Why do you think I keep disappearing?"

The ridiculously honest answer managed to diffuse Cain's anger. He barked a laugh. "So, the king of evasion wants to talk. Well Hail to the King." Cain gave him a mocking bow.

"No need for accolades." Lo returned the desk to its original position.

"Fine." Cain propped his ass on the corner of the desk. "I've got some questions I've wanted answered for a very long time."

"You misunderstand. When I said what I meant I will speak and you will listen."

"Then there will be no chat." Cain replied, stubbornly setting his jaw.

"You will listen to me." Lo demanded, unbelieving that Cain would dare to challenge him.

"No, but I will finish our fight."

"Oh, for the love of…" Lo sighed dramatically. "I will allow you one question. Then you will listen to me."

"Are you shitting me? No, I want five questions and no bullshit. The truth. You are capable of telling the truth, aren't you?"

"You're dickering with me, really? The world hangs in the balance and you're behaving like a merchant trader."

"Yup." Cain waited for Lo's answer.

"No, I will not agree to it. Too much knowledge could bring about a disastrous outcome. I would essentially be tampering with your free will. That is something I am forbidden to do."

Cain counter offered. "Three or nothing. You can just poof your ass outta here and leave me the hell alone."

"Done." Lo agreed. He realized Cain meant what he said. There would be no further negotiations. If this was what it took to get Cain back on track so be it. "Ask your questions."

Cain was struck temporarily mute. He had honestly never expected Lo to agree. All things being equal in Heaven and Hell if you made a deal it could not be broken. Lo would have to answer and answer truthfully.

"How did I survive the flood?" Cain blurted. "I should have gone down with the rest of the world. Why didn't I?"

Lo looked like someone just spit in his umbrella drink. "You're kidding right. That's your first question? I could think of a thousand questions better than that. Why didn't you ask me where Magnus is hiding? Or what is the meaning of it all? Hell, what about the ratio between hot dogs and buns?"

"I don't need to know where he is. Magnus will come crawling out of his hole and come after me. When he does, I'll be ready. I've already come to understand that there is no meaning to it all. And I don't eat hot dogs. Now answer the damn question."

"That was before my time." Lo evaded.

"But you know something don't you?" Cain pressed.

"Stories, rumors…"

"And…"

"Michael." Lo answered. "He took it upon himself to make sure you survived the flood. I have no answer as to how he did it."

That blew the top of Cain's head off. He sure as shit was not expecting that name. This just dredged up more questions. "Why would Michael save me?"

"He needs you." Lo answered. It was technically not a lie. More of a half-truth. The Order was forbidden from telling Cain any details.

"Yeah, needs me alive to prolong my torment."

"That's two questions honestly answered. You have one question left. Make it a good one."

Cain swallowed the lump in his throat. His palms were clammy.

So, this is what fear felt like. He had not felt this since the day he was cursed. There was really only one question that mattered. The one that woke him up in a cold sweat and motivated every decision he made. He had not really needed three questions. Now that he was so close to an answer, he was not at all sure he could bear to hear it but he knew this was the only opportunity he was ever going to get.

"Will he forgive me?"

Lo felt his uncertainty, his pain, and fear. It was so strong it slammed into his chest like a living thing. This was the question he had been expecting. The one he did not want to answer. The one he could not answer.

"I don't know." Lo answered simply and sincerely.

Cain was silent for a moment. He lowered his head. "Thank you for your honesty."

Furious on Cain's behalf Lo snapped. "Don't you dare be humble with me. I know that each single life is sacred. You have saved countless lives. Keep doing what you do. Be humanity's champion. Believe the forgiveness they are granted is for everyone. Most of all grab happiness where you can find it. If you find love wrap yourself up in it like it's a warm blanket on a frigid night. Open yourself up to the people who care about you. These are the things that will keep you on the right path. These are the things that will save you."

"Damn Dr. Phil."

Lo poofed himself out. Cain stood stupefied. He had always believed Lo had his own agenda. He still believed that, but maybe he also had a heart.

Cain blinked. A pinprick of light bounced around the office like a drunken Tinkerbell coming to a halt an inch from his nose. It spoke. "You still owe me a chat." It disappeared with a tiny pop.

Cain laughed. He laughed until his sides hurt. When he was finished, he had a new determination.

"Time to go be Humanities Champion."

Maybe he should consider getting a cape.

Was there anything better than fresh coffee? Cain stood behind the bar blessing Juan Valdez while emptying the steaming mug in his hand. This, he decided, was mankind's greatest discovery.

Across the room he could see signs of life beginning to stir. Their captive was awaking. It was time to get down to business. He took a seat in front of the demon and placed a syringe of Holy Water on the table beside him.

Micah's body jerked. Colorless eyes opened wide as they confronted the fiery ones trained on them. Cain scooted his chair closer. "Sleeping Beauty is finally awake. We've got some business to take care of. I want some answers."

Cain clamped his clawed hands around the demons bound wrists. He brought his face closer. "You're going to give them to me."

"I know nothing Murderous One."

"Liar." Cain squeezed on Micah's arm. Claws dug into tissue thin flesh leaving behind weeping puncture wounds.

"I know nothing. I swear it." The demon whined.

Cain snatched the syringe off the table. He waved it in front of the demon's nose. "Wrong answer."

Cain drilled half the contents into its neck.

Micah's body went into convulsions. Cain sat watching stone faced. He knew how far he could take things before physically harming Micah permanently. That did not mean he didn't feel gut sick over what he was doing. When the jerking subsided, he found himself looking into the confused blue eyes of Micah.

"Cccain." His voice trembled. "Wwwhat's happening to me?"

Cain sucked back his anger. The bastard demon was having a high old time fucking around in the kid's head. Now he was allowing Micah to surface in an attempt to screw with him. Cain had been expecting it. He wanted to speak to Micah. Anything Micah could tell him would be to their advantage when the time came to expel the demon.

"You've been sick." Cain stretched the truth.

"I feel like, um, something is scratching around in my head, my brain. It won't stop. What is wrong with me?" Micah's voice became a high-pitched wail.

"Calm down kid. I'm trying to figure it out. You've got to pull it together and talk to me."

"My skin is crawling." Micah jerked around as if trying to shake imaginary creatures from his body.

"Fight it Micah. Concentrate on my voice. I've got to ask you some questions so I can help you."

Cain watched as Micah fought for control. His handsome face was ravaged. His chin was bruised from where Cain had hit him. His skin color was a sickly grey coated in clammy sweat. Dark purple circles surrounded his puffy red rimmed eyes.

"What do you, ah, what do you need to know?" Micah struggled.

"What's the last thing you remember? Your last clear memory."

"Closing…last night. Um…Talking to Mom and Pop. We … uh, we were waiting for a call about…Sam's baby."

Shit. That meant Micah had been totally under the demon's control for over a week.

"Think back. Did anything out of the ordinary happen? Did you have a bad fall? Get hit over the head? Get into a fight?"

"Everything's so sketchy." Micah seemed to strain, fighting to recall recent events.

"Take your time." Cain encouraged him.

"Jami." He remembered. "I walked Jami home a couple of days ago. Coming home I got jumped. After that I started getting headaches."

"That's great kid. That's what I need to know."

"Cain I'm scared." Micah slumped in exhaustion.

"Don't worry. I got you. I'm gonna take care of you. Close your eyes. You'll feel better."

Micah nodded weakly and did as Cain asked. Cain hit a pressure point that sent a slight current through the nerve. Micah was out in an instant.

Doing the math Cain figured Micah had been fighting the demons influence for about a month. This was not going to be an easy fix. The demon had made himself at home in Micah. It was not going to give up without a fight. This exorcism would be a full-fledged fight for Micah's soul.

Cain emptied the rest of the syringe into Micah. It was time to wake the sleeping demon. It came back with a snarl, its teeth bared, and its white eyes glowing. The demon started rocking the chair trying to free itself. Cain grabbed it by the wrists again and held it firm.

"Bastard." It hissed.

"Welcome back." Cain smiled.

Jami located Cain planted on his usual barstool sipping coffee. She spent most of her time upstairs lying awake worrying. She had seen exorcisms performed on t.v. and in movies and was pretty sure this would be much, much worse. Micah was a pain in the ass but he was her brother. She loved him and wouldn't wish what he was about to go through on anyone certainly not her own brother. She had also heard that exorcisms could fail and the person being exorcised could die. She was putting her faith in Cain and Ennie. They knew what they were doing. They would not allow anything to happen to Micah.

An hour ago, she gave up any pretense of sleeping. She took a much-needed shower then headed downstairs. She felt the last few days had drawn her and Cain closer together. Jami had come to discover that just being in his presence kept her calm and centered. She drew strength from him.

Cain knew as soon as the door closed it was her. She smelled like Ivory soap and apple scented shampoo. He turned to look at her. Dressed in her brother's sweatpants and an Archer's tee shirt she still managed to look hot. He felt his body respond.

"Hi." She said shyly.

Cain struggled to remember how to work his vocal cords. How had he missed the transformation? She had grown to beautiful women right under his unsuspecting nose. "How did you sleep?"

"I didn't." She admitted. "Too worked up to sleep."

She walked toward him. Her body language saying all she could not. She stopped in front of him and waited. She had made it clear what she wanted. He would have to make the first move. She knew what she wanted. Did he?

Hell, yes, he did. Despite what he knew in his head that this could be dangerous for the both of them he still wanted her. But he always had been a selfish bastard.

Cain cupped her face. He took notice of the softness of her pale skin as he rubbed his thumbs along her jawline. Leaning forward he kissed her soft and slow.

He slid his tongue between her parted lips. She tasted of cinnamon toothpaste. The male in him wondered what the rest of her would taste like. The thought made him burn. Fisting his hand in the thick damp waves of her hair he deepened the kiss.

Jami moved in closer to stand between his legs that straddled the barstool. She wrapped her arms around his neck. She shivered as she felt his erection through the thin material of the sweatpants they both wore. Jami leaned into the hardness wriggling until the erotic friction pulled a needy moan from her throat.

Cain slid his hands under her tee shirt and up her rib cage. He paused just beneath his goal. She had neglected to put on a bra after her shower. If he allowed himself to go an inch higher all bets were off. He would have her on his lap riding his cock.

"Cain." She whimpered, urging him to touch her.

The huskiness in her voice pushed him over the edge. Reaching up he palmed her breasts. He lightly pinched her nipples so they punched out for him more than they already were. It wasn't enough. He needed to taste her. He released her long enough to pull the shirt up exposing what he wanted. He took a quick bite at her nipple loving the goose bumps rose on her skin. At last, he took her into his mouth swirling his tongue around the taut pebble. Jami's back bowed wanting him to take more. She whispered his name pulling his head closer.

Jami could not get enough. Her body was begging for him. She reached down between them. With one hand she cupped his balls. She pulled the other hand from his bowed head and wrapped it around his cock. Damn, she thought, He is huge. She started to gently squeeze and stroke.

Cain growled. Jami looked at him from under heavy eyelids. His eyes were glowing ruby fire.

They both froze at the sound of a nervous giggle. Faith clapped a hand over her mouth. Grey gaped.

Cain hissed quickly covering Jami. Her hands sprang away from his erection. He kept her standing in front of him until his already deflating erection finished the process.

There were a few moments of awkward silence then Dore spoke up. "Who's ready for an exorcism?" She asked with a shit eating grin.

Tearzahn curled his full lips in disgust as he raked Magnus over the coals. "You're hiding in a cellar like a rat?" His amber eyes swept the dirt hole Lucifer had just dumped him into. "You've got to be shitting me."

"Unfortunately, the comfortable home I had acquired was compromised when my assistant was taken hostage."

"Make a place for me to sit." Tear commanded.

Magnus did what he was told, although he would have preferred to rip the enforcer's throat out. At least he would not have to put up with his shit for long. Lucifer's time restriction had taken care of that. Things were coming to a head at last. Lucifer could hardly blame him if Tearzahn were killed in the heat of battle.

He grabbed some wooden crates and began stacking them into a couch like formation. When he was satisfied with his labors, he draped his cashmere coat over the lot.

"Better than sitting on dirt." Tear grumbled. The crates creaked under his weight as he took a seat. His chestnut suede trench coat swirled around him. He stretched his long legs out crossing them at the ankles. The tops of his ostrich skin boots stuck out from under a pair of faded jeans. He steepled his violently nimble fingers at his waist. All ten fingers were adorned with a silver ring topped with a single sharply pointed spike.

"Now." He began. "Tell me what I need to know."

Magnus was pacing as he began to speak. "I was sent to seduce an innocent. When her soul was compromised, I would send her to Lucifer."

"Stop!' Tear barked. "I didn't ask for a damn dialogue. Tell me who we need to hit. Where to hit them and when they will all be together."

"Cain, the witch of Endor, Faith Martin, and the three Archer siblings, Grey, Micah, and Jami who is a novice witch."

"Where do we find them?"

"They will gather at Archers Bar." Magnus answered. "By the way, my apprentice is still residing in Micah Archer."

"That means what to me?"

"I believe they will soon be attempting an exorcism. They will want to free Micah Archer from the demon that is controlling him."

"Again, that means what to me?"

"They will all be together. "Magnus snapped, incredulous at Tears attitude.

"I need a little me time first." Tear responded, not giving a shit about Magnus' over eagerness.

A rat scurried past. Tear blasted it with a blink of an eye. Magnus decided it was best to keep his opinion of Tear's attitude to himself.

Tear lowered his amber eyes. The cellar began to fill with a slow-moving fog. Magnus could not see his hand in front of his face. A few minutes later the fog swirled away. The musty cellar had taken on the guise of an elegant bedroom. Tear now lay back on a king size bed hung with chocolate covered silk and decked out in matching chocolate silk sheets. Five-foot-high candelabra each holding seven cream colored taper candles sat at the four bed posts casting a mellow glow against the now creamy walls. It was all an illusion. Sill, Tear preferred the illusion to the reality.

"You will go now and get me food, a large quantity of good alcohol, and a half a dozen willing sluts. While I relieve my hunger, my thirst, and my lust you will keep an eye on our targets."

Magnus risked speaking up. "Lucifer has given us only forty-eight hours to bring this to its conclusion."

"My brother will get what he wants. After I get what I want. Now go. You've got work to do."

Magnus vanished.

Tear relaxed. He figured he had about twenty-four hours to get his groove on before he had to stop Magnus from fucking up even more than he already had. His brother's promise of shore leave was pure bullshit. He had been with the Father of Lies since before the world had been created. Lucifer would pull his ass back to hell as soon as the mission was complete. Tear would have one mortal day to satisfy his urges. Magnus had better move his ass.

CHAPTER SEVENTEEN

Ennie was totally indifferent to the awkwardness in the room. She bounded over to the sexed-up couple as if they had been having a cup of coffee rather than on the verge of doing the nasty.

"I'm recharged and ready to go. How about you?" En asked, as bubbly as a glass of champagne.

"Yeah, sure." Cain grumbled.

Grey and Faith hung back both with identical Holy Shit expressions on their faces.

Irritated with his old friend Cain glared lasers at her. She simply grinned in return. Cain noticed her eyes were too bright. She was fidgeting like a kid with ADD after a sugar binge.

Now concerned he questioned her suspiciously. "You sure you're okay? You need to eat or something"

"Nope. I'm good." She insisted. "Let's get moving. What are you waiting for?"

"Fuck." Cain groaned with sudden clarity. "Your power drunk. What the hell did you do?"

"None of your damn business." En snapped back.

Jami ducked out and made her way over to where Faith and Grey stood. They kept their distance as the two powerful Immortals stared each other down.

Cain glowered at En. She met him stare for stare her jaw set stubbornly.

"The hell it's not my business."

"I'm fine." She snarled.

"I'm not stupid. Your power is zapping off me like static electricity. Somehow you have supercharged your magic."

"I may have borrowed some energy from the Spirits." She admitted.

"You siphoned energy off of the ones waiting. What were you thinking?"

"I am the Witch of Endor. I will do as I damn well please."

"You're a damn idiot is what you are. I told you Ladocia was watching us. He made another appearance earlier. The Bloody Seven are watching every move we make. Why would you take a risk like that?"

"I was told to do it. A voice called to me telling me I would need the power."

"And of course, you always do what some random voice tells you to do."

"It was a voice of light asshole. I have learned to tell the difference. Give me a little credit for surviving this long please."

"Lo?" Cain wondered.

"I don't know. It does kind of make sense though. If he is trying to help us without getting directly involved."

"I guess all we can do is play it out." Cain concluded.

"Back to business." En corralled the others.

"Hold up." Jami stopped her. "Who is Lo and what are the Bloody Seven?"

"Woof." En exhaled. "That's a very big question. Cain is better acquainted with them than I am. I'm going to let him field this one."

Cain walked over to a table and sat down with his coffee. The others followed. They took seats and waited for Cain to speak.

He began to lecture. "The Order of the Key aka The Bloody Seven. The heads of the Churches of the provinces of Asia. They were reborn and given Angelic powers. Seven Assassins whose sole mission is the guard The Key to the Gates of Hell. You threaten their Key, you die."

"Revelations." Faith spoke with awe.

"Correct." Cain nodded at Faith and continued. "Each member of the Order took on the name of his province. Ladocia was here while you were all upstairs sleeping. For some reason our situation has pinged their radar."

"Where is the Key?" Jami asked.

"Who the hell knows who, what, or where the damn thing is except the Order."

"I think I met him." Faith spoke. "At the Memorial. He seemed so nice."

"What did he look like?" Cain demanded.

"Um… Blonde hair, icy blue eyes…" She wasn't allowed to finish before Cain interrupted her.

"That sounds like him."

"Aren't Angels good?" Grey asked. "Shouldn't they be on our side?"

"One third of the Angels in Heaven fell with Lucifer. They are individuals with minds of their own. They are more powerful than you can imagine. An unstoppable force of Creation. The Bloody Seven will do anything necessary to ensure the Gates stay closed and they have the Swords of Solomon to back them up."

"Okay, now explain the Swords of Solomon." Grey interjected.

"You're going to tell us the Testament of Solomon is real and not total bullshit, aren't you?" Faith suspected.

"It was real and so was the ring." En answered.

"The ring?" Jami questioned. "What ring?"

"King Solomon was given a ring. It gave him control over demons. Before he lost his mind, Solomon had the ring and its stone broken up into seven pieces. Each sword contains a piece of the ring and a piece of its stone. If one of those swords so much as touches a demon it's vaporized. The swords work just as well on immortals and humans. Just in case you're curious."

"And these guys are watching us." Grey groaned. "Great."

"How bad is Micah?" En questioned Cain.

"As bad as we thought. We're going to have to go with your plan."

"Were really going to have an exorcism?" Faith shook her head, she had been hoping there would be another way to handle things. "Don't we need a Priest?"

"Nah. There were demons being cast out long before there was a Catholic Church."

Faith looked to En who gave a negative shake of her head.

"I can't do it. Neither can Cain or Jami. We are abominations. Only a pure soul can perform an exorcism."

"No way is Faith doing it." Grey laid down the law.

"You two are being cagey again." Jami surmised. "How about sharing with the group."

"All right, quick lesson on demon removal." En relented.

Her audience gave her their full attention. Cain left the peanut gallery to grab another cup of coffee.

He had played professor once today and that was enough.

"Demons 101." En began her speech "You have got two basic kinds of demons. The Fallen aka Legion. You are not remotely ready to go up against them. The Fallen followed Lucifer in his war against Heaven. They still have a lot of their angelic powers. They can come to this plane in their true form. When they do, they tend to dim down their powers so mortals can look upon them without getting their brains fried. They can also take a host, change their form, and alter our perception of reality. Very nasty."

"How do you fight something like that?" Grey wondered out loud.

"YOU don't, and we're not going to go there right now." En told him. She could clearly see the relief written on all three of their faces. "What were up against is the second kind. Made Demons. These are creatures created by Lucifer. There are different levels of these demons. Their strength depends mostly on their age and if they were once humans Lucifer chose to turn. In which case the viler the human the viler the demon it becomes."

"So, these are the demons they exorcise on television and in the movies? The ones who possess people."

Ennie answered Jami. "For the most part yes. Although that stuff on t.v. is bullshit. The way to handle these beasties depends on their strength and how long they have had influence over their host."

Cain picked up the conversation as he returned with his coffee. "I sent one back, shit, and two days ago. I'm losing track of time. Anyway, it was a lower-level piece of shit that just took up residence.

I shot him up with Holy Water and sent him back to the pit. Piece of cake."

"Why do I have the feeling that THING out of Micah is not going to be so easy?"

"Because you're smart. I had an informative conversation with our demon friend while you were upstairs. The thing has been in Micah for weeks. It's almost fully integrated. It does not want to leave. It's going to fight us tooth and nail."

Jami looked furious. Faith buried her face in Grey's chest. Grey was white as a sheet. Cain was worried he would have to get the kid something to vomit into. He knew they would all come through. This was just the initial shock. Hearing the words spoken that had until now not been put into words.

"What do we have to do to save my brother?" Jami ground out through clenched teeth.

"Grey." En caught his attention. "You're going to have to do it."

"Me? Why me? I don't know anything about this. I'm the most vanilla of us all."

"That's exactly why. Cain, Jami, and I are impure. Faith has been contaminated. You are the purest of us."

"What is that supposed to mean? Faith is not contaminated. I can't believe you would say that." Grey furiously defended his girl.

"She had contact with Magnus. Once a demon has gotten that close it's much easier for them to get back in. Only this time this demon could try to possess her. Do you want to put her at risk? I don't."

"I've got no fucking clue how to do an exorcism. Hell, I don't even remember Sunday School."

"Don't worry. I'm getting you some help." En assured him, giving what she hoped was a reassuring smile.

"Who?" They all asked at once.

"I'm going to help you channel Faith's father."

Lucifer lay on his stomach. Bed pillows were tossed around. Rumpled sheets fell over the side of the bed and onto the floor. Any observer would be aware that a wicked bout of hot sex had just gone down.

A fine sheen of sweat covered Lucifer's tawny skin. An evil smile of satisfaction lit up his devilishly handsome face. Having just fed his inner beast he felt almost content. He had no urgent desire to feed the furnace at the moment. Big step for him at any rate. The occupants of Hell were breathing a momentary sigh of relief.

Cyndahl slid her lithe body up his long legs kneading the hard muscles as she went. She stopped when she reached his firm ass and settled herself there. She leaned over tracing the magnificent tattoo that took up the entirety of his smooth wide back. Her slender fingers followed the flowing lines of the Tree of Knowledge. The colors were vivid. The artistry so realistic she swore she could feel the roughness of the branches and the velvety softness of each individual leaf. The trunk of the tree was formed to depict a male and female twined together in the throes of orgasm. The male was Lucifer. She had always assumed the female to be Eve.

"I've always been fascinated by this tattoo. It's exquisitely done. Who is the artist?"

"My Father." He admitted in a rare moment of honesty. "A reminder of what I did and what I lost."

"That would certainly explain the skill." She continued to run her hands over it. She didn't want to spoil the mood. He was never this relaxed and had never before answered any of her questions. "I've always wondered why it lacks the infamous snake."

Lucifer burst out laughing. Cyndahl bobbled up and down on her seat as his body shook.

"The snake is there he's just hiding out of sight. Stories get changed over the centuries. The truth is I showed Eve my snake. After she got a look at it she decided she would enjoy a taste of my forbidden fruit."

"You were lovers." Cyndahl chuckled deep and naughty. "I always suspected as much. That is why she is treated like a Queen in your realm."

"We still are lovers. I am Prince and she is my Consort." He rolled them over pinning her down with his legs.

Emboldened she asked. "What about Cain?"

"What about him?"

"Did you send Tearzahn to kill him?"

Lucifer cupped her breasts massaging them. "Why do you care?"

A wicked smile crossed his face before his even white teeth nipped at her dusky erect nipples.

"My Prince." She pushed at him playfully determined to get an answer.

Lucifer sighed in exasperation. Amethyst eyes glowed drawing a squeak from their target. He caught a handful of her hair pushing her face closer to his. "Your father has nothing to fear from me. For the moment."

Cyndahl released the breath she had been holding. "Thank you Great One."

Lucifer released her. He rolled onto his back. Closing his eyes, he began to stroke himself. "Ah, my little witch. You know how to thank me."

Licking her lips, she did.

A short, squat, Smurf blue demon waddled her way along the dank stone corridors of Hell. Her webbed feet made slapping noises on the smooth hard trodden stone as she moved forward with purpose. When she reached the chamber of the Masters Consort, she entered silently through a hidden doorway taking a seat without being noticed.

Eve relaxed immersed in her bath. Her toffee-colored skin glowed from the heat and jasmine scented bath oil she used in an attempt to mask the smell of brimstone. Her ebony hair was piled high atop her head secured with an amethyst clip. Twin pitch-black brawny demons adorned in white loincloths serviced her. One knelt on each side of her soaping her ample breasts. Her rich burgundy nipples stood erect a testament to her enjoyment of the bath. One of the attendants reached down to wash between her spread legs. Eve's berry lips parted as a soft hiss of anticipation emerged. Her own hand vanished under the water to guide the attendants as they found a rhythm water began to swirl lapping at the sides of the marble bathtub. The demon at her breasts began to pinch her nipples he sealed his mouth to hers biting her lips until blood was drawn it sucked the blood its white eyes rolling back into its skull. Eve's body shook with release. Her cry of pleasure lost inside the brutal kiss.

When she recovered she motioned for her attendants to depart. They left her knowing they would soon be called back. Once was never enough for the Prince's Consort.

"Nefer, fetch me a towel." Eve ordered her demon companion.

The stumpy demon was immediately by her side. Her compact fleshy arms outstretched holding the towel for her Mistress to step into. Eve allowed her most trusted companion to wrap the fluffy towel around her waist since Nefer could reach no higher. Bare from the waist up Eve walked to her dressing table and took a seat.

Nefer stepped up onto s stool and removed the clip from Eve's hair. The long flowing tresses feel like waves of silk down her back. Eve handed back a hairbrush. Nefer went to work easing the brush through the waving lengths.

Eve stared at her reflection in the ornately carved mirror. Her almond shaped honey eyes were vacant. They had been since the day her son was taken from her. Her berry lips no longer turned up in a smile. She was lovely beyond words but there was a coldness to her beauty now.

"Tell me my dear Nefer. Did your eavesdropping prove fruitful?"

The demon halted her brushstrokes. "Yes Mistress. I heard him tell Cyndahl that Tearzahn will spare your son."

Eve bowed her head. She knew better than to set her hopes too high. After an eternity as Lucifer's consort, she had learned that hope brought pain.

"He could be lying. It is what he excels at." Eve countered.

"We must try to believe that this time he is being truthful. That he did not send the enforcer for your son. Surely he does not wish to see Cain hurt."

"He cares only for himself." Eve spoke with grief in her voice. "That was a lesson I learned far too late. Ah Nefer, you believe for the both of us. I have run out of belief."

"He seems tender with the girl. It was wise of you to place her in his path."

"He has no tenderness in him. It is a momentary distraction. A game he enjoys playing. One I have had to learn to play."

Nefer could not bear to see the sadness of her Mistress. "Is there nothing I can do to help you?"

Eve placed her hand on the blue one resting on her shoulder. "You are a good friend. Send my attendants back to me. Then go back to your spying. I have a plan in mind to keep Cain safe."

The little demon jumped down from her stool. She kissed Eve on the lips then scuttled back to her spying.

Eve went to her bed. She laid back. The twin demons returned they opened their mouth showing their long pink forked tongues. Eve growled with lust and beckoned them to come to her. They approached with a cat like grace. Eve rose to her knees as they settled on the bed. She watched hungrily as they knelt before her and removed the loin clothes from each other. Eve marveled as their thick long cocks sprang free. They were not up to Lucifer's standards but they were impressive. She sat back on one taking the demons rigid penis inside her. The other demon bent down in a position of supplication. Its serpents tongue snaked out between her thighs licking her into a frenzy. Eve began to ride one demon as the other kept busy satisfying her with its tongue. It wasn't long until her shouts as she orgasam echoed through the chambers of Hell.

"What?" Faith yowled. "You're in contact with my Dad? How?"

"He contacted me for help. He sent me to Cain. By the time Cain called me for help I was already on my way."

"He was watching over me." Faith marveled at the thought.

"He still is. I'm going to open Grey's mind so he can speak to him as he speaks to me."

A round of shocked expletives rang out. Grey's overrode the others. "You've got to be out of your damn mind." He bolted from his seat and began pacing and grumbling.

"Do you want to save your brother?" Cain asked.

Grey spun around to face him. "Not by having Faith's father in my head." His face turned red as an apple from embarrassment. "We slept together last night. That's just too…arg…nasty."

The cat was out of the bag. Faith covered her face with her hands.

"Holy shit!" Jami blurted. "Damn Faith."

Faith uncovered her face. She glared at Jami. "Oh, you're a fine one to talk. Do I need to remind you what you and Cain were up to when we came downstairs?"

Jami's jaw dropped.

En clapped her hands. "Yee Haw. This just keeps getting better. Love is in the air."

"Shit!" Cain erupted. "Focus. What does it take to keep you people on track? I have never seen a group of people so easily distracted." He stood arms crossed with a look on his face of someone who's last nerve has been severed.

Ennie could not resist one last jab before smoothing over his irritation. "Love is important." She snapped, watching his eyes. "You are correct though. We don't have time to get sidetracked."

"Look." Grey picked up where they left off. "There has got to be a better way to do this."

"If there were do you really think I would be suggesting this?"

Jami picked up the argument. "I've already got one possessed brother. I don't need another one."

"This will not be possession. Were you possessed by Katie? He will just be able to speak to Grey." En explained.

"No." Faith dug in. "What if something goes wrong? My Dad didn't know anything about exorcism."

Cain spoke up, shamefaced and guilty. "Well, actually."

"What?" Faith demanded flatly. "Tell me. All of it. I've had enough with the secrecy."

"Technically I'm evil. I cannot perform the Rite of Exorcism. It was your Dad who did the exorcisms. He made me promise not to tell you unless I had to."

"He never told me." Faith whispered to herself. "I never considered the possibility."

"He didn't want you hurt. He knew that the knowledge would put you in jeopardy. He kept his silence to protect you."

"So he knew about you?"

"He suspected. He never asked and I never told him. It was safer for him that way."

"I didn't think anything could make me prouder of him. I was wrong."

She went to Grey. "My Dad was the strongest man I ever knew. You have got to do this. He won't let you down."

Grey took Faith's hands into his. He looked into her serious green eyes. "I love you Faith. I've loved you for as long as I can remember. When your Father is in my head that is what he is going to see."

"I love you too. I'll be right here waiting for you when this is over." She kissed him fiercely.

Ennie looked smuly at Cain. "Like I said love is important."

Grey and En sat at the table. The others had moved themselves over to the bar so they would not be a distraction.

"Take my hands." En guided him, reaching across the smooth surface of the table. Grey followed her lead. She flinched at the tension pouring out of him.

"Relax. The more relaxed and open you are the easier this will be for you."

Grey could not imagine relaxing. En was asking him for the impossible. Then he thought of his brother. Grey took a deep breath knowing he was his brother's best shot and did his best to chill.

"Look at me. Focus on my eyes." She instructed, pulling him in.

He gazed into her eyes. They were warm and clear. He listened to the sound of her bracelets jangling on her wrists. Grey thought of Faith. He brought a vision of her into his mind. Her face was bathed in sunlight. Her green eyes danced with happiness and her smile was soft and loving.

"Good, very good. Now hold that picture in your mind." En crooned.

In a remote corner of his mind he could hear En speaking. It was a lilting lullabye. The tingle of magic swept across his skin like a warm subtle friction. He paid little attention. Instead he kept focused on the face of the beautiful girl with the perfect smile.

CHAPTER EIGHTEEN

In the cellar bedroom mirage Tearzahn was partying like he could be sucked back to Hell at any second. Which unfortunately was a fact. After a meal of two rare steaks, four bacon cheeseburgers, six large fries, three bowls of chili, and four chocolate shakes his hunger for food was satisfied. Sam Adams had turned out to be an exceptional beer. He polished off a case. Jack Daniels made a damn fine whiskey. It was an excellent chaser for the food and beer.

His greatest discovery of this modern age was what the first woman he fucked had called waxing. The women of this time rid themselves of body hair. Angels, even fallen ones, have no body hair. Tear had always found it a furry smelly barrier when he was with a woman. He was now enjoying himself with his mouth buried between the slippery drenched lips of a luscious blonde.

A slick wet pussy bucked against his mouth as his tongue fucked her into her second orgasm. Now he was greedy for his turn. He gave her a final tongue tickle between her lips extracting another lusty moan. Pulling himself up him crushed her mouth with a kiss. His already hard cock turned to steel as she wantonly sucked her own juices from his lips.

The shameless female writhed under him rubbing her throbbing clit against his cock. The slip and slide she had going on was driving him crazy. She was more than ready for him. One hard thrust and his engorged cock was buried deep.

Her heavily painted eyes opened wide in astonishment. All of the Fallen were well hung. Tear grinned impishly at her surprised face. "Is that what you wanted?"

"Oh fuck yes."

The pleasures of the flesh, Tear thought. The most irresistible of all the indulgences the downfall of many of the Fallen. Well worth the fall. How was it humans did not spend every waking minute engaged in this wondrous activity?

Tear's hips began a slow steady roll. His dick thrummed inside the moist grip of his nameless lover. She grabbed his ass dug her fingernails into the firm flesh. He grunted slamming into her harder. He felt the orgasm roll through her squeezing him tighter.

Enough! His mind roared. Giving into his own pleasure he pounded in and out of her tight heat harder and more violently. Tear exhaled a growl as the brutal release rocked him. The girl under him lay sprawled in a boneless state of bliss.

Tear pulled out, sat up, and lit a cigarette.

The blonde grabbed his arm. "I want more."

"You've had enough and there is a waiting line." Tear pointed to the next girl in line crooking a finger for her to come to him.

The petite brunette pulled her lips from the girl beside her. Her skirt was rucked up around her waist. The pretty thing with hair the color of cotton candy removed her fingers from her new brunette friend and put them between her lips.

The brunette stroked herself as she went to tear.

"Hello, little dirty girl." He crooned when she reached him.

Tear put out a hand to help the blonde to her feet. The brunette was before him on her knees. Tear laid his free hand on her head as she licked her way up the length of him.

Magnus approached the well-used blonde then helped her to steady herself as she attempted to stand. She was the third girl Tear had been through and he was not showing any signs of slowing down. Magnus was growing adept at the exit routine. He pulled the top of her dress up and the skirt down. He then handed her her purse and shoes.

Magnus held out his hand. "Come with me."

Outside twilight was giving way to total darkness. The girl seemed lost standing barefoot holding onto her belongings.

She pleaded with Magnus. "I could wait. Maybe go back to the end of the line?"

"Why would you want to do that?" Magnus reached down stroking his burning erection.

The blonde smiled with hunger in her eyes. It did not seem to matter to her that they stood in a scrap of grass separating two buildings. She reached to the hem of her clingy dress and tugged it up and over her head. She stood naked before him in the moonlight.

Magnus moved swiftly capturing one of her overripe breasts in his mouth. They both made quick work of removing his clothes.

Magnus took them both down onto the prickly grass. "Get on your hands and knees." He ordered her.

She was quick to comply. From behind her Magnus slid his hand between her legs. Smooth and wet. Perfect.

He grabbed her hips roughly impaling her. She cried out relishing the pain. He rode her hard and fast. Her shrill cries of pleasure becoming incoherent.

"Do you belong to me?" Magnus whispered in her ear.

"Yesss." She hissed, assuming this was part of his sex play.

"Will you be mine? Body, mind and soul?" He prompted her, as he continued to thrust.

"Yesss."

Magnus bit into her shoulder. The pain sent an orgasm spearing through her which triggered his own.

After a moment Magnus stood. He tossed her the dress and began to gather his own clothes.

"Will I see you again?" She asked, pulling the dress over her head.

"I guarantee it." Standing naked in the moonlight Magnus reached out and grabbed his lover by the throat. A quick jerk of his wrist snapped her neck. As the sweat and sticky fluids from their sex dried on his body he watched as the Reapers from below pulled her soul clawing and screaming down to the pit. A lovely bonus for Lucifer and maybe it would score him a few bonus points toward making up for his delay on delivering Faith.

Grey was on an acid trip. Movement of any kind trailed out into vivid color bursts. There were figures gathered around him. He could not differentiate one wavy blob from another. He knew they were speaking. All he heard was wah…wah…wah… like a telephone call from a Charlie Brown cartoon. It made him giggle.

"What's wrong with him?" Faith anxiously questioned En.

"Give him some time. He's on sensory overload."

Grey started humming Purple Haze.

Jami barked a laugh. "Bro's trippin' balls." She leaned down into his face and started waving her hands back and forth on either side of his head. "You're running through the forest, really fast, faster. Faster…"

This sent Grey into fits of laughter.

"Stop it!" Faith hollered.

Jami stopped but turned her back to laugh. Faith was an only child and did not understand the need of siblings to screw with each other when an unexpected opportunity showed itself.

"Preacher." En called. "Can you help him out?"

Grey swayed in his chair. He shook his head to clear it. It wasn't long until he regained control of himself. When he was able to speak his first words were for Faith.

"He said to tell you he loves you and he is proud of you. He wants you to do what makes you happy."

Cain held onto Faith helping her through the shock.

"He's happy about us." Grey smiled at her. "He says to trust Cain. That he's a good man. He knows you're surrounded by love and you will have a great life. As soon as this is over he will be able to go home."

"I love you too Dad. You're right I am loved." She looked at the people around her. "I'll be just fine."

Ennie was sniffling. Jami was crying outright. Cain passed them a couple of bar napkins to dry their faces.

"He's ready." Grey announced.

Cain got them moving. "Okay boys and girls let's do this."

"Jami would you mind running upstairs to get my bag?" En requested.

"You betcha." She saluted, darting off.

"I'll start moving these chairs and tables." Cain volunteered.

Jami returned with En's bag. She joined with the others helping Cain to shuffle furniture into one of the corners.

"Scoot one table over this way." En directed.

Cain did as she asked placing a table not far from where the demon sat restrained.

Ennie began laying out implements she felt would be needed. Holy Water, a silver Crucifix, Communion Wafers, and a worn Holy Bible would be at arm's length when they were needed.

"Jami and Faith I want you behind the bar. I don't care what you see or here. You Do Not come out from back there period." Cain laid down the law.

Bobbing their heads in agreement they followed orders and got into position.

Ennie stood at the table explaining the contents to Grey. "I don't know why I'm telling you all of this. Preacher will help you. Cain and I will be only a few feet behind you if you run into trouble. Which you won't."

"Your right. I won't. I'm not the one doing this." Gray spoke solemnly.

A chorus of arguments rang out.

Grey held up his hands to silence them. "I won't be doing this Preacher will."

"What the fuck are you talking about?' Jami shouted from behind the bar.

"I can feel him. We are better off and Micah will be safer if I let Preacher take control. He knows what he's doing. There is a chance I could make a mistake. He won't."

Grey looked to En. "What do I do?"

"Just let yourself go. It will feel like something is filling you up. You will be aware but not in control. Hold my hands."

Grey gave himself a shake to loosen up. "Now what?"

"Before we begin, I want to ask you one last time. Are you totally certain you want to play it this way?"

"Yes." Grey answered. "It's the safest way for Micah."

"Alright. Close your eyes, feel him enter you, and allow him control." En instructed.

When Grey's eyes opened it was not him looking out.

"Hello Preacher." En welcomed him.

"Hello En." He returned. "Cain?"

Cain approached. "Hello old friend." They did the quick pat on the back man hug thing.

"Thank you." Preacher told his friend.

"Don't thank me. This was my fault. I didn't catch it quickly enough. I was almost too late."

"This is not your fault. They would have come after her sooner or later because of our work."

Before Cain could say any more Faith launched herself.

Jami said "Hi Mr. Martin."

Preacher smiled at her as he held his daughter. Faith released him and backed up. "This is so weird but I've got to say I love you Dad."

"I love you too. Now you and Jami get yourselves back behind the bar."

Both girls scrambled.

Preacher looked over at them." Instructions, you do not speak to it. You do not look it in the eyes. Pay no attention to what it says. It is a liar. Do you understand?"

Both girls answered, "Yes."

Preacher took the Bible. He got down on his knees in a silent prayer. When he finished he stood and looked to Cain and En.

"Ready?"

Cain gave him a shit eating grin. "Let's kick this shit."

There is a little known suite of rooms in Hell. The walls were cut from the same fire opal as the throne room. The ceiling a shifting pattern of blues done in turquoise made to depict a perfect summer sky. Every piece of marble, stick of furniture, or piece of cloth had been done in shades of white and gold. All created to enhance to the toffee colored skin of the creature who resided there.

Cyndahl's head was spinning. She laid upon silk sheets of the purest white in such an elegant room as she could never have imagined in her wildest dreams. Gazing up to the ceiling Cyndahl could almost imagine she was staring at the endless blue sky once again. She was certain she must be dreaming until her newest lover reached over to stroke her shoulder.

She was captivated. Never had she experienced such tenderness in the arms of a lover. Not when she was mortal and certainly not here in Hell. As she felt the soft palm of her lover caress her arm she was overwhelmed by the rush of joy that assailed her.

Adoringly she gazed into the honey eyes of the woman lying beside her. "Great one, I never guessed you cared for your own sex."

"Please do not address me so formally. Eve requested her voice smooth as the silk they had just made love on. "We are beyond that now."

"What would you like me to call you? I can think of nothing worthy of you."

"Your love?" Eve suggested seductively.

"Yes, you are my love."

Eve trailed her hand down Cyndahls shoulder to her breast kneading the soft flesh. "You are so beautiful."

Cyndahl mirrored her lovers touch. "You are perfection."

Eve took her mouth kissing her deeply. "Your mouth is sweeter than wine my Dahli."

A single tear slipped from Cyndahls eye. "No one has called me that since my mortal life. I thought never to hear it spoken in a loving way again."

"But you have never been completely mortal have you? You were born a very powerful Witch."

"Yes my love." Cyndahl responded, suddenly wary.

Eve sensed her pulling back. She saw the look of near freight in her eyes. She began placing tender kisses down the column of her throat until she felt Cyndahl's wariness melt away. When Eve teased her pert nipple with her tongue Cyndahl was lost. She lovingly stroked Eve's hair wanting the moment to last forever.

"You are Heaven to me." Cyndahl sighed.

"We are women. We know what women want. What we need. "Eve whispered in her ear. Eve's slender fingers made their way to Cyndahl's sweet spot. She rubbed and stroked with a practiced skill bringing her new lover to the edge.

"Whatever you need I will gladly give." Cyndahl moaned, then cried out her release.

"Really." Eve purred. She looked beyond Cyndahl's shoulder to where Nefer sat blending into a shadowed corner observing everything. Nefer nodded to her Mistress and silently slipped from the room.

CHAPTER NINETEEN

To Faith the world hung in the balance. Her lover who was carrying her father's soul was about to square off against evil in its physical form. She wished she had a few drinks in her as her hands shook. It was not an option. She had to be alert and on guard.

A few lights were on in the bar. The atmosphere made it feel like they were in a cave. The air was stilted and everything slightly out of focus. It was, she now realized the smell of brimstone she had heard the others talk about. It had become so strong that Faith, a mere mortal, found it hard to take a deep breath.

"Ennie will you wake him?" Preacher requested.

En walked over to them. Micah looked alien. His facial features seemed to have melted. His skin had an ashen pallor. Even unconscious lines of pain marred his once handsome face.

"Awake." She commanded, snapping her fingers in front of Micah's face.

His head snapped up. It was not Micah's eyes looking back at her but the dead white depths of the demons. En's stomach lurched. She exchanged the sickness for anger. It served her better.

The demon hissed at her. She flipped it the bird and returned to her seat.

This bit of sass enraged the demon. The chair shook as it thrashed against its bonds. Growls echoed off the walls of the empty barroom.

Preacher stepped forward drawing the creature's attention. It went still. Cackles off laughter emerged from its throat.

"You're going to have a bartender exorcise me. Ha. Bring me a Heineken boy. I'm parched."

The sound of its demented laughter sent chills up Faith's spine. She clung to Jami's arm as she fearfully watched the ones she loved going up against the demon.

Holding the Bible Preacher began to quote, "Our Father, who art in Heaven, Hallowed be thy name…"

"Yeah, yeah, yeah." The demon mocked. "You're Father, not mine."

"Thy kingdom come, thy will be done, on earth as it is in Heaven…"

"What do you know about Heaven? I serve in Hell and so will you."

"Give us this day our daily bread, forgive us our trespasses as we forgive those who trespass against us…"

"Forgiveness." It hissed. "Will you forgive the boy you're riding for fucking your darling daughter? I don't think so. I think you will make sure he has an accident before you finish this."

Preacher didn't as much as blink at the demons taunts. He refused to be sidetracked. He had done this many times before and knew the demons taunts would only more foul as they went deeper into the exorcism.

"Lead us not into temptation, but deliver us from evil…"

"Your daughter knows all about temptation and evil. Magnus said she loved to suck his dick. She wanted to lap up the evil in him."

"Nooo!" Faith wailed. "I never touched Magnus. He's lying."

The demon laughed deep and ugly. It locked its blank stare on Faith. He had not hit the target he aimed for but he hit one nearly as good.

"Keep quiet or go upstairs." Cain barked.

Preacher maintained through the outburst. He kept his focus on the demon. "For thine is the kingdom and the power and the glory, forever and ever. Amen."

The demon stayed riveted on Faith. "Look at her. She's a bitch in heat. Your baby girl is used goods."

Silent tears scalded Faith's flushed cheeks. Jami leaned in admonishing her friend. "Get it together. Do not let that lying nasty son of a bitch get to you. That's what it wants."

Faith turned away. She wiped her face on her shirt sleeve. Anger replaced the hurt and fear. When she turned again she met the demon stare for stare. She beamed at the damn thing waggling her fingers in a wave that was all screw you. Jami beamed proudly at her friends big balls taking on the demon.

Preacher stepped closer to the demon placing the crucifix against its forehead. Under the Holy object the skin burned. The demon screeched rocking the chair as it fought.

"Tell me your name." Preacher demanded.

"Fuck you."

"In the name of the One I command you to give me your name."

"You won't survive this. I'll rip out your throat just as I did sweet Katie's. She enjoyed it. She moaned in pleasure as I lapped her blood. You will enjoy it too. Then I'll drag you to the pit as a prize for my Master."

Preacher returned to reciting from the Scriptures. While he read the demon continued to belch its lies and obscenities. It continued on this way for over an hour. The four watchers unmoving caught up in the unnatural scene being played out before them. During it all Preachers confidence remained unwavering. The filth spewing from the demons mouth seemed to bounce right off of him.

Returning the Bible to the table Preacher exchanged it for a syringe of Holy Water. He went behind the demon and injected the full contents into the back of its neck. The demons mouth opened wide to scream its fury. Preacher took advantage of this opening. He got in front of the demon shoving a Communion wafer between its lips.

He clamped the demons jaw shut. Foaming bloody saliva oozed between Preachers fingers making his hands slip yet he held fast. The demon thrashed in the chair causing Preacher to hook an ankle around the chair leg to keep them both from crashing to the floor. At last the forsaken creature swallowed the wafer and the struggles ceased. With the Holy wafer churning in its gut and the Holy Water burning in its veins it had at least temporarily lost the will to fight.

It was now midnight. Everyone's nerves were jangled by caffeine and stress. They had taken two breaks for the bathroom and to keep the coffee flowing. They were now finishing up their third break and were preparing to begin again.

Jami and Faith were jumpy and strung out. Ennie had been chawing on a piece of gum so vigilantly Cain was waiting for her jaw to crack. They were all on edge but Preacher. He alone appeared unaffected.

Cain was aware the demon was wearing down. He was also aware of the physical damage being done to Micah's body. If things did not come to a head soon he would have to stop the exorcism before Micah suffered permanent damage or worse, it killed him. He, En, and Preacher knew they were pushing it. Exorcisms could last days, weeks, even months. With this one though they didn't have that kind of time.

Cain decided the girls needed a little pep talk before they got started again. He led them into the semi darkness of the kitchen.

Choosing his words carefully, he laid things out for them. "I know he looks bad. I know your starting to feel defeated. The thing is if I know this so does the demon. Believe it or not that matters. That thing feeds off negativity. We cannot allow it to get that boost. You have got to go out there and believe were going to beat this thing."

Jami stood up straighter. "You got it Coach."

Faith responded simply. "I can do it."

"Great, let's go get our boy back."

Lo and Sully sat at the bar. They had been observing the exorcism since it began. Cain and crew had no clue they were hosting uninvited spectators. No one ever saw them unless they wanted to be seen. Right now they were a no show. If Cain knew of their presence he would demand they take action. Insist they put a stop to the torture the boy was suffering. Lo was already walking a fine line to not do just that. With just one touch from him or Scully the demon would flee Micah Archer. The sad fact was, as usual, they had been forbidden to interfere.

Sully's Stetson had gone frisbee hours before. It now lay discarded in a corner by the jukebox. His pale blonde hair stood up at odd angles from his habit of running his hands through it when he felt frustrated. At this point it was a wonder he had not balded himself. He could feel the kid's life force wavering. He was shocked the poor sap had made it this far.

His foul attitude got the better of him and he lashed out at Lo. "So what's your grand fucking plan this time? Are we really going to stand here and watch another innocent die? Wasn't the girl enough for you?"

"Fuck you." Lo growled back at his brother.

"That's it? That's your plan? Fuck you. Wow that's incredible. I wish I had come up with that."

"What do you want from me? Whatever gave you the idea that I'm in charge? My hands are just as tied as yours are. This is what we signed up for."

"Then I quit."

"Fine quit. Give Lucifer my regards. I'm sure he will throw your ass a welcoming party. Especially since you sent how many of the Fallen to the Affa? I'll bet good ol' Lucy will be so glad to see you he will make you his new right hand man."

"Fuck you Lo. Fuck all of this. Just…Fuck."

"Well said."

Sully felt like a deflated balloon. All of his righteous anger gone like so much hot air. In a weary voice he asked Lo, "What do we do?"

Lo rubbed his temples thinking that if he were lucky his head would explode. "We wait it out. Right now that's all we can do. Maybe they will get lucky and pull this off."

"Or maybe we will be standing over another corpse."

Preacher plunged another syringe into the demon. He put the crucifix to its already burned forehead. The demon choked then spit a hock of bloody mucus into Preacher's face.

Preacher casually wiped the nasty stuff from his face and confronted the demon. "You're getting tired demon. All you have to do is give me your name and you can rest."

"Name, name, name, a rose by any other name would still smell like shit."

"Your name demon." Preacher demanded, as he held the crucifix before the demons face.

"Fred. I'm Fred the demon."

"I command you give me your name."

The demons head fell forward. When it snapped back up its white eyes focused beyond Preacher and trained on Ennie.

"Mama." A shaky female voice came from the demons lips. "Mama it's me Dahli. Help me."

En swallowed her gum. Her dark skin went as white as the demons milky eyes. "Liar!"

Cain looked at En like he had never seen her before. En refused to look at him instead keeping her eyes on the demon.

"Mama is daddy with you?"

"You're not my daughter. Shut your filthy lying face." Ennie's face twisted with pain.

"En, what the hell is this?" Cain demanded.

She looked at him with terror filled eyes. "It's a lying demon." Cain didn't believe that for a second. The demon had struck a nerve, but now was not the time to attempt to pry it out of her.

"Daddy is that you?"

Cain's eyes burned. "En?"

From out of nowhere Preacher yelped jumping like he had been goosed distracting everyone. He slammed the Bible down on its head.

Micah's once handsome face was battered. It wore a sinister grin as it winked at Preacher. "I was just getting to the good part. Won't you let me finish?"

"Silence!" As he began to pray all hell broke loose. Preacher was blasted off his feet and sent hurtling into Cain and Ennie. The three of them landing in a tangled heap on the floor.

Jami and Faith started screaming. Their eyes torn between their friends on the floor and the demon. The chair the demon was tied to, began to rise into the air. The bar erupted into chaos.

The three on the floor were falling over each other in an attempt to get to their feet. Jami and Faith were waving their arms shouting out instructions trying to help their friends. The demon cackled as he rose higher.

Cain was up and helping En to her feet when the first of the whoomps started.

Floating above their heads the demon was trying like hell to bash Micah's head into the thick ceiling beams. Everyone stared in horror as Micah's head hit leaving drops of blood to drop from his head onto the floor below.

Jami panicked as she watched her brother being murdered above her. Without realizing or understanding what she was doing she acted on instinct. She raised her hands and threw a blast of energy at the thing. She gasped as it crashed downward face and torso landing on the corner of a table top then thudding to the floor.

Cain got to the scene first. The body lay lifeless among splintered pieces of wood from the mangled chair. En moved to remove the ropes but Cain stopped her. They were no longer attached too much but still needed to remain intact.

En nodded to the girls. They raced over from behind the bar.

"No, no, no." Jami repeated, shaking her head in denial. "He's going to be fine. Right En?"

Micah's face was pulp. He left eyeball dangled from the socket. The back of his head was littered with tiny fragments of shattered skull that matted into his blood soaked hair. One hand nearly severed at the wrist lay limply beside him.

"You need to say goodbye to him." En broke it to her through her own tears.

"Stay back all of you." Cain roared. "The damn thing is still in him."

"Ahhh…nooo…" Jami cried.

Faith took her by the arm and pulled her back. "We have to let them finish. They have to free his soul."

"Why?" Jami snarled. "Who gives a shit anymore?"

"You don't mean that." Faith spoke indignantly.

"The fuck I don't. Fuck this shit." Jami ranted, unable to cope.

Ennie got to her feet. She slapped the girl she had come to love as her own.

Jami blinked, shocked. En stared her down.

"Shit." Jami acquiesced. "Finish it. Just finish it." She turned away.

The one milky eye left intact opened in a swollen slit. A few teeth showed through the ravaged flesh in a mockery of a smile. Cain fought the urge to vomit. He was grateful that Jami had turned away.

Preacher placed the Bible on the crushed chest. "In the name of the One I command you give me your name."

Blood bubbled from his mouth. "Sundrel." It croaked. Glasses fell smashing behind the bar. Liquor bottles burst their contents spraying amber liquid. "My name is Sundrel."

"I command you to return to Hell. I banish you Sundrel back to the darkness that spawned you."

A smoky haze rose above Micah twisting and coiling. Cain watched as Micah drew his final breath. Time stopped. Frozen.

Lo and Sully faced each other. The same What the Fuck look printed on both of their faces.

Sully was the first to speak. "What did you do?"

"Ummm, he's not dead yet."

"Yeah because you just stopped time. What the hell happened to we wait?"

"We waited." Lo blinked, shocked at himself. He was not really sure himself why he had done it. He only knew that at that moment he could not just step back.

"Oookay." Sully did not know what to say to his brother. Lo was always the reasonable one. For once he decided not to push. Lo seemed to be caught up in some inner struggle of his own. No way was he poking his nose into that. He would just keep his mouth shut and back his brothers play.

"They cheated. Sundrel was Legion."

"Well strictly speaking that's not exactly cheating. More like bringing out an elephant gun to shoot a squirrel."

"Does that seem fair to you?"

"Come on brother. Nothing about this shit is ever fair. Hey, does this feel like role reversal to you?'

Lo rolled his eyes at his brother.

"Just sayin."

"Well maybe this time I want it to be fair."

"Shit Bro, I'm right there with you. Maybe Lucifer has two job openings."

"Let's hope we don't need them."

Micah was looking through a fog bank. His body was weightless. He felt the way he did as a child floating on his back in the pool with the sun warming his face. "I must be dreaming." He thought muzzily, wondering if he had spoken out loud.

He could vaguely make out the shapes of people. No, not people, they didn't move. Statues of people. They were familiar to him.

A man appeared to him. He was outlined in a charcoal aura of smoke. He was tall and built like an mma fighter. The man had a completely bald head and glowing bronze eyes. Micah felt like he should know this strange man. They were connected in some way. He struggled to remember but was too exhausted to hang onto a coherent thought.

The man spoke to him. "Goodbye for now kid. We will be seeing each other again."

Then came a light so bright it hurt to look at. Two men stepped out of the light. Even with his eyes burning Micah could not turn his face away. He was reminded of walking into a movie theater halfway through the film and being at a loss as to who the characters were or what the storyline was.

"Sundrel." One of the men in white called the familiar man.

"Lo, Sully." He nodded to them. "What's up boys?" Sundrel greeted them with all the cockiness of one of the Fallen.

Sully snarled and allowed Lo to do the talking.

Lo looked puzzled. "I was just wondering why your boss would allow one of the Fallen to play lackey for a piece of shit like Magnus."

"Guess you will just have to keep wondering. I do my brothers bidding. I don't question the why's of it."

"Go home, Sundrel." Lo commanded. "You were cast out by your own name. You no longer have leave to stay here."

"What? That pathetic exorcism. I could have killed them all. They were lucky I was getting bored."

"Looked to me like you were enjoying yourself." Sully snapped.

"Okay, maybe just a little. I was actually thinking I might just stick around. Hop into another body and watch how the show ends."

"You always did enjoy riding a human. I guess you find shredding the body of an innocent more fun than wearing your own skin?"

"Yes, it is. Maybe this time I'll wear a hot young witch." He gazed lecherously at Jami. "You two sissy boys think you can stop me?"

"Hot damn." Sully hooted. A lethal gleam in his eyes he gripped sword that appeared in his hand out of thin air. An identical sword appeared in Lo's.

"Let me think." Lo hesitated. "I do believe two of Solomon's swords beat one fallen dickhead. Sully?"

"Yup." Sully agreed, a cheeky grin across his face.

"I'm not leaving without my prize." Sundrel snarled.

"He's not dead. You can't claim him." Sully reminded him.

"You ready to start a war Ladocia?"

Lo belly laughed. "I was born ready. You've got three seconds to smoke out of here or I let Sully have his fun."

Sully simpered. "Please stay."

"Fuck you. You don't have the balls."

"What is that I hear?" Lo asked Sully. "Hells Bells?"

"Satan's calling for you." Sully added, smirking at Sundrel.

Lo started counting while Sully played with his sword. "One, two…"

Sundrel turned to smoke then whistled through the floorboards.

This is one weird ass dream Micah thought. What the hell had he eaten before he fell asleep?

The man in white with cowboy boots? Stomped his foot. "Shit. Denied again."

The other one approached a statue of Grey. "Preacher." He spoke. A strobe of blue and white light appeared fluttering around Grey. "Go home now. It's over." The lights rose up circling around the statues then disappearing into the ceiling.

"I'll finish here." The one beside Grey told his friend.

Cowboy boots shimmered and vanished as well.

"Now for you." He said to Micah.

Lo crouched beside the confused and defiled boy. He cursed Lucifer and his Legion. Snapping his fingers he repaired the bar without taking his eyes off of Micah.

Micah found himself locked into the iciest blue eyes he had ever encountered. The voice that spoke to him was deep and gravley yet oddly soothing.

"You will not remember any of this. You will only remember what I'm going to tell you now."

Micah blinked his one good eye.

"You will tell Cain this. You remember being mugged. You hit your head. You feel fine now. While you were unconscious you dreamed of a drunken Tinkerbell. You may be a little confused about some things. That's all side effects from hitting your head. It's nothing to worry about."

Lo held both hands over Micah. An amazing warmth started at his head working its way down his body. It was such a glorious feeling tears fell from his eyes. He was warm and safe and all of the pain was gone. H did not want this feeling to ever end. Who was this man that he could do this?

When Micah opened his eyes the world was sharp and vibrant again. People were shouting and crying. He wanted to tell them something…what was it? He could not remember.

CHAPTER TWENTY

"He's awake!" Cain yelled to the others.

Jami beelined to Micah. Faith stayed with Grey who was on his back passed out.

Ennie stood rotating in a circle taking in the immaculately restored barroom. She marveled that even the smell of brimstone had been replaced by the fresh scent of lemon oil polish and clean fresh air. There was not even a whiff of alcohol or stale cigarette smoke.

"Cain?" Jami gurgled, as her brain worked to assimilate what she was seeing. Micah lay before her healed and healthy. He was looking at her with eyes that were no longer haunted. They were now as clear blue as a cloudless sky.

"Cain?" Faith wondered. She helped Grey to his feet. When he had opened his eyes and looked at her she could tell that he Father was no longer there.

"Cain?" Ennie questioned. She was hoping he could explain the bars instantaneous rehab.

"Cain?" Micah looked up at him.

Cain responded to Micah first. "How are you feeling kid?"

Micah replied verbatim as he had been instructed. "I was mugged. I hit my head. I feel better now."

"Do you remember anything else?"

"I dreamed." He began, a look of confusion on his face. "I dreamed of a drunken Tinkerbell."

Cain's eyes shot wide. He actually smiled, and so wide, he thought his face might crack.

"He's delirious." Jami diagnosed.

Cain looked at Jami's worried face and lost it. He laughed harder than he had in centuries.

"He's hysterical." En help me." Jami called.

En rushed to her aid followed by Faith and a wobbly Grey.

Cain looked into their concerned faces and laughed his ass off. He knew they all thought he had cracked under the strain and that made him laugh harder.

Ennie was shrewder than the rest and had known Cain a lot longer. She gave him the look. He fought for control knowing full well she was preparing to slap him as she had done to Jami earlier.

He caught his breath and told them. "Right now let's just be thankful for the gift we've been handed."

"Amen." En agreed wholeheartedly.

"Here's the deal. Since we don't have to stick around and clean up the mess we are outta here. Jami and En would you please pack up some gear for the boys? I'm not expecting anything until nightfall but I think it's in our best interest if we don't separate."

Jami and Ennie hustled upstairs to pack a bag.

Micah sprang up from the floor. "Why can't Grey and I stay here? We live here. Just exactly what do you mean by you're not expecting anything until nightfall?"

"All will be explained. Let's just get out of here first." Cain tried to placate him.

Micah was not thrilled with the answer but he knew it was all he was going to get.

Cain went to Grey. "How are you feeling?"

"Exhausted but good." He answered, smiling.

"Faith?"

"I'm great." She answered beaming at Grey.

"All right then. Here come the girls. Let's hit the bricks."

The amethyst eyes of Hells CEO were locked on his computer screen. Lucifer's office was where he spent the lion's share of his time. It was tricked out to rival the Oval Office. The antique mahogany desk top was burdened with parchments, ledgers, spreadsheets and dozens of post it notes. Twin bankers' lamps were the main source of light in the room.

The back and side walls were painted murals depicting an ancient forest. At first glance a serene setting to work in. But this was Hell and nothing was what it appeared. Take time to study the walls and you would discover the evil within.

Reptilian eyes slithered and skittered weaving in and out of breaks in rotted trees. Sluggy legless creatures burrowed out of the stagnant dirt winding their way through the dense vegetation. Small hairy rodent like critters poked long forked tongues from between fangs latching onto fellow forest dwellers pulling them in to feed from.

A suffocating miasma of putrid life seeping into the Wall Street chic office.

Lucifer glanced at the wall and hissed. The creatures withdrew further into their habitat leaving the walls to look as motionless murals once more.

The Son of Morning leaned back into his oxblood leather office chair resting his eyes. He drank in the oppressive atmosphere like a fine wine. His quiet moment was interrupted as heavy booted footsteps approaching his desk demanded his attention. Keeping his eyes closed, he asked, "Don't you knock?"

Bam, the heavy office door slammed shut.

"Shit." Sundrel cursed. He was standing outside the office door …again. Pissed off he hammered his fist against the panel.

"Enter." Lucifer sat forward waiting.

Sundrel stalked back inside and stood in front of his brother. "Bastard." He snarled.

"Correct," Lucifer agreed. "When did you return?"

"A bit ago."

"Did Magnus make you?"

"Are you kidding me? He is too full of himself. He believes he is much smarter than the rest of us. He totally believed I was a mindless underling you had sent to assist him."

Lucifer nodded his agreement. "Did you enjoy your time above?"

"Exponentially." Sundrel smiled cruelly.

The son of a bitch is almost as sadistic as I am Lucifer thought. "You have any information for me?"

"What can I say? You were right as always. The little prick intends to take him out."

"I've sent Tearzahn." Lucifer informed him. "He will finish this. If Magnus is stupid enough to make a move against Cain. Tear knows what to do. I need Cain broken not dead."

"I met up with some old friends."

"Really?" Lucifer remarked, intrigued," Who might that be?"

"Ladocia and Smyrna made an appearance after my exorcism. They denied me your tribute."

"Did they now?" Lucifer's eyes lit amethyst fire.

"They threatened me with the Swords of Solomon."

"Did you tremble in fear?"

"Hell yes." He laughed, pulling a chuckle from Lucifer. "They still don't have a clue."

"Good. I enjoy knowing they are doing my work for me."

"Fucking Boy Scouts." Tear snarled. "Michael keeps them chained like dogs. Wow, come to think of it that kind of reminds me of someone else."

"Watch what you say to me, Sundrel. The Bloody Seven serve their purpose and right now they are serving mine."

"Whatever." Sundrel shrugged, not really caring one way or the other. "You need me for anything else?"

"No, you did well. Go enjoy your reward."

"Is the girl hot?"

"Girls, my brother. Just arrived and pants pissing terrified." Lucifer elaborated.

"You are so the man." Sundrel mock bowed before Lucifer.

"No. I'm the Devil."

Other than the new and improved Micah it was a motley crew that trudged through the darkness along Main Street. While their feet shuffled an unsteady rhythm on the sidewalk Micah was given the Cliff Notes version of reality within their little circle. Since Lo had wiped Micah's memory of his possession Cain ordered that tidbit of information be excluded from the explanations.

Micah decided they were crazy and called them out on their bullshit. He was still busting their asses when they reached the house. Standing at the foot of the front steps Cain clamped a hand on Micah's shoulder. Micah turned and got a load of flaming eyes and fangs. He jumped squealing like a girl as he reached to pry Cain's hand off his shoulder finding claws where fingers should have been. Cain released him only to allow Ennie get shot at some fun. Their doubting Thomas levitated up the steps to land on his feet at the front door which proceeded to unlock and open in welcome. Everyone was laughing as Micah went inside speechless but now a believer.

Inside everyone sprawled on couches or the floor. The self-proclaimed period of sobriety was at an end. Micah was voted in as bartender since he was the only one who was not on the verge of collapse. Fifteen minutes later they were all feeling a little better with some alcohol in their system and the knowledge that they had crossed at least one major hurdle.

Cain learned a few things over his many years. One was that people with a bright future ahead of them would fight for that future. This was the reason he was making an announcement. "Before everyone passes out we need to have a meeting of the minds." This declaration was met with a round of groans.

"Can't we talk about Magnus after we get some sleep?" Jami whined.

"We will get to Magnus later. Right now I've got something else I want to talk about."

Cain thumped his empty longneck onto the table to make sure he had everyone's attention. "Micah I would like to offer you a job. Someone recently convinced me I need a personal assistant."

Cain looked at Jami. Her face was lit up that he had listened to her and taken her advice.

"How much do you pay?"

"Eight a week to start."

"If I screw up will you turn into a monster and eat me?" Micah asked, only half serious.

"Micah!" Jami scolded. "He's not a monster."

Cain shrugged it off. "Only if you forget to make the coffee."

"Cool, so what's the gig?"

"Always have a steady stream of coffee brewing. Cook once a day. I eat about five p.m. If something breaks or needs replaced take care of it or find someone who can without bothering me. You will be running errands and doing the shopping so you have the use of any of the cars…except…the Stingray. Touching that would be another eatable offense."

Micah's face fell. The stingray was the shit. He had been begging Cain to allow him to drive it since he got his permit when he was sixteen.

Cain continued. "You will have to live at the house. You will have the second floor to yourself. There are four bedrooms on that floor. Pick one. That includes a sitting room and an office, which you will be using. We will get you set up with a computer and whatever else you need."

"What about the ladies?" Micah asked, always a horn dog.

"Don't care. Just keep it to yourself. You will have plenty of room so that shouldn't be a problem. I don't want any taking up residence. Get em' in and out."

"When do I start?"

"As soon as this shit is finished."

"Sounds good Boss."

Cain felt a sense of satisfaction when Micah accepted. He would miss his cherished privacy but the kid needed some forward momentum. A fresh start, a new place, a sense of purpose and independence. Cain would just have to learn to live with sharing his space.

"Are we done now? We've got a Bar to open this afternoon." Jami reminded them. "You know Mom and Pop will stroke that we closed up even ONE night."

Moans and grunts came from her brothers.

Cain's face turned stoney. Reading his mind En tried to soothe him. "You and I will be right there to keep an eye on them."

Imitating Cain, Grey thunked his empty on the coffee table. "Next." He called out.

Grey took a small blue velvet box from his pocket. "I grabbed this from the safe earlier." He opened the box displaying the contents for Faith. "It was my Grandmothers."

Nestled in the box was an exquisite antique engagement ring. The center stone a quarter karat sapphire surrounded by diamonds. Faith stared wide eyed as Grey got to his knees at her feet.

"I have loved you for years. These past few days have taught me not to waste a second. You're brave and smart and kind. You're as beautiful on the inside as you are on the outside. I want to spend the rest of my life showing you every day that you are loved. Will you marry me?"

You could hear a pin drop as everyone anxiously awaited her answer.

"It took you long enough." She teased. "Yes, yes, yes." She threw herself into his arms. They both fell to the floor. Faith covered his beaming face with kisses.

Jami jumped to her feet. She whooped and hollered doing her version of the happy dance. Ennie was sniffling. Cain handed her a box of Kleenex.

Micah watched them. Their whole world was suddenly changing. Judging by the smiles on everyone's faces and the happy chatter in the room the changes were good ones. They were growing up and moving on to better things. This is what life is all about. "Congratulations!" He yelled over the din of voices.

"Anyone else?" En asked.

"No one spoke up so she thunked Cain's empty on the coffee table since she was still nursing hers.

"I may as well add my plans while we're at it. As soon as we wrap up this mess I will be taking Jami with me for a few weeks. After that power surge she threw out it is imperative she learns to control her powers."

Cain's face was unreadable. Jami knew En was right, but dammit, her emotions didn't care. She didn't want to leave now. How could she walk away when there was a possibility for a relationship with Cain? She had waited so long for him to notice her. Would it end before it even had a chance to begin?

"Wait!" Faith squealed. "I'm going to need you guys to help plan the wedding. You will both be in it. I can't do this without you."

"Darling we won't be gone long. I promise we will be in constant contact. There is no way in hell I'm going to leave you to your own devices and end up stuffed into some fuschia nightmare.

"What's wrong with fuschia?" Faith pouted, taking in her friends grimacing faces.

"Not a thing." Grey assured his bride to be. This statement earned him raspberries from Jami and En.

"But you two would look beautiful in fuschia Scarlett O'Hara gowns." Faith threatened with a sparkle in her green eyes.

"You wouldn't." Jami shuddered.

Faith smiled menacingly.

"This will have to be a short trip." En whispered to Jami.

Cain was relaxed. A Marlboro dangled between two fingers. He was enjoying watching the girly drama. He took a last drag then put his cigarette out. Watching them all so happy was a good thing. It was a memory they would all need to hold onto. Magnus would not wait much longer.

Faith climbed off Greys lap and went to Cain.

"It would mean a lot to me if you would give me away." She beamed a beautiful smile at him.

Cain's handsome face went blank. He was struck dumb. Holding his hand out to Faith she placed her delicate hand on his. He was blown away by her smile. She was radiant with the promise of a bright future. He was determined she would get that future.

"I would be honored." He accepted. Faith wrapped him in a hug.

"Well brother." Grey turned to Micah. "What do you think about being my best man?"

"Are you sure?" Micah asked. "What about Sam? You were the Best Man at his wedding."

"I want you." Grey spoke emphatically. "Come on brother. This is important to me."

"Yeah." Micah looked pleased. "I would love to." The brothers hugged.

Faith returned to her man. Grey held her in his arms while dropping kisses on her cheek.

Ennie reached over to Cain. She was sniffling again.

"I just gave you the box." He reminded her.

En glanced down to her side. She seemed surprised to find them there. Pulling out a tissue she blew her nose, loudly.

Cain was starting to choke on the emotions clogging the room. "It's almost daylight. We're all going to need a few hours of shut eye. Who knows what fun and games tonight might bring? We need to have clear heads."

Faith and Grey were the first to bolt. They all but ran up the stairs to Faith's room leaving the rest to crack on them for their hurry. They left no doubt as to what they would shorty be occupied with and it had nothing to do with sleeping.

Ennie gave Cain a questioning look. Satisfied with his vague response she grabbed blankets to put on the couches for her and Micah.

Jami stood at the bottom of the stairs. If she was going to have to leave him soon there was no way she was going to bed alone. After his response to her at the bar she knew he wanted her as much as she wanted him. She motioned to him with her index finger. Jami held her breath until she heard his footsteps coming up behind her.

As Cain walked past Ennie she called out a goodnight to both of them. She had a very smug smile on her face as she watched him go up the stairs.

Micah watched Ennie stretch out on the sofa. She yawned and wriggled under a soft old quilt. She had a muzzy sleepy expression on her exotic face that reminded him of a woman's expression while making love.

There was no way he was sleeping anytime soon. He had a giant gap in his memory and he was the only one who seemed concerned about it. He knew they were not telling him the whole story. Hell, what they had told him was damn hard to digest. Every time he tried to remember he saw nothing but a dark void. He finished off his beer debating whether or not to get a fresh one. He decided what the hell maybe another one or three would help him get some sleep. When he returned to the living room he already had the freshie half gone. He sat down and noticed Ennie wasn't sleeping either.

"Sorry." He apologised. "I didn't mean to keep you awake."

"Not your fault. I'm too strung out with excess energy to sleep."

"Need to burn some off?" He asked, giving her his best bad boy smile.

En chuckled seductively. "No."

"We could always just talk." Micah offered suggestively.

"Uh huh."

"You know you're the most exotic sexual woman I've ever met. I would give anything to make love to you."

En's sense of humor kicked in. "I believe you darling. The truth is as handsome as you are you lack the experience to satisfy me."

"Teach me. I'm highly teachable. You will find I'm a very fast learner."

The conversation came to an abrupt halt. Grey and Faith were directly above them. They were energetically celebrating their engagement. The squeak, squeak, squeak of bedsprings was clearly heard through the ceiling.

Micah decided to just tell the truth. "En?"

"Yes."

"I'm freaked. Everything you told me, showed me. I'm feeling head fucked. I don't understand what happened to me. I'm not totally sure what's going on here. I know were in deep shit. I just don't want to be alone."

Ennie lifted the quilt in invitation. As Micah crawled in with her she heard him singing Hot for Teacher. She chuckled to herself as a vision of poor dorky Waldo popped into her mind.

CHAPTER TWENTY ONE

Cain stood unnoticed in Jami's doorway. He was fresh from the shower wearing only a towel draped around his lean hips. His damp raven hair was brushed back and left to air dry. His toffee skin glowing in the light of the hallway after the heat of the shower.

He stood watching her. She was seated at her vanity table pulling a brush through silky ash blonde waves. Her silhouette appeared as a finely crafted cameo in the light of the jar candles she had placed around the room. She was correct, the damn things did smell good. Her thoughts appeared far away. Cain gave himself over to the simple pleasure of observing this quiet feminine side of her he had never seen before.

Jami had no idea she was being admired. She was lost to her memories.

As a child Cain had been a superhero to her young imaginative mind. Tall, strong, and handsome he was John Wayne, Superman, and the Terminator all rolled into one. During her adolescence he became her school girl crush. All dark and brooding. Not to mention movie star handsome with his black hair, and muscles showing under the tee shirts he usually wore. Now, as a woman, she was lost to him. The mystery of him intrigued her. His rare smiles melted her. The loneliness inside him broke his heart. She had stood as an unhappy witness to his unending stream of one night stands. Although it devastated her it was also obvious that none of the women meant anything to him. Jami had long dreamed of being the one who broke through his defenses and claimed his heart. She wanted to be the woman who took away the loneliness she saw every time she looked into his crimson eyes.

Cain stepped into the room. A floorboard creaked under his weight. Jami swung her head toward him. She got to her feet. Cain only now noticed she had changed into lacy white panties and a matching camisole. He felt his penis stir to life under the towel. A whisper of a sigh escaped her lips.

"Penny for your thoughts." Jami asked him, feeling suddenly unsure of her own thoughts.

"I think you can do much better than me."

"Why don't you let me be the judge of that?" His remark touched her. Jami walked behind him and closed the door.

The woman before him tugged at something he thought he had lost long ago. He was unworthy of the gift she was offering him. It was more than just sex. She was prepared to give all of herself holding nothing back.

Jami was the one who closed the distance between them. She reached out her hands resting them on his smooth hard chest. Looking up into his scarlett eyes she smiled showing no fear. Cain could not deny himself. He needed this the way a man lost in the desert needed water. Leaning down, he took her mouth kissing her slowly savoring the sweet taste of her. Her arms went around his neck. She pulled herself closer leaning the soft curves of her body into the hard plains of his.

His body heated as their kisses became increasingly urgent. Jami's hands dropped to his shoulders clutching him. Cain grunted as her nails dug into his skin.

"Why don't we take this to the bed?" He suggested.

She answered by taking him by the hand and led him to the spot where she had often imagined him.

Jami crawled to the middle of the bed and sat on her knees waiting for him to join her. Her blue eyes were heavy lidded with passion and her lips puffy from their kisses. Cain's dick hit totem pole status. The loose towel at his waist hit the floor. His enormous erection sprung free.

Cain joined her on the bed. He reached to her camisole pulling it up and off. Running his hands up her ribs he cupped her soft ivory breasts rubbing his thumbs over the shell pink pebbles. He watched as her eyes closed with pleasure. He leaned her back against the pillows then captured one of the delicate morsels with his mouth. Using his tongue to swirl around her nipple and his teeth to gently nip he took his time tormenting her.

He was making her crazy. She was twisting with the need for more. "Cain please."

"What do you want baby?" Cain asked, his voice gruff with lust.

"Touch me. She grabbed his hand and drew it down between her legs.

At first it was just a soft brush of his hand over the lace. But she wanted more. She urged him with her hips. The friction of the lace rubbing against her clit was driving her mad. His strokes became bolder. Jami whimpered with wanting.

Cain hooked his forefingers on both sides of the lace. Jami raised her hips allowing him to slide the panties off. He spread her open kneeling between her legs. Putting his hands on her knees he slowly slid his rough palms up the silken skin of her thighs leading to her pouty lips. As much as he wanted to dive down and take her with his mouth he held back continuing to torment her.

With one finger she teased her running it lazily down her slit. She moaned. Cain took his finger and thumb working her clit until it was swollen and begging for for him. Lowering his head he nuzzled her teasing her even more with his whiskers. Then with painstaking slowness he ran his tongue up her hot center barely touching her with the tip of his tongue. Softly he blew over the path his tongue had taken. Her whole body shivered. Cain chuckled enjoying her reaction.

Out of her mind Jami growled at him. "Put your mouth on me. Fuck me with your tongue."

Cain was more than ready to take it up a notch. He licked, sucked, and stroked. He took her clit between his lips sucking her off while his fingers plunged in and out of her heat.

Jami ground her wet pussy against his face as she teetered on the brink. "Harder Cain. Suck me harder."

Cain gave in giving them both what they wanted. Jami cried out as the orgasm shook through her. As she came in his mouth Cain had the satisfaction of lapping up her creamy sweetness as she shuddered against his mouth.

Now that she was ready for him Cain couldn't hold back. Rising above her Cain filled her warm tight sheath in one hard fluid stroke. Jami cried out in a combination of pain and pleasure. Cain held rigidly still giving her body time to adjust to the size of him.

"Holy shit." Jami gasped. She had seen the size of him, even felt it in her hands, but feeling it inside her was something else entirely.

"Did I hurt you?"

"No, I just wasn't expecting so…much. Don't stop. I want you."

Cain started an easy slide in and out. Long deep strokes. Jami's body instinctively adjusting to the way he filled her completely.

"You want more?" He asked, his voice gravelly with lust.

"Yes, fuck yes."

Cain's rhythm grew more aggressive. His cock pounding into her harder. Jami dug her nails into his ass matching him thrust for thrust. Her head thrashed wildly as she called out incoherently while another orgasm ripped through her.

Cain clenched his teeth. Blood pooled in his mouth as his fangs punctured his bottom lip. He didn't give it a thought. His mind was on the feeling of Jami as her orgasm pulsed around his cock. He nailed her hard one last time as he found his own shuddering release.

They lay in the aftermath of mind blowing sex. Jami rested her head on Cain's broad chest. Her body was boneless with satisfaction. She had become so quiet Cain began to wonder if she was having second thoughts about them being together.

"Are you having regrets?"

"No." She snapped. "Just the opposite. I was wishing we could stay like this forever."

"Forever is a long time. Don't you think you would get tired of me?" He joked, attempting to stay away from the serious stuff.

"Never, here with you I feel happy and safe. When we leave this bed we will have to go back to the real world. I'm afraid Cain."

So much for staying away from the serious stuff. "I will not let anything happen to you."

"That thing in Micah scared the shit out of me. I can't even imagine what Magnus is like."

Cain scrooched up on the bed pulling her along with him so that they were both relaxing on the pillows. She had left an ashtray and his pack of cigarettes on the nightstand. He lit up. Pulling her into him she rested her head on his shoulder allowing herself the comfort of his strength.

"I've sent LaMech back to Hell more than once. I'll do it again."

"Can you tell me what started all this between the two of you."

"It's not a pretty story." He warned her, hoping she would not want to hear it.

"I don't expect it to be."

Cain took a deep drag from his smoke. If he told her she may very well hate him. But she was caught up in this mess and deserved to know the truth no matter the outcome.

"La Mech is my great, great, grandson. He is the reason I am who I am today. His death was my turning point."

Jami looked up at him. His eyes were on fire but he was far away back in time. She stayed quiet and let him tell his story.

"I was a killer. I took pleasure in it. I spent more than a thousand years as a paid assassin. When I got news there was to be another birth to my bloodline I returned to my people."

Cain extinguished his cigarette and lit another. Then he continued.

"I was there when he was born. I watched helplessly as his mother died in childbirth. It was an omen."

"Physically he grew to resemble my brother. There was nothing I could deny him. All he had to do was ask. It was the first time in my cursed existence I cared about anyone. I stayed as long as I could but eventually, as always, I had to leave. It was seven hundred years until I saw his face again. People lived a lot longer in those days. In my absence the man I knew had changed. Not for the better."

"As I made my way back I stopped at familiar communities. La Mech's reputation had a far reach. As I heard tales of his tyranny and cruelty I refused to believe my ears. At the last settlement I stopped at before reaching his home I heard the worst of it. La Mech had followed in my footsteps. He had taken an innocent life."

"Upon my arrival I found that his two sons had deserted him. I was taken into the shelter of his home by his two wives. They were exquisitely beautiful. They attempted to seduce me. I could see by their eyes that they were demon whores, succubus. They had been playing with him for years. He was already cursed being of my bloodline. They just needed to push him a little to bring the killer in him to the surface."

Cain paused to take a breath and put out his cigarette. He was shocked he could still be affected by the events that took place so long ago.

Jami casually stroked his chest. It was all she could do to comfort him.

"I tried to reason with him. He called me a hypocrite. Why was it okay for me to be a killer but not for him? He was a true son of my blood. He refused to listen to a word I said."

"La Mech had also been cursed for his murderous ways. Just as I had done he took pride in it. His curse had been tenfold. The killer of La Mech would face vengeance seventy fold."

Jami gasped but otherwise remained silent.

"When he turned a deaf ear I slayed his demon wives before his eyes. He cursed at me as they turned to smoke and were drug back to Hell. He turned on me with every intention of killing me."

"La Mech was seven hundred and seventy seven years old when I slit his throat and took on the penalty for taking his life condemning myself even deeper."

Jami had listened quietly. She knew she would have to choose her words carefully before she spoke.

"I'm falling in love with you." She spoke honestly." Your past means nothing to me. I love the man you are now."

"What?"

"You heard me. I love you. You will find your redemption. This is not your fault. Magnus or La Mech or whatever he wants to call himself embraced evil. You did what you did to stop him and you will do it again."

"How can you say that after what I just told you?"

"Because I can look into your eyes, your beautiful cursed ruby red eyes and see the goodness inside you."

Before he could argue anymore she leaned in and kissed him. If he could not believe her words maybe he would believe her actions. They made love again. This time it wasn't with the urgency of their earlier lovemaking. It was the sharing of two people each wanting nothing more than to please each other.

That afternoon, all of the women wore a rosy blush while all the men smiled smugly at each other. Given the inadequate amount of sleep they all had it was a perky bunch that bustled around the house preparing for the evening and what they might encounter.

Last night their talk had been of the future. Now they focused on the present. It had been unanimously agreed upon, from this point forward, until they sent Magnus packing there would be no more splitting up. They would go to Archers en masse. There was no disputing the fact that there was safety in numbers. The odds were on their side. They had Magnus outmanned six to one. Confidence was high. Their biggest concern was for unsuspecting bar patrons.

They got a lucky break. Weather forecasters were calling for a balmy spring evening. Grey had suggested they keep the doors at Archer's propped open. This would allow an unhampered exit at the front and the rear of the bar if things got ugly.

Grey would be at his position behind the bar. Jami would be on the floor waiting tables and Micah would be in the kitchen. Cain would be on his normal barstool while Ennie and Faith sat at a corner table where they could observe most of the bar. The plan was simple, wait for Magnus to arrive and send him back to Hell.

Cain entered the kitchen to find Ennie loading up a duffel bag of magical implements and weapons. She stopped what she was doing when she got a look at his stoney face.

"You got something on your mind?" She huffed, not liking the look on his face.

"Yeah, I do." He spoke seriously.

"Well I don't want to hear it."

"Ennie."

"No, go away."

He reached out and took her by the arm. She tried to pull away with no success. "You're the only person in the world I can say this to. Now stop acting like a kid and listen."

She settled down with a huff. Now she knew for certain it was something she did not want to hear.

"If anything goes wrong I'm leaving you in charge. All that I have is yours and the kids. You will have to watch over them. They will all be wearing targets. If Magnus walks away from this I want you to find Ladocia and beg him for help. If Magnus manages to take me out he will not be satisfied until you are all dead."

"May I say something now?" En snapped.

Cain shrugged. "If you must."

"You have kicked his ass how many times now? Why should this time be any different?" She argued with him defiantly.

"I wasn't invested like this before."

"That should make you fight even harder."

"Trust me I'm going into this full boar. I fully intend to rip the son of a bitch to tiny pieces. Anyone can slip up though. Even me. This time I have got the added distraction of trying to keep everyone else safe."

"You leave that to me. You concentrate on Magnus. I will concentrate on keeping the kids out of the line of fire. You are Cain. You will squash him like a bug." She spoke with a sassy conviction.

He kissed the top of her head. "I appreciate the faith you have in me."

Jami poked her head in the doorway. "Time to go."

Ennie zipped up the duffel. Cain took it from her and they headed out.

Cain was the last one to leave. He watched as they strutted down the sidewalk filled with the confidence of youth. He grimly wondered who if any of them would be returning.

Tearzahn lay snoring under the heavy coat he had taken from Magnus. Out cold, he was sleeping off the overindulgence of food, booze, and sex. He was not a happy Fallen Angel when Magnus barked at him to wake up.

Tear threw out a hand. The action sent Magnus hurling through the air backwards. Magnus "Hoofed" in pain as he slammed into the decaying wall.

"Fuck off." Tear grumbled rolling over to go back to sleep.

"No, you fuck off. I didn't ask for your fucking help. I don't need it. Keep sleeping. Believe me when I tell you I would love for you to sleep through the whole damn thing."

Tear hissed flashing his fangs at Magnus. Struggling to sit up he groped blindly until his hand captured a half full bottle of Jack. He took a long greedy pull rubbing his hand over his bleery amber eyes. "What's got your nuts in a knot?" He garbled, then cleared his raw throat. Tear could really give a shit less about whatever it was that had Magnus all fired up. Reclining against the wall he took his time polishing off his bottle.

"It's time. They have surfaced. The lot of them just went into the bar. This is the opportunity I have been waiting for." Magnus exploded.

He was being driven by bloodlust. He wanted his revenge. Magnus was sick of all the waiting and scheming. Screw delayed gratification. The Fallen Angels disinterest was intolerable. Magnus was ready to go for his jugular. It must have shown. Tear's bored face came to life with the raising of a single eyebrow.

"Have a drink with me." This was an order not a suggestion. Magnus hesitated.

"Take the stick out of your ass. Grab us each a bottle and sit." Tear offered again. His tone clearly insinuated if Magnus refused he was screwed.

Temper cooled down Magnus was smart enough to understand that he did not want a smackdown with Satan's enforcer. He grabbed two unopened bottles from a case on the floor. He handed one to tear opened the other and slugged some down. He reluctantly took a seat next to Tear. They sat drinking in silence while Magnus impatiently waited for Tear to speak.

"Patience." Tear spoke at last.

Magnus opened his mouth to argue. Tear shut him down with the same raised eyebrow.

"Listen to an experienced warrior. You're an Incubus. You play your games with women. You get some pussy. You taint a soul. It's a simple drain and drag. Warfare is something else altogether. Waiting is good for us and bad for them. They are already shitting their pants waiting for you to make your move. We wait until their tired, frazzled, and jumping at shadows. The longer it takes the better. Then when they start to think maybe tonight is not going to be the night that maybe they can let their guards down. That's when we hit them."

Magnus hated to admit it but Tears lecture made sense. He could handle a few more hours of waiting. The knowledge that he would be bathing in Cain's blood before dawn would be worth the wait.

"Do you have a plan?" Magnus asked.

"Kill."

CHAPTER TWENTY TWO

Beelzebub roared outside the door of Lucifer's man cave. There was no reply and no wonder. The music thundered out vibrating the stone floor so hard Beelzebubs teeth were knocking together. Lucifer's right hand was pissed. He pounded on the door with a ham sized paw.

The Master of all things evil was enjoying some down time. His golden head was propped on the end of a red leather couch. His bare feet dangled over the armrest of the opposite end. A solid silver tray lay across the crotch of his frayed jeans. A remote, a half ounce of weed, and a pack of papers scattered across the tray. A six pack of Corona sat on the floor by his right hand for easy access. His pointed pink tongue snaked out to lick the paper. Picking up a beer he carelessly chugged some down allowing a bit to dribble from his chest to his stomach. He ignored it and lit up. This was the way the Light Bringer was supposed to live. Arg, he was sick of work and responsibility.

Avenged Sevenfold's Nightmare drowned out the screams of souls as the hit the flames of his furnace.

Lucifer looked more like a high school senior whose parents were gone for the weekend than the ruler of Hell. Lost to the bliss of a sinister guitar riff Lucifer did not hear Beelzebub until he stood right beside him and roared in his ear.

Lucifer sprang up cursing. His tray went flying scattering his shit all over Hell's creation. "What the Fuck B!"

Beelzebub growled gearing up for another roar. Lucifer zapped his jaws shut. He picked up the remote and turned the tunes off.

"Wheres Eve?" He demanded. "I told you to bring her back. I need a little fun B." Lucifer undid his zap so Beelzebub could answer.

Still pissed off at the Boss B refused to speak out loud. "I can't find her." He shot into Lucifer's head.

"Bullshit." Lucifer bitched. "She's here somewhere. Go look again."

"If I say she is not here, she damn well is not here!" B finally spoke with a growl.

"She is not permitted above." Lucifer reminded his brother.

"I cannot sense her there. You are closest to her. I think you should try." Beelzebub suggested.

Lucifer opened himself up. He looked wildly at B. I cannot sense her anywhere. It's like she has vanished." A confused frown creased Lucifers forehead.

Beelzebub rumbled. "Or a Witch has cloaked her."

Lucifer's body shook with rage. "Cyndahl." He ground through clenched teeth. "B, go fetch my little witch."

Chyndahl stood shaking bug eyed with fear. The room she had been dragged to have been reduced to rubble and ash. Looming before her stood a vision of uncompromising malevolence. Truly the thing in front of here belonged in this burned out shell for the thing resembled a charred corpse. The beast looked nothing like her lover and yet she knew it was Lucifer smoldering before her.

"Come to me." His voice was deep, echoing, bone chilling to her ears, not the smooth silken purr of her memories.

Paralyzed with fear Cyndahl could not force her feet to obey his command.

"What's wrong? Do you no longer find me appealing?" The hellish beast demanded as the crisp blackened skin of his face cracked leaving burning bloody trails of puss oozing down its face.

She opened her mouth to voice the denial of his words but was incapable of speech.

Beelzebub used his great lions head to push her forward. Cyndahl fell to her hands and knees being forced to crawl to her devilish lover by his most loyal brother.

Lucifer struck out. Snatching a fistfull of her long inky hair as he dangled her so she was forced to look into his sizzling amethyst eyes. She hung in his punishing grip not daring to utter a squeak of pain. Her body quaked as her mind screamed out images of the torture tactics Lucifer was known for. She dropped her eyes from his unable to maintain the contact only to have them fall on his fangs. They were longer than she had ever seen them. Ivory daggers that he stroked with a long curling tongue. Perhaps he would make it quick and simply rip out her throat. She dared not pray that he would.

"Where is my wife? You are the only Witch in Hell strong enough to have hidden her from me."

"Please…" Her frightened voice pleaded. "She only wanted to help my Father. I could not deny her."

"Yet you pair of bitches dared to defy ME." His voice caused ashes to whip about the rubble. The stone walls vibrated and cracked.

"No Great One. That was not our intent. We simply wished to be of assistance to you."

"Am I so inept that I need help from whores?"

"We meant no disrespect. We did it out of love for you."

"Pull her home now." Lucifer roared making the walls tremble. Blood seeped from around his eyes quickly turning to ash from the heat from the heat generated by Lucifer.

"I can…nooot…" Cyndahl stammered bursting into tears.

Lucifer shook her like a dog shaking a rat. She was unable to hold back a scream of pain as she felt the hair being ripped from her head.

"The spell." She cried. "It lasts only twenty four hours. She will then be pulled back willing or not."

Lucifer seethed in frustration. He snapped at Beelzebub. "Throw this whore to my hounds."

"Pardon, my brother." Beelzebub spoke cautiously. Even he was in danger of feeling Lucifer's wrath when he was in this frame of mind. The Lucifer he faced now was the Greatest of the Fallen. The Angel who had been arrogant enough to declare war on Heaven. "If you kill her it could disrupt the spell adversely. There is the potential that without the Witch who cast the spell here as an anchor your wife may be stranded above. She could be locked powerless in whatever mortal she is inhabiting."

"A stay of execution for you." Lucifer snarled.

Cyndahl sagged in momentary relief.

Lucifer laughed. He shook his head magically bringing back his handsome angelic face. "My darling you look pale."

She sighed with joy that he had become his old self. "You frightened me."

Lucifer beamed bathing her in radiant light. "B, escort my precious girl. I want to see her strung up over the pit. They should put some color back into her pretty cheeks."

He dropped her to the floor. She wrapped her arm around his ankles. Her tears fell on his bare feet. She begged for his mercy.

Lucifer bent down roughly jerking her chin to look him in the eyes. "Do you mistake me for the Son? You shed your tears upon my feet and believe I will forgive your sin. Will you dry those tears with your hair harlot?"

He barked a laugh sharp and cruel as broken glass. "I am Lucifer. I hold every evil, putrid, bit of filth imagined within me. The very breath I expel is tainted. Serial killers, rapists, and Leaders of Nations, pray to ME. I happily corrupt and defile all that is pure. I whisper lies into the ears of those without hope. Do it. I will free you of your pain. Then I watch with amused satisfaction as the pit devours their souls. I make sure the dope fiend gets his next fix the one that will send him into my arms. I assure the weak minded always have a strong psychopath to lead them. Their destruction is my pleasure. You ridiculous bitch. I am the Death of forgiveness." Lucifer brutally kicked her away.

"Take her. String her up. I'll enjoy watching her dangle after I wash her whore's stench from my skin."

Beelzebub shook his full flaming mane. He wrapped his tail around her throat and drug the unconscious woman from the room.

"B, when your done there find that fucking smurf of a demon that Eve keeps close to her. That little spy had to have a hand in this. When you find her keep her. You've earned yourself a new chew toy."

Beelzebub roared his thanks.

Cain sat perched on his usual barstool nursing a warm beer. He glanced at his watch for the tenth time in the last hour. It was one a.m. Last call was still an hour away. So far all was quiet.

It was a Friday night and the bar was still hopping. The usual crowd was in residence. At last check the pool tables were still cracking. A gaggle of one more beer and maybes were bent over the jukebox in their miniskirts. They were working it for the boys at the bar trying to give them a good show before closing so they wouldn't have to go home alone.

Jami had gotten nervous and sent the part time girl home hours ago. Now she was scrambling back and forth between the bar and tables trying to keep up with the crowd of frustrated drunks.

Grey was busy behind the bar. Everyone was ordering up trying to get the last few in before going home for the night. His eyes were constantly on the move darting around the crowd but stopping a second every time they landed on Faith.

Faith and Ennie sat at a table keeping an eye on things. They tried to look like a couple of friends out for an evening of fun. The edgy looks on their faces said otherwise.

Micah was the only one out of sight. He was frantically working to close down the kitchen so he could get out to the others.

Grey had just handed Cain a cold one when the pain exploded in the base of his skull. As the pain dissipated he heard the racket. His heightened hearing allowed him to catch the new noise over the din of the bar. It was the sound of thousands of tiny nails scrambling across hardwood floors. Cain leapt up and ran straight towards the small stampede.

Coming up from the cellar in rippling waves of hairy bodies and bald tails were rats. Hundreds of them. All with filmy white eyes.

Micah blasting curses from the kitchen had Cain back stepping. Pandemonium erupted. Cain was nearly plowed over by the mini skirt set as they flew past him like a herd of cattle making their way to the rear exit. He made it to the kitchen and if the situation had not been so serious he would have laughed.

Micah stood on top of the butcher block table having a whopping good time. The kid held a thirty pound fire extinguisher. He was gleefully hosing the nasty critters as he shit talked them. A nasty sea of foamy rats was already ankle deep around the table. Seeing that he was holding his own and having a good time Cain left him to it.

The beady eyed bastards were clawing their way up his jeans. As he made his way back to the barroom he peeled them off grabbing them by their heads and snapping their necks then throwing them to the floor. All the while he did a crazy boot stomping dance while crushing their skulls beneath his boot heels.

The bar was under attack. The rats ran along the bar top spilling over drinks. There was not a clear place to step on the floor. People were covered in the damn things. Cain pulled one from a girl's hair before it took a bite out of her scalp. He grabbed another from off a guy's back who was trying to stop one from gnawing on his girlfriend's bare leg.

Tables were overturned in the frantic rush to get away from the attackers. Glass coated the demon rats as they scurried across the floor looking for people to bite. Cain ran to a girl who had fallen and was fast vanishing beneath a blanket of the beasties. He pulled her up and all but threw her out the front door.

Ennie and Jami were blasting the rodents to oblivion. Piles of furry bodies were evident as their teamwork started paying off. Grey and Faith shot them with Super Soakers full of Holy Water. It was like an acid bath for the damn things leaving behind squashy flurry blobs on the already treacherous terrain.

Cain grabbed two more guys who were too inebriated to find their way out and hauled them to the door. Returning to the fray he was shocked to see the tide of the battle had turned. The last of the nasties were fleeing out the door. It looked like they had won the first round with limited casualties.

Micah ran in whooping. "Hot damn. We kicked some demon rat ass."

No one else spoke they were too busy trying to catch their breath.

Grey found two bottles of Jack that had somehow managed to survive. He cracked them and passed them around. Everyone drank straight from the source since all the glasses were either broken or too gross to drink from.

"Well at least it's over." Micah spoke naively.

"Don't get too excited kid. That was just the opening act." Cain brought him down to reality.

"You mean it's going to get worse?" Micah blurted.

"Of course it is you silly boy." Magnus answered, with a grisly chuckle.

Six heads swung in the direction of the voice.

"Faith my darling. Did you enjoy playing with my pets?" Magnus stood by the cellar door. His smile was maniacal. Any trace of the handsome face had been replaced by a demonic look of madness.

Faith kept silent. Grey held her while Micah took a protective stance on her other side.

Magnus had eyes only for Cain. "I've waited an eternity for this."

"Glad to hear it." Cain shot back. "I've been looking forward to killing you …well…since the last time I slit your throat."

"Six against one. That hardly seems fair. Let's try this instead." Magnus vanished. In his place appeared more than a dozen demons.

The new arrivals stood about four feet tall. Their skin was a leathery gray. They had the now familiar tell-tale milky eyes. Overbites exposed tiny jagged teeth. They stood on cloven hooves. Long arms hung nearly to the floor ending in hands that tipped with three clawed fingers.

"Cannon fodder. Just another attempt to wear us down." Cain told them.

"How do we fight them?" Jami asked, grimacing at the ghoulish sight of their new adversaries.

"Go for the throat." Cain instructed.

"They don't look very intelligent." En commented.

"What they lack in intelligence they make up for in tenacity and brute strength." Cain told them. "I've encountered them before. Strong as a bull but uncoordinated as hell."

"Let's do this." Ennie waved dramatically at the broken jukebox.

The Final Countdown began to play.

"Cain glared bloody daggers in En's direction. Everyone started shouting and bitching. The demons tried to cover their ears as they screeched.

Ennie cut the music. "Oh all right." She looked at them all disgustedly. She found the song quite appropriate under the circumstances.

"Are you finished?" Cain ground out.

"Not quite yet." She snapped. She pointed back to the machine. This time the music roared. "Let the bodies hit the floor…let the bodies hit the floor…let the bodies hit the floor…let the bodies hit the floooor…."

"Now." Cain ordered.

The room erupted with violence.

Cain carried his own weapons. He opened himself up allowing the killer inside to emerge as his curse fully took control. A demon rushed him. He used the deadly talons on his fingers. With cold blooded accuracy they sliced through the demons leathery neck spraying Cain with viscous black blood.

Jami and Ennie were right beside him. They threw blast after blast at the demons holding them back until the others could get their bearings.

Micah tried sprinting through the muck of dead rats only to slide and fall on his ass. He drug himself until he reached the bar then jumped up and vaulted over. He grabbed a kitchen knife used for cutting fruit for drinks. Fortunately the demons were not having much better luck navigating the floor. Cloven hooves and rat innards did not make for easy stepping. One of the damn things did manage to corner Micah behind the bar. In the tight space Micah's shorter arms were an advantage. He plunged the knife into the demons chest ripping and tearing until it fell still.

Faith frantically picked her way across the room to where the abandoned duffel lay behind an overturned table. She groped inside for another gun of Holy Water. With her back to the room she did not see the demon as it came up behind her. It grabbed a fist-full of her hair jerking her head backward. The demon swung out with its arm preparing to bring its claws around to slash Faith's fragile throat.

Grey jumped into the air, landing in a slide hitting the demon like it was home plate. The thing released its grip on Faith's hair throwing its head back in an ear splitting shriek. Grey moved in grabbing onto its head and slitting its throat.

Faith yelped as she wriggled out from under the disgusting dead thing. She got to her feet with a minor amount of slippage.

"You okay?" Grey asked.

"Yup." She answered. In each hand she held a Super Soaker. "I'm thinking a June Wedding. I know it's a cliche' but what the hell we've earned it."

Grey gaped. His girl was covered in noxious black blood and rat guts. To him she had never looked more beautiful. He gave her a quick peck on a clean spot he found on her forehead. "Sounds perfect. You ready?"

"You betcha'."

Jami was shooting blanks. She didn't have half the strength of Ennie. She was slipping to her knees almost totally drained.

Micah saw his sister going down. Fear for her safety won out over self-preservation. He moved to go to her. A demon caught him with his guard down. Snaking an arm out it wrapped around Micah's torso sending him flying across the room into a pile of broken chairs knocking him out. Faith and Grey covered him. Keeping the demons off him. Faith shot them with Holy Water while Grey sliced and diced with a large meat clever.

Cain witnessed Micah's failed attempt to reach Jami. He made quick work of the demon he was fighting. When he reached her he found her pulling a switchblade from her boot.

"Stop!" En shouted. She was turning in a circle. "They're dead. We took them all out."

"Holy shit." Jami blurted from her place on the floor.

"Is everybody still in one piece?" Cain asked.

"We're all good except Micah. He's out cold." Grey relayed.

"Wake the kid up would ya." Cain told him.

Faith shot him in the face with the Super Soaker. He came to sputtering and spitting water. He was the only one with a clean face.

En's twisted sense of humor bubbled up. "That was fun. What's next, flying purple monkeys?"

"Who cares? I just want a hot shower." Faith grouched as she pulled her slimey shirt away from her body. "It's going to take a whole bottle of body wash and shampoo to get me clean."

"Don't worry I'll make sure you don't miss a spot." Grey teased.

"I second the shower suggestion." Jami chimed in, as cain helped her to her feet.

"Amen to that." En agreed.

"Where did Grey go?" Jami asked.

"I sent him to the office to get some chairs for you lovely ladies to sit on that are clean." Cain answered.

"Why can't we just go home?" Jami groaned.

"Because this isn't over. I've got to finish it."

"Before Jami could question Cain Grey returned. He had no chairs with him but he did have one unwanted guest. Magnus had him by the back of the neck and was pushing him into the room. When he was satisfied everyone had noticed his presence he shoved Grey away sending him stumbling toward Cain.

"You ready to fight me like a man?" Cain taunted. "Or do you have some more tricks up your sleeve to pull out?"

"No more tricks. This is between you and me. You owe me."

"I owe you more than you think."

"What is that supposed to mean?" Magnus snarled.

"At first I thought you were trying to play me. Then I realized you really do not know."

"Cain." En grabbed his arm. "Do not do this. Not now."

"I know what I'm doing." He snapped. "Now get the kids back and keep them back whatever it takes."

"You're a fool." En growled. She stormed away waving at the others to follow her.

"Just what is it I don't know old man?" Magnus demanded.

"After I killed you I took out a little insurance policy."

"And did it pay off?"

"The benefits were immediate. You see to make sure something as foul as you didn't keep popping up every few centuries I looked up your sons. Then their sons. I took out your bloodline. MY cursed bloodline."

"You murdered my sons." Magnus roared his face blood red with rage.

"I killed them all until the flood came along and finished them off for me. I made certain my blood would never again be a plague upon humanity. When I'm through with you my job will be complete. We both know Lucifer will never allow you above again after your colossal failure this time. Your punishment this time will be far worse than a cell in the pit."

Magnus bellowed until the window glass shattered. He glared at Cain. "When I'm done with you they will all die screaming."

"Not gonna happen." Cain spoke with absolute certainty.

"Are you ready Old Man?"

"Absolutely Son. Let's finish this for good this time."

Jami wanted to scream, "What the fuck!" Was Cain telling the truth about killing off his entire bloodline? She had a sinking feeling that he was. Why in the hell would he be throwing this shit at Magnus now? Magnus already wanted him dead. Cain's remarks had just given him a greater incentive to rip him to pieces. Not to mention Jami did not doubt for a second Magnus would make good on his threat to kill them all. She could only hope Cain knew what he was doing.

Cain and Magnus stood facing each other. Cain's face could have been chiseled from stone it was so emotionless and unmovable. Magnus' face was dead opposite. His appeared contorted with barely leashed rage.

When the first attack came Jami held her breath. She could not believe what she was seeing. This was not a powerful Immortal up against a supercharged Demon. It was a bloody fisted street brawl. Two royally pissed off men beating the ever loving shit out of each other. They seemed to need the feel of fist's striking flesh.

They fought hard. Punch for punch. Cain broke Magnus' nose. Magnus split Cain's lip. Still the fists flew. They both had blood dripping down their faces. It was a boxing match with no bell and no rules.

Faith kept her hands over her eyes. Ennie, Grey, and Micah were shouting out encouragement. Jami was certain Cain was oblivious to all of them and she was glad for it. Cain's mind stayed utterly focused on Magnus just as it should. He was unaware of anything other than the violence he unleashed.

Jami stood on her own away from the group. Her eyes riveted on every punch thrown. As the fight ramped up it did not take long before it became a supernatural smack down. Both of the combatants trading fists for fangs and claws.

Magnus struck out dragging his claws down Cain's torso. Cain's blood splattered shirt hung in ragged strips. Crimson slashes now added to his assortment of wounds. A cheshire cat grin dominated his grubby swollen face. He laughed like he was having the time of his life.

Cain's laughter incensed Magnus who let his guard slip. Cain used the advantage to rake his claws down the side of Magnus' face leaving him with only one useful eye.

Jami watched powerless as Magnus made another run at Cain. Things began to move quickly now as claws shredded and fangs punctured.

The whole thing reminded Jami of dueling guitars. Starting slow then building faster. Drawing you in chords and notes battling each other for dominance. Building up into a throbbing pulsing thing of beauty until you felt a part of it. Bringing to voice a magnificent song that rode you on a wave until at last it erupted into a mind-blowing explosion.

The music ended when Cain went down. Magnus had managed to dislocate Cain's shoulder then knock his feet out from under him. Magnus had Cain on the floor digging his claws into Cain's injured shoulder. Magnus knew he was about to deliver Cain's death blow. One last strike and his vengeance would be fulfilled.

Magnus looked down at Cain. He smiled. "At last it's over. I beat you old man. Die knowing that I received my revenge while your pitiful mortals watched."

"Don't you want to know your son's last words?" Cain taunted.

"Why? So you can tell me they begged for their lives?"

"No, they never begged. They thanked me. Thanked me for killing them before they became like their father."

Magnus roared. His scream was cut short when Cain reached up impaled Magnus under the chin with his claws dragging them down his neck until he hit the breastbone.

"Now it's over." Cain finished, as he spit Magnus' black blood from his mouth.

CHAPTER TWENTY THREE

Tearzahn watched it all from a shadowy corner. It was one hell of a fight. He had been certain of the outcome before the first punch had been thrown.

His true orders had been to make sure Cain came out on top. He was not to interfere unless Cain was in danger of being killed. Tear knew warriors. He knew when Cain was down he would have a trick up his sleeve. Magnus had never had a chance. Like he had told Lucifer it was a babysitting job. If not for the sex it would have been a total waste of his time.

It had been a cake assignment. Until…he saw the occupants of the room freeze in place. "Aww shit."

Lo bent down and rolled the corpse off of Cain. He clapped a pair of handcuffs on Magnus. The cuffs were not standard police issue. They had been forged Hell to bind demons. Lo had come across them when he killed a demon bounty hunter centuries before. They had come in handy. Magnus was lying dormant in his host. The cuffs assured his demonic essence could not escape the body he inhabited. The body itself was ruined. The human it had once held unsalvageable. Lo stayed where he was silently absorbing the outcome. Then he acknowledged the Fallen One.

"Show yourself Tearzahn. I know you been skulking around waiting for the outcome."

When Lo stood he was not surprised to find Tearzahn beside him.

"Did you catch the fight? Better than anything on pay per view."

Lo chuckled wearily.

"Lucifer wants him. I've got to take him back for punishment."

"Not gonna happen. You're going to have to give Lucifer my apologies on this one. He stays here."

"Come on Ladocia. You know what will happen if I don't deliver him. My boss will give me the devil of a time."

"Yeah well my boss is a real Angel and he is just as easy going as yours."

"Your right. I know him well." Tear reminded Lo.

From out of nowhere Lo asked. "Do you ever get tired Tearzahn?"

Tear was shocked that Lo would ask him such a personal question. "More often than not." If Lo would lower himself to speak to his enemy the least he could do is answer honestly.

"You're really going to risk your ass over this piece of shit?"

"Damned if I do. Damned if I don't. I've got my orders."

Lo put his hand on the hilt of his sword. He didn't want to fight. Why couldn't the Big Guns just let it end here?"

The bar filled with an ethereal light banishing the darkness brought by the demons. The scent of hyacinth washed away the smell of death and brimstone. The bodies of the gray demons turned to dust.

A being appeared from the light. He stood at a height that rivaled Lucifer and was every bit as terrifying and beautiful.

Matte black biker boots added to his already impressive height. Long muscular legs were encased in form fitting black leather pants. His broad chest and ripped abs were shown off to perfection in a tight black tee shirt. Straight blue black hair hung to his waist. Eyes glowed sapphire blue from a face of porcelain delicacy. Lips of deep red were set in a flat line of annoyance. This was the Archangel Michael …and he was not pleased.

Michael knelt by Magnus. He wrapped his hand around what was left of the demons throat. Magnus stirred, his white eyes opened wide in terror at the vision before him.

"You know who I am?" The deep gravelly voice spoke to Magnus. Magnus could only blink in return.

"Then you know what I do with you cannot be undone."

Magnus blinked again.

"Ladocia." Michael called. "I want you to take this piece of shit demon and deliver him to the Affa."

Lo pulled Magnus to his feet. "You want me to dump him in there whole? Still in this body?" He asked incredulous.

"I'm certain I spoke clearly."

Magnus rolled his eyes toward Tear. He tried to scream but only managed to produce a bubbling foam of bloody mucus from his throat.

Tear shrugged. He might have to face Lucifer but right now it was Michael standing before him and he sure as hell was not going up against Michael. He had no desire to help Magnus anyway so what did it really matter.

Lo nodded to the others then disappeared with Magnus.

Tear faced off with Michael. Tear was afraid of Lucifer. He was pants pissing terrified of Michael. He managed to keep a bland look on his face. He had a reputation as a badass Fallen to protect. Tear had been on the battlefield with both of them. It was Michael who whopped Lucifer's ass and sent them all to their new home in Hell.

They had been inseparable once. Lucifer with his golden beauty, Michael's deadly darkness, Tear's fiery temper, and Beelzebub's fierce loyalty. That was before the time of man. Now they were on opposite sides and Tear kept those memories of brotherhood buried deep. He wondered if Michael ever thought of those halcyon days. No use thinking about it now. Michael would soon destroy him. He may as well go out fighting.

"Thanks a lot Brother." Tear sneered. "Do you have any idea of what you've just done?"

"I'm aware."

"Yeah, why should it matter to you if Lucifer flips shit and fries my ass?"

"Why did you allow the humans to live? The Fallen Tearzahn is a merciless killer. Satan's enforcer. He leaves no one to tell the tale."

"Your boy Ladocia interrupted me." Tear snapped, not at all pleased with Michael's innuendos.

"Michaels black brows arched as if to say bullshit. "You've been here in the shadows all night. You could have killed them at any time."

"I was busy enjoying the show."

"That I believe." Michael snarked. "I have an offer for you."

"Can't wait to hear it. Let me guess you kill me quick so I can avoid whatever torment Lucifer has planned for failing to bring back Magnus."

Michael was unamused. "You can return to Lucifer in failure or you can stay here and work for me under my protection."

Tear barked a laugh. "I don't remember you having a sense of humor."

"Then you have an excellent sense of recall."

"If that's the case, you're fucking with me. What's your angle?"

"This is an honest offer. I'm going to be needing someone with your particular skill set." Michael explained.

"Fine, I'll bite. What's the job?" Tear questioned the fearsome fallen Angel, still wary of his motives.

"Be a Watcher. You remember how to do that don't you?"

"Why me? You've got literally a host of Angels to do your bidding."

"Like I said skill set."

"You want your own enforcer. Your assassins have a conscious. I don't."

"Honestly, yes." Michael admitted. "You will have to fight your own kind."

"Ahhh... That's the way of it. I have one qualifier."

"Qualifier?" Michael's face showed mild amusement but then Tear had always been brazen and utterly fearless.

"I will not raise a sword against B."

Michaels sapphire eyes burned. If Tear didn't know better he would think it was pain causing that blue fire. "I know that B is broken. If it comes down to drawing swords I will be the one to go against him. Unlike Lucifer I understand brotherhood. I would not ask it of you to go against Beelzebub."

Whoa, sore spot. Tear dropped the touchy subject. "Who's the target?"

"Target? You mean the innocent."

"Yeah, that's what I said." Tear offered him a snarky smile.

Michael sighed. "Faith Martin."

"Yawn." Tear griped, opening his mouth wide and patting his hand to his lips. "She has got to be the most boring human on the planet. This is not my definition of enforcer. Why don't you just slap my ass in a Nursing Home?"

"Do you accept my offer or not?" Michael demanded, quickly losing patience with Tear's smart mouth.

"Sounds dull as a doorknob but it sure as hell beats the alternative."

"It will liven up. You know Lucifer is finally making his play for the Key. This little town is about to become Ground Zero."

"Now that's what I'm talkin' bout." Tear grinned, at last showing some excitement.

"I'm so glad you won't be bored."

"So I take it Cain still doesn't know?" Tear inquired.

"That he is the Key. No, it's not time to reveal that little tidbit. Less than twenty four hours ago he was on the verge of going dark side. Ladocia talked him down but he's still not ready for the whole story. We can't take the risk. Especially now that Lucifer is ready to make his move."

"Who makes these damn rules anyway?" Tear bit out with annoyance.

"Someone a lot more powerful than the two of us."

"Before we swear to this new alliance I need to know the rules you expect me to play by esiasch."

Michael made no comment when Tear called him brother. Even on opposite sides they still were brothers. That was why he could go to Tear and ask this of him now. "Well first of all Cain is not to know he is the key. As far as the Order is concerned you a private contractor working for me."

"I can go along with that. I doubt they want me in their Boy Scout Troop anyway."

"Michael grinned. "What's wrong Tear does the thought of them not wanting to play with you hurt your feelings?"

"I don't have feelings. Good or bad." Tear responded his voice deadpan.

"I know." Michael agreed with the truth of the statement. "Okay, rules. You kill only demons. You will not kill, maim, or otherwise hurt, or injure any human without a direct order from me. Also, you are forbidden to reveal your true identity to mortals or Cain for that matter. I will cloak you so that Cain cannot recognize you for what you are."

"You take the fun out of everything."

"I've never heard that one before." Michael said sarcastically. "Now, do you swear to aid and follow me and all that I have set down this night?"

"I swear." Tear dropped to one knee and kissed the sapphire ring on Michael's finger.

Michael turned his hand over. Lying on his open palm was a ring. It was identical to Michaels with one exception. The stone in the ring was amber. The exact color of Tear's eyes. The ring had only been worn on the finger of one being, Tearzahn. When they lost the war and were banished from Heaven their rings had been forfeit. Now Michael was offering him this treasure he had thought he would never see again. Tear recognized this as a turning point. Michael was offering him more than a job. He was giving him a chance to earn his trust back and maybe his place in the order of things again. Tear trembled with the emotions he had just declared he no longer had.

Tear could not let this unwarranted opportunity pass by. He stood. His hand shook. He feared if he touched the ring it would vanish once again. He looked into the blue depths of Michaels eyes. His brother gave an affirmative nod. Tear reached out and returned the ring to its rightful place on his finger.

"Thank you my brother." He spoke softly.

Michael put a strong hand on Tear's shoulder. "It belongs to you does it not?"

"Yes it does." Not wanting to show further emotion Tear asked, "What now?"

Michael reached into the pocket of his leather pants. He pulled out two items a cell phone and a key. He handed them to tear. "My number is in the contacts."

"The key?"

"It's for a house on Main Street. It is located two doors down from Faith Martin and Jami Archer. The house is furnished. You will find cash, credit cards, bank information, identification, keys to a vehicle, and other necessary items in a kitchen drawer."

"Damn, I'm loving this already." Tear grinned. "Question?"

"Yes."

"How did you know I would say yes to your deal?"

Michael just smiled. "One last thing. Notify me immediately if and when Beelzebub surfaces."

"I don't see that happening any time soon but if he makes an appearance you're my first call."

"I suggest you leave before I rouse them."

"Later brother." Tear walked out of the front door and into the night.

Michael snapped his fingers and vanished.

Six people were stupefied.

Jami was the first to recover and comment. "Who stole our dead bad guy?"

"I'm guessing the Powers that Be." En answered.

"Who is that?"

"Your guess is as good as mine."

"But he is gone, right?" Faith wanted conformation. "It's over?"

Cain looked at the dried inky blood on his hands. He caught the scent of hyacinth. "Yeah, it's over."

"We whooped Magnus' ass." Ennie gloated merrily.

"La Mech." Cain muttered.

"Whatever." They all chimed in.

"Ding dong the demons dead." Jami sang.

"Anybody want a drink?" Grey looked around. "Uh…if I can find anything."

Affirmative shouts followed his suggestion.

Grey made his way to the stockroom.

"I'll help you forage bro." Micah called out following Grey.

Jami looked around the bar. There was nothing left that was salvageable. The bar was finished.

Grey and Micah passed out bottles of warm champagne. Corks were popped. Everyone tossed back their heads in celebration. They drank calling out toast after toast until Micah was forced to go for more bottles of Bubbly. No one wanted to be the one to stop the celebration.

Finally as things wound down they became more aware of their surroundings. "This place is totaled." Jami groaned.

"Were screwed." Micah added.

"We've got two days before the parents come home to fix it up." Grey spoke, ever the optimist.

"Like I said, were screwed."

The door to Archers creaked open then whomped closed. Heads turned. Six bodies stood rigid with fear as yet another smack down became unavoidable. This one destined to be more overwhelming than the last.

From the entryway a voice boomed. "Grey Goose, Jameson, Michelob Archer. What in the hell have you children done to my bar?"

Mom and Pop Archer had just arrived home earlier than expected and shit hit the fan. For an instant Cain wondered if this was the shitstorm Lo had told him was coming.

"They named them after alcohol?" En whispered to Cain.

"Pop named the kids after whatever he was drinking when Mom went into labor." He whispered back.

"My babies!" Mom cried out when she caught sight of her bruised and battered children who were covered in some kind of filthy black slime.

"Your babies." Pop screeched. "Woman look at my bar." His five foot six inch frame vibrated with anger. His enraged face turned the same shade of scarlet as the bowling shirt he wore. He stormed further into the bar his tennis shoes sinking into the muck while his wife did her best to tiptoe carefully behind him.

Glaring at his children he threw out a challenge. "Which one of you is going to be man enough to tell me how you destroyed my livelihood?"

Jami shook her head and pointed to her breasts clearly indicating she was in fact not man enough. She then stuck out her thumb directing it at her brothers. She had no qualms about throwing them under the bus. Especially when that bus was Pop Archer with a full head of steam ready to mow them all down.

Grey and Micah cowered awaiting the next verbal onslaught. Pop was not even close to wearing down yet. They knew he could go on for hours if he wanted to. The destruction of his bar could likely last for days, weeks even.

"The first vacation we have taken in years. I took your dear Mama to see her first and only grandbaby. This is what we come home to. You children show no respect."

Mom went to stand with Cain and Ennie. "I expected you to control these foolish children." She chided him gently. Cain looked at her shamefaced.

"Do you have any pictures of the baby?" En asked, distracting the proud grandmother.

"Ennie." Mom squealed in delight, pulling her in for a hug. "I haven't seen you since the children were babies. You haven't changed a bit."

Mom whipped out her phone. She began showing En countless pictures relating a cute story with each of them. En politely commented on the beauty of the baby as she heard all about its sleeping patterns, intelligence, and what a good disposition the baby had.

"Hon." Pop scolded.

"Not now dear. Can't you see I'm visiting with Ennie? She agrees the baby is the prettiest one she's ever seen."

"Hello Ennie. I didn't see you over there behind Cain. It's nice to have you back. I'm sorry you had to be a witness to this. A fine welcome home our children have given us. I swear we did our best to raise them right. I guess it just didn't take."

"Why are you home?" Grey ventured bravely. "And at four in the morning."

"Why?" Pop barked. "When none of you could be bothered to answer the phone for three damn days your mama got worried and insisted I bring her home. You children nearly worried her to death. Did you think of that? No, of course not. Why would you take the time to worry about your mama when you're so busy tearing my damn bar apart."

Cain threw himself on the sword speaking up to take the heat off of the kids, he hoped. "It's my fault. There was a broken pipe. I called my plumber in for the kids. He broke through the wall. Rats spilled out. They were everywhere. They must have been breeding in the walls."

"Rats!" Mom wailed. "Oh my babies are you okay. Did they bite you? Were they rabid? Oh sweet baby Jesus."

Pop went to her. "Calm down dear. They are all on their feet. I'm sure they didn't have rabies." Pop looked to Cain for backup.

"They showed no sign of rabies." Cain shook his head. "No, none at all."

"See, Cain said no rabies." Pop assured her, gently patting her back while he sent a scowl at his children for upsetting their mother.

"Look, don't worry about a thing. I'll cover all of the renovation costs. You just hire someone and give me the quote. I'll take it from there."

"The hell you'll pay. The kids will pay. They can work the rest of their lives for free and hope their mama will feed them."

"I'm responsible (no lie there). Consider it payment for damages as well as a gift to celebrate your first grandchild. Keep Archers going for the next generation."

Mom got all sniffly as she wrapped Cain in a big hug. "I'm sorry I scolded you earlier. You were just trying to look after them. Forgive me?"

"No, don't apologize. You were right I should have been watching after them better. I should have had them call your plumber. My mistake."

Pop's face was blank. That was his normal expression when he was seriously pondering a question. Slowly a silly grin took over his face. "A partnership." Pop offered. "That way it stays in the family. What do you say?"

Now Cain's face was the one to go expressionless. He did not know how to respond. Family. His emotions scrambled. Mom had a hold of his arm and was smiling up at him. Pop was beginning to look anxious over his lack of response.

Ennie was overcome as well. She knew what that one word meant to her friend as she had been the only person he had ever allowed to get close to him. She got weepy again. This time it was Mom who reached into her purse and handed her a tissue.

The kids sat across the room with glory hallelujah smiles. They had always thought of Cain as part of the family and for them moment Pop was not raising hell with them.

Cain found his voice. "I guess I say…you got a deal."

Pop clapped him on the back. "Well alright then."

"Such a good boy." Mom stood on tiptoe to kiss his scruffy cheek. "You need to shave."

Cain chuckled at her. Soon the champagne was being passed again to toast the new partnership. Cain was all up in his head marveling at the way things had ended.

Mom let loose a loud yawn. "Lunch at the house tomorrow. I will be expecting the whole family. That means you too Ennie. Now I'm going home to get some sleep in my own bed. I'm exhausted and it looks like we're going to be busy around here with remodeling the place. Go home." She ordered.

Everyone began filling out the door. Pop caught Cain by the arm. "So son, what do you think, a stage for bands on the weekend? We will need a dance floor. Oooh, a disco ball. So, how about it?"

"Gotta love a disco ball Pop." Cain cringed inwardly. "Anything you want. The sky's the limit."

"Do you think we could get Disturbed to play?"

"I don't know if they do disco balls Pop but I'll damn sure give it a shot."

"That's my boy."

Mom and Pop went to their house next door to the bar. The rest of them started the walk to the house.

It was a clear night. The stars were bright in the sky. They walked in pairs. Grey and Faith leading the pack. A friendly argument broke out over who would get the first shower. En was demanding to know who planned on feeding her claiming that her stomach was positively hollow.

Grey was practically carrying Faith. She clung to him. All of the fear and tension of the last few days had drained out of her leaving her wiped out but happy to be in the arms of her man.

A shadow stepped down from the porch to stand in the spotlight of the streetlamp. There stood a woman well known by anyone who watched the local news.

"Miss Martin." She called out. "It's Jessica Landry. I've received information that there was an altercation at Archers Bar tonight. They say that several people were injured. I was informed that you were in attendance at the time of the incident. I would like to ask you a few questions."

Faith looked helplessly at Grey.

"No questions." Grey told her firmly.

"Miss Martian, please. It would only take a few minutes. My viewers would love a direct quote from you." She persisted.

Grey was amazed at the audacity of the woman. It was nearly five in the morning. Had the crazy bitch been sitting on the porch half the night just waiting to ambush them? It was time to put a stop to this, now.

"For shit's sake lady you have got to be kidding me. You need to back the fuck off." Grey pushed Faith backward into Ennie's waiting arms. He stalked forward to confront the tenacious reporter.

"Faith has nothing to say to you. You need to leave before I call the police."

"Mr. Archer, would you care to comment. I believe you were questioned as well in connection to the murder of Miss Shepard."

"That's it. I tried to be decent." Grey spat. He pulled out his phone and waved it as a warning. "I'm calling the police now."

Cain had hung back allowing Grey to play the hero for his woman and dispatch the pushy reporter. He had his own woman to worry about. From the moment Jami had seen Jessica Landry she had gone into a tirade ranting about the flipping K.G. wannabe. She had plans to knock her on her fat ass a second time. Cain was doing his best to keep her under control when the pain blasted his skull. It was strong as hell this time and sharp enough to have him releasing Jami to grab his head. One look at him and she shut her mouth. She had never seen this before and didn't know how to try to help him.

The pain passed. Cain jerked his head up and came in contact with molten gold eyes. The demon was too quick and Cain was too far away. Things appeared to move in slow motion. It was over before Cain could react.

The demon went for Grey. All it took was a quick slash with one clawed hand for her to slit Grey's throat wide open.

Grey fell to his knees then his body slumped over. Cain reached him just as he hit the sidewalk.

Faith pulled free from Ennie who was too stunned to stop her. She ran to Grey falling to her knees beside Grey who lay on the cold abrasive cement. Faith wailed a single, "Noooo." She pulled Grey into her lap oblivious to the blood still pumping from his throat and covering her with wet sticky warmth.

His curse now in full control Cain lunged for the demon. Riding the fury he grabbed it by the shoulders prepared to tear its throat to shreds with his fangs. He wanted to taste blood for this death. The demon began to shudder. Thunder surrounded them all as the ground under them quaked. Cain paused long enough to hear the demon utter, "Ozien nor." It was the first language. The speech of the Angels. It meant, "Mine own son."

The demons eyes faded to a warm honey gold. Cain recoiled releasing the demon. It fell to the sidewalk the familiar oily black smoke rising from the body it had inhabited. With a force Cain had never witnessed before the demon was violently sucked back to Hell leaving Cain to wonder what the hell he had just witnessed.

Cain stood transfixed staring at the spot where the demon had vanished. Only the trembling voice of Faith calling his name brought him back to the here and now.

"Cain, fix him. You can make him better." Faith pleaded, as her terrified eyes locked with his.

"Oh baby, I wish I could do that for you. I can't. I don't have the power over life and death."

"Ennie?" She looked up her eyes imploring. "Please help him. You can do anything."

Ennie knelt down beside her. She put her arm around the shivering girl. "I'm sorry honey but I don't have that kind of power either."

Micah stood holding Jami. She had been so strong throughout all of the mess they had just come through, but this broke her. She sobbed in her brother's arms while Micah stood dried eyed disbelieving.

Faith sat there rocking Grey back and forth as if he were a child in need of comfort. Her eyes never leaving his face as if she were trying to memorize the sight she knew would soon be lost to her forever.

Needing an outlet for his anger Cain stepped in and took control of things. "En call 911. I'll call Mom and Pop."

Cain sat on the porch where he could watch the others. His mind was a tilt a whirl of anger, disbelief, and sorrow. How could he have been so careless as to let down his guard? He should have suspected one last surprise. Didn't the dead bad guy always seem to pop back up at the end of the movie for a final scare?

The demon had said, "Mine own son." The eyes when they had faded were the color of his mothers. How was it possible? Lucifer had created the Empty for his parents. He hated Adam for keeping Eve from him. He hated Eve for for refusing to go to him and instead choosing to stay with Adam. The Affa had been their punishment. At least that was what he had always been led to believe. Cain did not have the time to puzzle it out now.

Flashing lights from the ambulance were making their way down Main Street followed by the flashing lights of the police. Mom and Pop were hurrying down the sidewalk to their children. And here he sat useless. Oh he would take care of things. He would handle all the questions and make all of the arrangements. It wasn't enough though. He had let down his guard and been blindsided. Now one of their own was lost. Ultimately he had failed them and didn't that just make him the Mother Fucker of the Year.

Tearzahn reached a hand into his new, well new for him, refrigerator. He pulled out a Bud sucked down half of it then reached for another to take along with him. What the hell had just gone down? He had been standing out on his porch tossing one back while checking out the sights of his new neighborhood when he caught the drama going down with Cain and his crew. A sonic boom from hell shook the whole damn town. It threw him back knocking him on his ass.

He hit the living room dropping his ass on a nappy old plaid recliner. The remote to the big boxy television sat on the end table beside him. He picked it up hitting the power button. I Love Lucy came up on the screen. Hells bells at least the show was even older than the furnishings.

No way was he bitching. He had a pretty good set up here. The way he saw it right about now all hell was cutting loose in Hell. Tear had recognized that puff of smoke as Eve. She had just had her ass hauled back to Hell hardcore. Lucifer did not want that woman anywhere near her son. His old boss would be on a rampage. Tear was damn glad he would be nowhere around when the repercussions from that shit hit the fan. The one sure fired way to to turn the Light Bringer into Satan incarnate was to fuck with Cain. The pit would burn bright for the next century from Lucifer venting his fury over Eve daring to leave Him.

Tear did not as much as blink when he felt the blade at his throat. He knew that if he did his head would be rolling across the floor.

"Cozy place you got here." Ladocia spoke in a cordial tone of voice.

Oh shit, Tear thought as Sully popped up before him. Sully put the tip of his blade dead center in the middle of Tear's chest. He grinned flashing his pearly whites. The assassin obviously relished his job.

"So you just thought you would stay above, move on into town and make yourself comfortable did ya?" Sully asked.

Tear held his hands up, silently asking how they expected to get an answer when he had Lo's blade kissing his adams apple.

Lo removed his sword since Sully had the Fallen covered. He came around to stand with Sully in front of Tear.

"Don't you have somewhere else you need to be?" Lo asked.

"Nope, I'm real comfortable where I am."

"You need to get your ass back to the Pit where it belongs now or were going to have to send you on your way. More fun for us but I'm guessing you like your head where it is."

"I take it you have not spoken to your boss lately. He's the one who set me up in this fine town and gave me my comfy new digs. I suggest you take it up with him." Tear reported, clearly enjoying the looks of disbelief they both displayed.

"Bullshit." Sully spit. "Michael doesn't play well with your kind."

Tear held his right hand up waggling his fingers. The amber in his ring caught the light giving off a warm glow.

Sully immediately recognized the ring as one that could only be worn by an Archangel. "No fucking way. How the fuck did you get that?"

"You already know the answer to that. Only one being could have restored my ring to me. Well two actually, but only one would suffer me to be in their presence."

"He's not lying." Lo pulled Sully's sword arm back. "Only Michael could have given that ring to him. It would have had to be brought down from Heaven."

Sully growled. "I don't trust you. Ring or no ring you're still a filthy demon to me."

Tear snickered. "Then you've got more of a brain then I would have given you credit for."

"Why?" Lo needed to understand what could have made Michael come to this unprecedented decision.

"Faith Martin. Michael does not seem to think Lucifer is done with her yet."

Lo shook his head. "After what that demon just did I would not be too worried about that poor girl. She is probably going to end up in an institution cutting out paper dolls and finger painting on the walls."

"Demon." Tear grinned smugly.

"You know something we don't?" Lo glared at him accusingly.

"Quite a lot actually." Tear flashed his ring again. "Remember I was here since…In the beginning."

"Asshole." Sully grumbled.

Tear made a kissy face and blew a smooch at him. Sully growled and went for his sword again. Lo held him back.

"Awww come on esiasch. Were on the same team now." Tear smirked.

"Were not brothers." Lo ground out, angry that he would use the enochian term. "If you are deluded enough to think we would ever trust you at our backs you have lost your demon mind."

"How about this. You boys want answers. As a show of faith I'll tell you where to find them."

"What makes you think we want answers or anything else from you?" Sully stormed.

"One, because you didn't have a clue who that demon was. Two, because I know your boss. He is a tight lipped son of a bitch. He didn't even bother to tell you he was putting me here."

"What do you think you've got that would be worth our time?" Lo demanded.

"A book. I don't have it but I know where to find it."

"And what's so special about this book?"

"It's the Gospel of the Lightbringer. Written by the legend himself. I'm not talking about some Anton La Vey shit. I'm talking about the gospel according to Lucifer."

"That's a myth." Lo doubted him.

"Please, do you really believe that with his ego he did not write his own story? I've seen it. I watched as he wrote the damn thing. From our creation to our fall to the creation of Hell. It's all there. Written in his own blood."

"How does this do anything for us if you don't have the book?"

"There's the rub. It's in Eden."

"Could this fairy tale get any more outrageous? Eden was destroyed." Lo argued, rolling his ice blue eyes.

"Not entirely. Lucifer has very fond memories of the place. He had it relocated to Hell. Naturally, Hell has befowled it. It's not quite the place it used to be. I guess you would call it the Anti- Eden. The only way in is through the wall in Lucifers office. The book is hidden inside the dying Tree of Life."

Sully's mouth fell open. Lo burst out laughing. When he caught his breath he had a few words for Tear about his ridiculous story.

"You're telling us that to find a book we have zero proof even exists we have to go to Hell. Then get into a decaying Eden by strolling into Lucifer's office, locate the dying tree of life, steal the book and escape Hell unnoticed. You expect us to believe this bullshit?"

"Believe it. Don't believe it. Your call. But let me tell you this. If you're serious about keeping your precious key safe the best way to do it is to get your hands on that book. Lucifer wants your key. What you need to stop it can only be found in that book. Those of us who were there can never speak of it. The punishment would be worse than anything Hell or the Affa could dish out."

"Well that almost sounds like a challenge."

"Take it any way you want to. Now that I'm up top I don't want to see those Gates sprung. I'd like at least a couple of centuries to enjoy myself first. Michael has given me a pretty sweet deal and I intend to take full advantage of it."

Lo looked thoughtful for a moment weighing Tear's words for any sign of truth. He decided he could not trust the bastard. That did not mean he would not be checking into things as soon as he got the chance. If a Gospel written in Lucifer's own hand, own blood, did exist someone other than this Fallen had to know about it.

"Come on Sully. He is full of shit. We can't touch him now. He will fuck up sooner or later. My guess is sooner. Then we do our job and kill him."

They vanished.

"Thanks for stopping by." Tear yelled after them. "Feel free to pop in anytime. Next time bring some beer. This was a piss poor excuse for a housewarming party."

Tear knew he had peaked their curiosity. If they managed to get ahold of the book it could work out well for him. He might be able to find a way to get his ass out from under Lucifer and Michael. He may be free now but that freedom came with a noose around his neck.

The events of the past week were a blur in everyone's memory. The loss of Grey felt more unreal than any of the other things they had just been through. After a quiet ceremony Grey had been laid to rest in the Archer plot behind the wrought iron gates of the town cemetery.

Mom and Pop Archer were in a state of shock. They went through the motions of life but inside they were shattered. Mom had noticed the heirloom ring on Faith's finger. Faith told her the truth about the engagement. It was the only time Cain had seen Faith cry for her lover. Faith had tried to return the ring but Mom refused to hear about it. Faith continued to wear it. In her mind she was now a widow. Everyone walked on eggshells around her trying their best to be careful of her feelings. Only Cain saw the rage that boiled behind her dry eyes.

Renovations on the bar were set to begin in a few days but no one's heart was in it. Micah was handling that end of things. He was hoping once they got started on the bar Pop would begin to take an interest. Micah was feeling like a deserter by leaving them to work for Cain. He had been the one to pack up Grey's belongings when he moved his own to Cain's home. Grey's boxes now took up space in Mom and Pop's attic. The apartment over the bar sat vacant.

Cain and Ennie had been the ones to deal with the authorities. Between Cain's friendship with the Mayor and Ennies magic there had not been many questions. Faith was no longer a person of interest in the murders of Katie and Miss Myrtle.

Jessica Landry was now a patient at the Wernersville Mental Hospital. She claimed to have no memory of the twenty four hour time period leading up to Grey's murder or of the murder itself. It turned out that Jami was wrong. Jessica Landry's ambition had paid off. Her face was all over the National News.

Jami woke up snuggly cradled in the warm of Cain's strong arms. He had been lying awake for hours watching her sleep. He had never felt this close to any woman before, not even Ennie. He held her while she cried for her brother. Listened to her scream as the pain turned to rage. Made love to her when she needed to feel alive. Now it was time to let her go.

"Good morning." She smiled up at him.

"Good morning to you too." Cain reached over to grab a cigarette. "Are you all packed?"

"Yeah, I finished last night." Jami replied. She sat up beside him dragging the sheets with her to cover her breasts. "Ennie said we will be driving to her place in Manhattan. We will be there for two or three days while she takes care of some business then we will fly to London. We should only be gone a few weeks."

Cain knew better but refrained from saying so. She had things she needed to do and so did he. He was determined to solve the mystery surrounding his mother. If, in fact, it was his mother. Why after all this time did she decide to make contact? Or, was it just another demon with a more imaginative way to fuck with him? Then there was the shitstorm Lo told him was heading his way. He couldn't complain immortality was boring.

"En will work your ass off. It's going to be good for you to get away from here and see what the world has to offer. You need to experience life outside of Lancaster County P.A." Cain told her. He had to stop and wonder if he was trying to convince her or himself.

Jami could feel the distance growing between them. She hated it. The closeness they had shared had turned to awkward tension. She was afraid to speak about it for fear their parting would end in an argument. She wanted to hang onto what they had in hopes they could pick up where they left off when she returned.

"I guess I should get in the shower. Ennie wants to get an early start." She mumbled, moving to the edge of the bed.

Listen a second." Cain took her arm and turned her to face him. "What has been going on between us has been really great. You're going to meet a lot of new people. Don't miss out on something that could be good for you because of me."

"So that's it. Thanks for the fun but now it's done. I'm glad it meant so much to you." Jami snarled tossing out her resolution not to start an argument.

"It did mean something to me. You mean something to me. That is exactly why I want you to leave without worry or guilt over leaving me behind. I've had centuries of life. You need to go with no strings hanging on you. I will be here when you get back."

"Yeah, okay. I'm going to get my shower now." She turned from him.

"I'll go down and see about breakfast. Meet you in the kitchen."

"Sound good." She agreed, as she turned her back and headed for the shower. If she were lucky she could have a quick cry before she had to say goodbye.

Cain hit the kitchen his mouth salivating over the scent of fresh coffee brewing. If there had ever been a morning he needed coffee this was it. He knew he hurt Jami and it tore him up. She needed to be free from all of her attachments here so she could live and grow in her life and her magic.

"Kid, you're a saint." He praised Micah as he reached for a mug.

"Just doing my job and trying to make sure you don't eat me." Micah teased.

"You have been going above and beyond. I appreciate it. Anyway, you don't look very tasty."

"It's better to keep busy, ya know." Micah said, keeping his eyes lowered.

Micah started scrambling eggs. Frying bacon was spitting hot grease across the stove top. The kitchen smelled like a home. Cain thought maybe it would not be too bad having his privacy invaded.

Ennie joined them her nose twitching gratefully at the smell of food. Cain handed her a napkin. She frowned at him. "What's this for?"

"To wipe your mouth. You're drooling."

"Look who bought a sense of humor. How much did you have to pay for it?" She teased. "But I've got to admit that does smell good."

"You are ruled by your stomach."

"Better to be ruled by stomach than…" She let the smart crack hang dropping her gaze to his crotch.

"Somebody's sassy this morning." Micah joined in flashing her his dimpled smile.

"Feed me and the sass will vanish. Can I help?"

"Toast?" Micah suggested.

"I'm on it." En pulled out the toaster and went to work.

Faith arrived on the scene. "Good morning." She spoke in the quiet way that had become her new tone of voice.

En and Micah both turned to greet her. They were equally stunned by her appearance. Her golden hair had been cut to just below her chin. Silver crosses hung from her ears and on a chain around her neck hung the silver cross that En had given her. She was dressed in a black tank top and black jeans. Her face pale from grief appeared translucent from the dark makeup that now circled her lifeless green eyes.

"Did someone come in the night and steal all the pink?" En quipped, trying to coax a smile from the girl.

"Just wanted a change, you know? Maybe it's time for a new direction."

En exhaled heavily. "A makeover is always fun before traveling."

Faith did not bother to reply just sat down at the table. Cain plonked a mug of coffee down in front of her. She gave him a nod of thanks and took a drink.

Ennie started setting out plates of food. Just as everyone took their seats Jami arrived.

Jami grabbed herself a seat. As soon as she got a look at Faith she exploded. "Holy shit! What the hell have you done to yourself?"

Faith rolled her eyes at her best friend and bit into a piece of bacon. She had been expecting Jamis reaction and didn't have the strength or energy to argue.

"I think she looks hot." Micah commented, trying to stop a fight before it started.

"That's one way to put it." Jami snapped at her brother, giving him the evil eye.

"Jami." En warned.

"I'm sorry. It's just so drastic. I wasn't expecting it."

"It's okay." Faith assured her, not really caring what her friend thought of her new look. There was an awkward silence around the table that seemed to grow by the second.

Jami couldn't stand it. She wanted to scream but decided the better way to go would be to ignore it and act as if everything was normal. "I'm glad you're coming with us. You need to get away from here for a while too." Jami told her, trying to be understanding.

"I'm not going." Faith spoke firmly.

"Excuse me. "Jami growled. "We already decided this Faith. You're coming with me and En."

"No, we did not decide. You and Ennie decided. No one ever asked me what I wanted. I don't want to get away. I'm staying here and I'm going to help Cain. I'm going to train to do exorcisms and take over where my Father left off."

"So now we're back to the daddy issues. You doing things you think he would want. Are you ever going to live for yourself?"

"Go to hell Jami. This is not about my Dad. This is about doing something for all of the innocents the demon sons of bitches kill. Innocent people like Katie, and Grey. Innocent people who get taken over like Jessica Landry. I'm staying and Cain is going to train me. He may not be able to perform exorcisms but he can teach me. He can also teach me how to fight. I will not be helpless ever again. Lucifer was worried about me doing well in the world. The son of a bitch can keep on worrying. He tried to take me out and failed. I plan to keep fighting."

"You knew about this." Jami accused Cain, her face flushed from their betrayal.

Cain held his ground. "We talked about it. I think she's right. En needs to concentrate on you. I can train Faith and keep her safe. I promised her Father."

"So you two just decided this?"

"It's my life. My decision. It's not up for debate." Faith stated flatly.

"Sis." Micah spoke tentatively. "I'll be here too. If Cain doesn't mind I'll train with them. I need to learn too. Now that we know what's really out there we need to be ready for it. Don't you trust us?"

"Arrr." Jami groaned. "It's not that. It's just…"

"We have always looked after each other. Maybe it's time we both started doing something for ourselves." Faith tossed her words back at her. "You do things your way I'll do things mine."

Jami looked sheepish. She knew Faith had a point. It was just strange to have Faith being the one to lecture her. "But I'll miss you."

"I'll miss you too. Right now I need to work on me. We will be together again and we will always be best friends."

They both got out of their chairs to embrace each other.

"Well now that that's settled." En spoke up. "We need to get on the road."

After Goodbyes were said En hung back while the kids loaded the car. "You good." She asked Cain.

"Good as I ever was." He answered. "It's better this way."

They were both looking out the door at Jami. Faith and Micah were teasing her. She teased back tugging at Faith's short new hair and warning Micah to be careful with the girls. Cain thought to himself how young and carefree they appeared.

"Enjoy your self-inflicted misery." En broke into his thoughts.

"En…" Cain started. "Keep her away. It's going to get ugly around here. Encourage her to move on. She deserves a happy uncomplicated life."

"I know and I half agree with you. I will stay in touch and I expect you to do the same. If things do get ugly call me. I can always leave her working on some project and get back here if you need the help of a good Witch."

Cain put his arm around her shoulders and they walked outside to join the others.

Ennie grabbed Faith squeezing her tight. She planted a smacking kiss on her cheek. "You know all you have to do is call my name." Ennie sighed, grabbed Faiths shoulders. "I love you. Life will get better. If you're going to fight these things do exactly what Cain tells you and you fight hard. You understand me?"

Faith nodded. A tear fell down her cheek. She swiped it away and gave En a watery smile. She didn't think she could cry anymore. "Take care of my best friend. She's a knucklehead."

"Hmmm… Pots and kettles." En muttered just loud enough for Faith to hear.

"Micah." En snapped. He went to her, bent her over backward. And kissed her long and hard.

"Now that is a Goodbye." She sassed.

Back in the house Cain, Faith, and Micah worked to clean up the breakfast mess. It did not take long with all three of them working at it. They spoke of trivial things. It was comfortable and easy.

"Looks like it's just the three of us." Micah commented, loading the dishwasher. "What happens now?"

"We train and get ready." Cain answered.

"Get ready for what exactly?"

"There's always something and it's always nasty." Cain informed them. "I've got it on good authority something wicked this way comes."

"How long do you think we've got?" Faith asked.

"Hard to tell. The waiting is the hardest part. But we've got plenty of training to work on in the meantime."

"Well then I suggest we get busy." Micah said.

"No time like the present. What do you think Pops. Ready for our first lesson?"

"Meet me in the gym in five." His smile suggested he was not going to go easy on them.

"Why am I more worried about Cain's training methods than the demons coming our way?" Micah whispered to Faith.

"Because despite what people may think about you actually are pretty smart."

"No, if I were smart I would have left with Jami and En." He replied so seriously Faith burst out laughing. She looked into Cain's eyes as he smiled down at her. She wondered if he realized his eyes had remained crimson since Grey had been murdered. His incisors had become pointed as well. Whatever the reason, Faith had no fear of Cain and never would. He had stood by her and protected her through the worst and she would always give him her trust and loyalty. After all, didn't all of the Creators children deserve a second chance?

EPILOGUE

Lucifer reclined in his office chair. His long curling hair hung like a golden cascade catching the light. His beautiful face was an empty mask. He could be in his new man cave mulling over his recent losses but lately he had become drawn to watch his office walls. Staring for hours at the dying Paradise of Eden was the only thing that soothed him. He was bored. He was lonely. He was a horny little Devil who's appetites could not be satisfied these days.

Beelzebub had been trotting out the hottest pieces of ass Hell had to offer for his brother to sample. None of them had pleased him beyond the moment. They were all too eager. Each wanting to become his new favorite. He wanted more. There was just no pleasing the Devil.

Traitors and their betrayal had brought him low. His brother Tearzahn who had fought by his side since the time before time was counted had abandoned him to be Michael's newest lapdog. His women, Eve, he had waited for her. She had begged him to allow her to live out her mortal life and care for her children before she came to him. He had granted her that. Then for one glimpse of her first born she had betrayed him and fouled his plans for his heretic son. Cyndahl, daughter of Cain, had helped her with her plot against him. She too had turned her back on him for his disobedient offspring.

He knew he was a jealous beast but this kind of defiance was beyond endurance. After all, everything he had done was designed to bring his son home. Only when Cain sat willingly by his side would the Gates be unlocked. He had to break Cain's will to turn him back to the killer he had been. Back to the time when the lust for blood motivated him not the foolish need for His forgiveness. Then and only then could he be reunited with his only son and they would rule together. If only his betrayers knew they had all played their parts like puppets on his string. Lucifer laughed, he was always a step ahead of them and always would be. His pawns were lined up awaiting his next move. Time to bring his son home. In the meantime there was business to attend to.

Lucifer sighed, what was Hell coming to? He had become too soft and trusting. Never again. The flames of hell burned bright with the punishments he had been handing down. For fucks sake he was the Dark Lord. It was time he got back to being the Evilest Badass in Creation. The residents of Hell needed to be reminded of how he had earned the position and right now he was more than happy to show them the evil that dwelled inside him.

Swiveling his chair to face the wall he watched the cause of his current misery. Eve and Cyndahl frantically pounded their fists on the opposite side of the wall. Their urgent cries for help gave him tingles of pleasure. Their clothes now in filthy tatters hung limply from their still beautiful bodies. Their faces that once smiled at him with love were now dirty and twisted with fear. Still he felt their punishment was not severe enough. He could not send them to the Affa. He would have need of them to fulfill his plans. So he would leave them where they were until the time came they would once again prove useful to him.

Lucifer lapped up their misery taking pleasure in their fear. There they were under the very tree where he had seduced Eve and in her lust for beauty she gave herself to him. The soft grass he laid her on was gone now. Instead she stood upon the rotted decay of corpses. He briefly wondered how long Eve's wiley mind and Cyndahl's magic could keep his pets at bay.

Beelzebub growled fiercely making his presence known. Lucifer drug his eyes away to look toward his brother. Ah, he had brought another lovely distraction. Maybe this one would be able to hold his interest.

"Thanks B. You're the only one to show any sympathy for the Devil."

B rolled his eyes and walked away having no desire to watch Lucifer's sexual exploits.

Standing at the entrance to the room a petite redhead with creamy skin and wide green eyes stood awaiting his pleasure. She smiled boldly at him without a trace of fear. Lucifer found himself unwillingly intrigued. It looked like this one had a little fire in her and Lucifer loved the heat.

He summoned her to come to him.

Full breasts swayed as she sashayed across the room to stand nude before him. She was lush and curved in all the right places. With a wicked grin she knelt before him lowering her head in supplication. "Stay on your knees." Lucifer smiled wolfishly, lowering the zipper of his red leather pants.

Lucifer heard her gasp and then purr as his huge cock sprung free. He fisted her thick red hair and shoved her face into his lap.

As she took him into her mouth and started to work him Lucifer let his eyes drift back to the wall. He blew his ladies a kiss.

Lucifer chuckled as his women screamed from their side of the wall. "It's good to be the Prince…of Darkness."

www.ingramcontent.com/pod-product-compliance
Lightning Source LLC
LaVergne TN
LVHW040045080526
838202LV00045B/3502